## DEATH OF AN ITALIAN CHEF

Randy slowly turned his head toward Hayley. "She doesn't believe me. She's not going to do anything."

"Let's just wait and see," Hayley said, moving closer to the bed. "It's her job. She's a police officer."

"I wish Sergio was here," Randy lamented. "He would investigate." He then reached out and grabbed Hayley's hand and squeezed it. "Will you do it?"

"Will I do what?"

"Find out who came in here last night and killed Chef Romeo! I did not dream this, Hayley! He was murdered!"

She could see him starting to stress out.

His blood pressure and heart rate began rising on the digital monitor next to the bed.

She just needed to calm her brother down, and she knew there was only one way to do that.

"Yes, Randy, I will find whoever did this. I promise."

She just hoped it was a promise she could keep . . .

# Books by Lee Hollis

*Hayley Powell Mysteries*

DEATH OF A KITCHEN
DIVA

DEATH OF A COUNTRY
FRIED REDNECK

DEATH OF A COUPON
CLIPPER

DEATH OF A CHOCOHOLIC

DEATH OF A CHRISTMAS
CATERER

DEATH OF A CUPCAKE
QUEEN

DEATH OF A BACON
HEIRESS

DEATH OF A PUMPKIN
CARVER

DEATH OF A LOBSTER
LOVER

DEATH OF A COOKBOOK
AUTHOR

DEATH OF A WEDDING
CAKE BAKER

DEATH OF A BLUEBERRY
TART

DEATH OF A WICKED
WITCH

DEATH OF AN ITALIAN
CHEF

*Collections*

EGGNOG MURDER
(with Leslie Meier and
Barbara Ross)

YULE LOG MURDER
(with Leslie Meier and
Barbara Ross)

HAUNTED HOUSE
MURDER
(with Leslie Meier and
Barbara Ross)

CHRISTMAS CARD
MURDER
(with Leslie Meier and Peggy
Ehrhart)

*Poppy Harmon Mysteries*

POPPY HARMON
INVESTIGATES

POPPY HARMON AND
THE HUNG JURY

POPPY HARMON AND
THE PILLOW TALK
KILLER

*Maya & Sandra Mysteries*

MURDER AT THE PTA

MURDER AT THE BAKE
SALE

**Published by Kensington Publishing Corp.**

# DEATH of an ITALIAN CHEF

## LEE HOLLIS

**KENSINGTON**
PUBLISHING CORP.

www.kensingtonbooks.com

KENSINGTON BOOKS are published by

Kensington Publishing Corp.
119 West 40th Street
New York, NY 10018

All Kensington titles, imprints, and distributed lines are available at special quantity discounts for bulk purchases for sales promotion, premiums, fund-raising, educational, or institutional use.

Special book excerpts or customized printings can also be created to fit specific needs. For details, write or phone the office of the Kensington Sales Manager: Attn.: Sales Department. Kensington Publishing Corp., 119 West 40th Street, New York, NY 10018. Phone: 1-800-221-2647.

The K logo is a trademark of Kensington Publishing Corp.

First Printing: July 2021
ISBN-13: 978-1-4967-2497-7
ISBN-10: 1-4967-2497-6

ISBN-13: 978-1-4967-2498-4 (ebook)
ISBN-10: 1-4967-2498-4 (ebook)

10 9 8 7 6 5 4 3 2 1

Printed in the United States of America

# Chapter 1

Randy stabbed at a clam nestled in his plate of linguini and then popped it in his mouth. He chewed and swallowed it, and then put down his fork and sat back in his chair, discomfited.

Hayley, who was twirling a healthy portion of her spaghetti carbonara onto her own fork, instantly noticed. "You okay, Randy?"

Randy nodded, tiny beads of sweat beginning to form on his brow. "Yeah, I'm just feeling a little under the weather." He placed the palm of his hand to his forehead. "I hope I'm not coming down with something. I knew I should've gotten that flu shot at my last physical."

Bruce gulped down a glass of red wine. "Well, you can't get sick now. You need to look after my wife while I'm out of town."

Hayley picked up her glass of chardonnay to wash

down her pasta and smiled. "You know, Bruce, it's a re-markable thing, really, but before we got married, I actually was quite adept at looking after myself whenever you weren't around."

Bruce chuckled and then opened his mouth wide to take in a large spinach-filled ravioli. He snapped his mouth shut like a crocodile, closed his eyes, and moaned rapturously. "Oh, that's good."

They were dining on a Saturday night at Bar Harbor's newest Italian hot spot, Romeo's, owned and operated by its namesake Chef Romeo—no last name, just Romeo—which was part of his shtick, apparently, although officially he claimed that according to his birth certificate his full name was Romeo Russo. A self-described world-class chef by way of Naples, where his family emigrated from in the 1950s and New York, where he lived most of his life, Romeo was a portly, gregarious, loud, larger-than-life character fond of big, crushing bear hugs whenever he greeted his guests. He had taken Bar Harbor by storm from the moment he first blew into town. His restaurant had only been open a few weeks now, but business was booming, mostly due to its simple, no-frills, but tasty, traditional Italian fare that the locals were eagerly lapping up. There was something in the marinara sauce, some kind of special ingredient that he claimed was his true secret to success. Romeo insisted his restaurant be a throwback, complete with checkered tablecloths, Chianti bottles with melting candle wax, and even an accordion player on Friday nights who would float through the restaurant playing "That's Amore."

Randy lowered his hand from his forehead. "It doesn't feel like a fever, but it's awfully hot in here, don't you think?"

Bruce stopped eating and shrugged. "Seems okay to me."

Hayley looked at her brother Randy, slightly concerned. "Are you sure you don't want us to drive you home?"

"No, I've been going stir-crazy with Sergio back in Brazil for the next three months. I've really been looking forward to this dinner out all week."

Once a year, Randy's husband, Bar Harbor police chief Sergio Alvares, made the long trek down to South America to visit with his family at their farmhouse outside Curitiba. Randy had considered leaving his bar, Drinks Like A Fish, in the capable hands of his manager Michelle and join Sergio like he had last year, but in the end he decided to stay home because he had not been feeling himself, and was afraid if he traveled, he might get sick.

Bruce went to refill his wineglass, but Hayley snatched the wine bottle away before he had the chance. "It's no fun flying with a hangover."

Bruce scoffed. "I'm not flying all the way down to Brazil to see Sergio, I'm just going to New York." He gently extracted the wine bottle from Hayley's grasp and poured himself some more.

Bruce was leaving on an assignment for the *Island Times*, where he worked as the crime reporter. Normally his stories were exclusively local—house break-ins, bicycle thefts, domestic disturbances—but a high-profile court case in lower Manhattan was about to kick off, and it involved a wealthy summer resident on the island who had been accused of defrauding investors in her multimillion-dollar company headquartered in Manhattan. Given the massive public interest in the case, plus the fact that the defendant had a sprawling waterfront estate in Seal Harbor, and was known by just about everyone on Mount Desert Island, editor-in-chief Sal Moretti thought it might serve the community well if Bruce covered the story as it unfolded right where it was happening in the Big Apple. Bruce had jumped at the chance to go, excited about finally having a meaty, high-stakes story to write about.

Hayley crinkled her nose in judgment as Bruce filled his glass to the rim and defiantly belted it back. "Come on, it's my last hurrah," Bruce said. "I have no idea how long I'll be stuck down in New York."

Hayley turned to Randy and sighed. "Just listen to him. *Stuck*. Please, I've never seen him so excited to be covering a story. He can't wait to get to New York City."

Bruce grinned. Just the mention of NYC had him buzzing and all keyed up.

"Randy, you look pale," Hayley said, frowning.

Randy lifted his red cloth napkin off his lap and patted the sweat off his brow. "Maybe we should call it a night so I can get home to bed." He dropped his napkin back down in his lap and pushed his barely eaten plate of linguini in clam sauce away from him.

Lenny, a big, lumbering local kid working as a busboy at Romeo's, suddenly appeared at Randy's side.

"All finished, sir?" Lenny asked.

Randy nodded half-heartedly. "Yes. Thank you."

Suddenly, like the Tasmanian devil in a whirling burst of energy, Chef Romeo bounded up to the table after seeing Lenny clearing away Randy's plate of food. "What's going on here? He's not finished with his dinner!"

"He—he said he was," Lenny stammered, obviously in fear of his thundering, frightening, gigantic boss.

"But he's barely touched it!" Romeo wailed. "What's

wrong with it? Too much garlic? I've heard that before from some of my customers, to which I always say: How can there be such a thing as too much garlic?"

"No, it's delicious, Romeo, I'm just . . ." Randy said, trying to avoid insulting the prickly chef. He then turned to Lenny. "You know what? Can you wrap that up for me to go?"

"Yes, sir," Lenny said, scooting away toward the kitchen with the plate of linguini.

"It tastes even better the next day!" Romeo boasted.

Romeo noticed Bruce scraping the last of the marinara sauce off his own plate with a spoon, causing him to break out into a wide, satisfied smile. "I love a man with a hearty appetite!"

"Best ravioli I've ever tasted!" Bruce crowed.

Romeo clapped his hands together, then his eyes dropped on Hayley's plate, which still had a few remnants left of her spaghetti carbonara.

Hayley threw her hands up in the air. "Before you say anything, it's absolutely delicious! I just couldn't possibly eat another bite. I probably shouldn't have gorged on all the garlic bread earlier."

"What did you think of it? I bake the bread myself every day," Romeo said.

"Buttery perfection," Hayley answered.

Romeo eyed Hayley suspiciously. "Is that what you will write in your column tomorrow?"

"I beg your pardon?" Hayley asked innocently.

"Come on, Hayley, you can tell me," Romeo said, leaning closer, his ample belly nearly moving the table a few inches. "Is this just a casual night out with your husband and brother, or is this a *professional* visit? Are you here to review my restaurant for the *Island Times*?"

She was caught.

There was no point in denying it.

Hayley nodded sheepishly.

"I knew it!" Romeo exclaimed, pounding his fist in the palm of his other hand.

"Well, you can rest assured that my review will be glowing. Our entire experience here this evening has been nothing short of five stars," Hayley promised.

"Well, I am sure there is always room for improvement. I've had many haughty New York food critics remind me of that fact over the years," Romeo said with a laugh. "So tell me, what didn't you like?"

Hayley sat frozen in her seat, suddenly put on the spot. "No, really, everything was—"

"Come on! There has to be *something*!" Romeo roared.

Hayley knew she could continue to dodge the question, or risk insulting the chef and be totally honest. It finally came down to the fact that he would never allow them to ever leave, even though the dining room was almost cleared out at this point, if she did not at least come up with something to lightly criticize.

"Is my house salad dressing too salty and vinegary?"

"No, it was perfect, and like Bruce said, the spinach ravioli was outstanding, world-class—"

Romeo zeroed in on Hayley's plate. "Aha! You're focused on Bruce's entrée, but what about your spaghetti carbonara? You've had better, haven't you?"

Hayley vigorously shook her head. "No, it—"

"You can admit it! This helps me, Hayley! I'm always looking for ways to make my food better! I'm not one of those overly sensitive chefs who become personally offended if someone criticizes one of their specialty dishes even the tiniest bit!"

"Okay," Hayley sighed, finally giving up. "Although your spaghetti carbonara is without question very flavorful and yummy . . ."

Romeo leaned in even closer, his round stomach right in front of Hayley's face. "Go on . . ."

"I like mine better," Hayley squeaked.

Romeo exploded. "What? You're crazy!" He threw a pudgy hand over his heart as if a dagger had just pierced it.

"I knew I should have kept my mouth shut," Hayley muttered to Bruce and Randy.

Romeo was on a tear. "That's my great-great-grandmother Gabriella's recipe, handed down for generations in Naples! There must be something wrong with your taste buds! You should go see a doctor!"

Hayley knew the bombastic chef was half joking, but she could also tell he was clearly rattled by her comment, so she felt the need to blather on. "But again, your spaghetti carbonara truly is scrumptious—"

"Don't patronize me!" Romeo roared, dismissing her with a wave of his hand. "If you think my spaghetti carbonara is second-rate, you're entitled to your opinion!"

"I *never* said second-rate—"

Lenny returned with a container wrapped in a plastic bag and set it down in front of Randy. "Here you go, sir."

"Thank you," Randy said to Lenny before looking up at Chef Romeo, and in an attempt to diffuse the tension, picked up the bag of leftovers. "I cannot wait to devour this tomorrow. The clam sauce was exquisite."

Romeo just blew past the comment, remaining focused squarely on Hayley. "What are you doing on Monday?"

"Working," she said.

"I mean after work!" Romeo shouted.

"I—I don't know . . ."

"I want you to come here and make me some of your spaghetti carbonara right here in my kitchen!"

"Oh, Romeo, please, I wish I had never said anything—"

"But you must! If somebody makes better carbonara than my dear old departed great-great-grandmother Gabriella, well, then I need to know about it!"

"The last thing I want to do is compete—"

"It's not a competition! I just want to find out what makes your spaghetti carbonara taste so special!"

Hayley opened her mouth, ready to give the spiraling chef a definitive *no*, when suddenly he grabbed his busboy Lenny by the shirt and barked, "Bring them more wine and some cannolis on the house!"

Well, that was it. There was no point in protesting any further, because Hayley was going to be preparing her own recipe for Chef Romeo Monday afternoon. If she knew one thing about herself, Hayley Powell knew she could easily be bought with a complimentary dessert and free-flowing wine.

# Chapter 2

Hayley sat at her kitchen table, staring wistfully at her phone as Bruce and her daughter Gemma, who now lived and worked in New York City, breezed across Washington Square Park at dusk, the majestic arch at the foot of Fifth Avenue in the background, both their faces pushed in close in front of the camera phone.

"I wanted to take him to an awesome spaghetti joint I'm obsessed with in Little Italy, but he said he's had his fill of Italian lately, so we're going to my favorite French place on Bleecker Street," Gemma yelled into the phone. "Then we're going to go see Conner's show uptown."

Conner was Gemma's fiancé, an up-and-coming Broadway actor who was currently enjoying success in a revival of *Fiddler on the Roof* playing the Russian student Fyedka, who romances the lead character Tevya's daughter Chava. He had perfected a Russian accent, which he eagerly showed off to Hayley during a number of Zoom calls.

"I promised Gemma I won't nod off like I usually do during any kind of long musical," Bruce said.

"Just make sure you stay awake during Conner's solo. He knows exactly where we're sitting, so I'm sure he'll have his eyes trained right on us." Gemma laughed.

"I'm jealous," Hayley sighed. "I wish I was there with you two right now."

"Me too, babe," Bruce said with a wink. "What are your big plans for tonight?"

"Liddy and Mona are on their way over for dinner. I'm doing a dry run preparing my spaghetti carbonara before the face-off with Chef Romeo tomorrow afternoon," Hayley said. "I need to get the dish perfect, or I will never live it down."

"I'm not even going to pretend to know what you're talking about, Mother," Gemma said, chuckling.

"I'll explain everything over dinner," Bruce said.

"We're coming up on the restaurant now. Bye, Mom!"

Hayley waved at them. "Goodbye! Enjoy! Love you both!"

"I'll call you after court is dismissed tomorrow," Bruce promised, waving back.

And then they were gone.

Hayley felt a little lump in her throat.

With her husband and daughter gallivanting all over Manhattan, having a wonderful time after months of painstaking worry about Gemma and Conner's safety there during the pandemic, Hayley found this moment bittersweet. She, of course, was excited to see Gemma thriving in the big city, her wedding plans with Conner restarted, her career as a food critic and columnist back on track, and she was happy for Bruce to be covering possibly the biggest assignment of his career, but at the same time, she felt stuck at home alone, missing out on these memorable moments.

But instead of feeling sorry for herself, Hayley stood up from the kitchen table and got to work on her spaghetti carbonara, whisking the eggs and cheese together in a bowl and frying the bacon in a pan on the stove until brown and crispy. She popped open a bottle of Pinot Grigio, which, in her opinion, was the perfect companion to her pasta recipe, and as if on cue, Liddy and Mona ambled through the back door, hands out for glasses of wine. By the time she had stirred in the garlic, pasta, egg mixture, and was seasoning with salt and pepper to taste, the three women were on their second glass. Doling out a healthy portion of the carbonara for all of them, they sat down at the dining room table, Hayley anxiously awaiting the verdict.

"Well?" Hayley asked, eyeing both of them as Mona shoveled a forkful into her mouth.

"Oh, Hayley, it's divine," Liddy cooed.

"Thank you, Liddy, but you would say that no matter what. Mona is the one I really trust because she never holds back punches."

Mona swallowed, stared straight ahead, and then slowly nodded. "Not bad."

"High praise indeed," Liddy cracked.

"No, you don't understand," Hayley said happily. "Coming from Mona, that's a rave review."

Mona's mouth suddenly dropped open, her eyes watering, and she quickly buried her face in her elbow and erupted in a giant sneeze, startling both Hayley and Liddy.

"I'd go easy on the pepper next time," Mona suggested.

"Noted," Hayley said.

Liddy twirled some more spaghetti on her fork and shook her head. "I don't understand why this Chef Romeo is making you jump through hoops to prove you make a better spaghetti carbonara. What's the point?"

"He's very competitive and he's used to being the best, so when I challenged him . . . well, his ego couldn't resist calling me out to prove it," Hayley said, before taking another bite of her dish, savoring it. "It is really good, isn't it?"

Mona reached for the bottle of white wine and up-ended the rest into her own glass before slamming it back down on the table. "Got any more of this?"

"Yes, in the pantry," Hayley said, standing up from the table and removing the empty wine bottle from the table.

Mona gulped down the rest of her wine.

"Don't you have to be up at like four in the morning to haul your lobster traps tomorrow?" Liddy asked, eyebrows raised.

Mona shook her head. "Is that your way of saying I'm drinking too much?"

"No, that goes without saying," Liddy quipped. "I'm just asking."

Hayley was in the kitchen uncorking the bottle of wine, but could still hear their exchange.

"Well, my boys are covering for me for a while," Mona muttered, not exactly overjoyed to be sharing this news.

"Why? Are you taking a vacation?" Hayley asked as she returned to the dining room with the fresh bottle of wine.

"Nope. They keep yammering on about how they're grown men now and can run the business, and how it doesn't make sense for their dear, aging mother to be doing so much hard labor," Mona snorted. "Can you believe that nonsense?"

Hayley poured Liddy some more wine.

Liddy swished it around in her glass as she spoke. "Yes, I can! Your sons are big, strong, strapping men now, fully capable of the physical demands of running a successful lobstering business. Why should you and your tired, crumbling old bones be out on that rickety, leaking boat in the icy waters of the Atlantic every day at some ungodly hour?"

"It's all I know!" Mona wailed.

"You can still run the business from home," Hayley said. "Take orders over the phone, look after the books . . ."

"You both know I flunked every math class they made me take in high school. Besides, my daughter Clara's much smarter than me when it comes to numbers. I let her keep track of all that. If I stop hauling traps, I won't know what to do with myself."

"Find yourself a hobby," Liddy said.

"I'm not the knitting circle type, okay?" Mona moaned.

Hayley reached over and lightly touched Mona's hand. "Look, all we're saying is, maybe it's time to take a step back, just a bit. Relax and enjoy your life a little more."

"I'm bored already just thinking about it," Mona spit out, glowering.

"You should be grateful you can afford to do it," Liddy said. "The real estate market has been in the toilet lately. I haven't had a sale in months; I'm bleeding money; I have credit card payments overdue; I am close to the point of having to augment my income with a second job. Maybe I should be the one out there hauling traps."

Hayley and Mona exchanged a look, then busted up laughing.

"All right, it sounded just as ridiculous to me as I heard myself saying it, but I'm going to have to do something soon or I'll be filing for bankruptcy. I can just hear my mother now if it comes to that!" Liddy wailed.

"You could try living on a budget," Mona suggested.

There was a tense silence in the dining room before Liddy exhaled a long breath. "I am just going to pretend you did not say that."

Mona lifted her glass, toasted Liddy, then gulped down the rest of her wine.

Hayley sat back in her chair. "My whole adult life I have always been on the lookout for ways to make more money, but over the last couple of years all of that has suddenly changed. Marrying Bruce essentially doubled our income; I've got an empty nest with the kids gone and on their own; and well . . . financially speaking, things have gotten easier, but . . ."

"But what?" Liddy asked.

"I don't know. Something's missing. Don't get me wrong: I never expected to get married again, but I love being married to Bruce. That's not it . . ." Hayley sipped her wine thoughtfully. "I guess I wish my job at the *Island Times* was more fulfilling."

"You can't quit your column!" Liddy cried. "Do you know how many people all over the island can't wait to read you every day!"

"It's not the columns! That's my favorite part of the job. It's the office managerial duties. They've become so monotonous and, not to be too dramatic, but a little soul-crushing. I'm so tired of handling customers' subscription complaints, and even more demeaning, keeping the coffeepot full throughout the day."

"Sal would be lost without you," Mona remarked.

Hayley nodded. "I know . . ."

"So what are you going to do?"

She shrugged. "I have no idea. The only plan I currently have is to kick Chef Romeo's butt tomorrow with this spaghetti carbonara recipe! Which reminds me—there is enough for three more helpings."

Liddy threw her hands up in the air. "Ladies, we all know excessive carbs solve nothing!"

Hayley collected their plates and headed back to the kitchen, overhearing Mona say, "No, a salad solves nothing. Spaghetti carbonara solves *everything*!"

# Chapter 3

Chef Romeo opened his mouth wide and shoveled the forkful of Hayley's spaghetti carbonara into his mouth, a few long noodles dangling behind, so he pursed his lips and sucked them in. He chewed slowly, methodically, his twinkling blue-green eyes darting back and forth wildly as he let his taste buds get to work.

Hayley took a deep breath, nervously awaiting the final verdict. Romeo's eyes stopped flitting about and he zeroed in on Hayley as he swallowed. There was an agonizingly long silence, and Hayley began to tap her foot restlessly. It looked as if Romeo was on the verge of blurting out his final assessment of her dish, when he suddenly slammed the fork back down on the plate and began twisting it violently, winding more noodles around and around like a ball of yarn until he had so much on there that he had to drop his jaw even wider to fit the entire mound of spaghetti into his mouth. He snapped his lips shut, a dollop of cream caught in his thick black beard, and repeated the entire process, chewing, considering, chewing some more, before dramatically swallowing and slamming the fork back down on the table yet again. Hayley was on pins and needles, not sure she could endure the time it would take him to eat another bite.

Chef Romeo closed his eyes and sighed as he grabbed a cloth napkin and lightly patted his lips and beard. He had not done that before, so Hayley hoped they finally might be close to some kind of proclamation. She was dead tired from a long day at the office, having been up late for girls' night with Liddy and Mona.

After rushing over to the restaurant when she was finished with work, armed with her covered dish, she had found Romeo alone in his kitchen, scribbling tomorrow evening's specials on a chalkboard since the restaurant was closed on Mondays. She was hoping the whole food challenge initiated by the chef would be short and sweet, and she would be home in time for the local news, a winner or a loser. Either outcome would be just fine by her, if truth be told.

"Yours is better!" Romeo blurted out.

"*What?*" she gasped.

"Honestly, I'm amazed, just stunned," Romeo said, shaking his head in disbelief. "How can you take a dish that's so easy to make—let's face it, at the end of the day it's just spaghetti, with eggs and cheese and a fatty cured pork—how can you take something so simple and turn it into something *this* special?" He scooped up his fork to go at it again.

"I'm thrilled you like it," Hayley said, beaming.

"*Like* it? This puts my family recipe to shame. My great-great-grandmother is, right at this moment, spinning around in her grave. You're not even *Italian*!"

"No, I did that whole AncestryDNA thing where you mail in some of your spit and get a whole readout of your family history. I thought for sure I must be part Italian, given how much I love pasta and wine, but the results came back zilch. Nada. Nothing. I'm mostly English with a dash of Scottish and Irish thrown in for good measure!"

"Blasphemy! How can you be descended from the people responsible for steak and kidney pie, not a drop of Italian blood coursing through your veins, and come up with something as *bellissima* as this?"

Hayley assumed the question was rhetorical, so she just smiled and accepted the compliment.

"I want you to come work here!" Romeo declared.

Hayley giggled, assuming he was joking.

"I am serious, Hayley. I need someone to help me in the kitchen. We're getting busier by the day and I can't handle it all myself. Of course, my name is on the door, so I will still be head chef, but I will give you credit on the menu board. We can start tomorrow with Hayley's spaghetti carbonara, then introduce more specials as you create them. I will give you free rein; you can prepare whatever you want."

"I'm flattered, Romeo, really, I am, but—"

"How much are you making at the paper?"

"It's not about the money—"

"I will double your salary!"

Hayley nearly choked after swallowing the wrong way.

She had always dreamed of receiving an offer like this, but never seriously thought she would ever hear the words *I will double your salary*. That only happened in TV shows and movies. But maybe this was a sign. Just hours earlier, she had declared to Liddy and Mona that she wanted to do something more fulfilling than just being office manager at the *Times*. And now this opportunity was presenting itself out of the blue.

Still, would it be worth the huge increase in pay to work alongside the mercurial, egoistical, demanding Chef Romeo, who had not been in town for very long but had already cemented a difficult reputation? Taking this job could very well turn out to be her worst kitchen nightmare.

"It's a very tempting offer, Romeo, but—"

He smashed a pudgy finger over her lips. "Don't say no. Not yet. Just take some time to think about it. There is no rush. I'm not going anywhere. We just opened."

Hayley nodded, then Romeo removed his finger from her lips and used it to sop up some cream left on the plate and slurp it off with his tongue. "But fair warning: I will not stop. I will wear you down until you tell me your secret ingredient!"

"I'm not the world's greatest spy. All you need to do is ply me with some of your homemade spumoni and I'm sure you'll get me to talk."

Romeo closed his eyes and threw his head back as he erupted in laughter. He reopened his eyes while catching his breath, and his broad, happy smile slowly faded as his eyes fixed upon something behind her.

Hayley spun around to see two men entering the

kitchen. She recognized both of them. Vic Spencer, short and round, bald head and a thick, graying goatee, a local contractor with a sour disposition, twice divorced, and for good reason, Hayley suspected. He was there with his head foreman, Chuckie Rhinehart, relatively new to town, a tall, muscular kid, kind of brutish and angry by nature, with a shaved head and a similar goatee, as if he was trying to emulate his boss and bond with him. But poor Chuckie couldn't quite grow any facial hair properly, so he was left with a patchy attempt that looked as if he had trimmed it either drunk or blindfolded.

"How you doin', Hayley?" Vic said with a sneer.

"I'm fine, Vic, thank you. Hi, Chuckie," she said.

Chuckie seemed surprised that she was addressing him at all and grunted an unintelligible reply.

"Chef, I was wondering if we might have a word with you . . . in private?" Vic inquired, eyeing Hayley with a dismissive scowl.

His answer was emphatic. "No."

Hayley made a move to leave. "You know, I should be going anyway . . ."

Before she had the chance, Romeo stepped forward ahead of her, unintentionally blocking her exit from the kitchen.

The chef poked Vic in the chest with the same pudgy finger he had used to lick the last of Hayley's carbonara sauce off his plate. "You and your two-bit thug here can turn around and leave my restaurant right now because I have nothing to say to you!"

"You owe me," Vic seethed. "Fifteen hundred bucks! That's your remaining balance. I got the invoice right here!" He reached into his shirt pocket and yanked out a folded-up piece of paper, shoving it toward the chef. Romeo slapped it away and it floated to the floor. Chuckie bent down to pick it up and hand it back to his boss, but Vic testily waved him away.

"*Niente*! You get nothing! Not one cent!" Romeo bellowed, his face suddenly flushed with anger. "I already paid you over twenty grand to remodel this kitchen and you botched the job royally!"

"I stand by my work," Vic growled, insulted.

"Oh, really?" Romeo scoffed. "First of all, you finished two months later than you originally stated in the contract! I had to push back my opening, which cost me thousands of dollars in lost revenue."

"You can't fault me for unexpected delays!" Vic barked.

"How about shoddy work, then?" Romeo roared before pointing to a wall of cabinets. "You nailed those storage cabinets in place instead of screwing them so they're loose and unwieldy, not to mention cheap-looking. And how about the new floor? You ran it up to all the appliances but not underneath them! So you cut corners whenever you could, and let's talk poor drain connections and unsafe and illegal electrical work! Should I go on?"

"You signed the contract," Vic warned. "You need to pay in full for services rendered. Don't make me get my lawyer involved."

"Go ahead, sue me. I don't care. I will take this all the way to the Supreme Court if I have to! You are not getting another dime out of me! It's already going to cost me a hell of a lot more than fifteen hundred dollars to repair the mess you made in my kitchen!"

Chuckie lumbered forward, breathing hard through his nose, chest puffed out, fists clenched. "We're going to get paid one way or another," he said in a low, intimidating voice.

Romeo glared at Chuckie for a moment and then busted out laughing again. "You think you can scare me? What a joke! Chuckie, you're about as intimidating as a baby penguin! Now get out of my kitchen!"

Chuckie held his ground, pouting. Then, in a burst of anger, he thrust out his giant flat hands, pushing Romeo, who stumbled back in surprise.

Romeo roared like a wild animal and lunged forward, this time surprising Chuckie, and the two began grappling with each other.

"Stop it! Both of you!" Hayley heard herself screaming.

Neither man heeded her order.

Fists were flying.

There was lots of grunting and cursing.

Crashing into pots and pans.

Romeo got in a good kick to Chuckie's shin, causing him to lose his balance, which he seemed to regain by wrapping his giant mitts around Romeo's neck to steady himself and squeezing as hard as he could.

Vic stood back, watching the brawl with a self-satisfied smile slapped on his face.

Hayley yanked out her phone and thrust it in the air. "I'm only going to say this once! Don't make me call 911!" She poised her index finger over the phone screen, prepared for action.

That seemed to finally get their attention.

None of the three men were eager to get tossed in the slammer, and so the rumble came to an end as quickly as it had begun.

"This isn't over by a long shot," Vic spat out, turning on his heel and stalking out.

Chuckie, chest heaving, out of breath, wiped his nose with his hand, then slowly limped away after his boss.

Hayley finally lowered her phone.

Chef Romeo brushed himself off, and then with a wink, cracked, "You sure you don't want to come work here? I can promise you it will never be dull!"

# Chapter 4

After devouring the rest of Hayley's spaghetti carbonara, Chef Romeo was still on a tear about his unwanted visitors, Vic Spencer and his flunky Chuckie, and the shabby, unacceptable job they had done on his kitchen.

"How does he think he can get away with something like this? It's a small town, word gets around, and believe me, I have the biggest mouth for miles!" Romeo roared.

Hayley thought better of nodding in agreement.

Romeo began opening cupboards. "Just look at these flimsy shelves. The nails are already loose—this whole thing could collapse at any moment and hurt one of my employees! It's ridiculous! And he actually thinks I am going to pay him *more* money? What an imbecile! That guy doesn't even deserve to have a license to do business! He's a menace to the community!"

Hayley observed Romeo's face turning beet red as he worked himself up into a wild frenzy. "Romeo, you should calm down . . ."

"I am calm! Do I not look calm?" Romeo shouted.

"What would you say *calm* looks like? Because right now what you're doing doesn't look calm to me," Hayley said softly.

"Can you believe he had the nerve to threaten to sue *me*? Who does that idiot think he is? I'll tell you one thing: I'm a Brooklyn boy, born and raised. We're tough as nails, a lot tougher than the ones he used to hammer that cupboard into place, and we don't take guff from nobody!"

Suddenly Romeo stopped screaming and clutched his chest, sweat pouring down his face, mouth agape, bottom lip quivering.

Hayley took a step forward. "Romeo, are you all right?"

She noticed his hand at his side trembling.

"I'm fine!" Romeo insisted.

"Do you feel a tightness in your chest? Is there a pain shooting down your arm?"

Romeo waved her off. "It's nothing to worry about. Just a little indigestion. I promise not to blame your carbonara."

Hayley had been around long enough to recognize the signs of a heart attack. "Do you have shortness of breath?"

Romeo firmly shook his head *no*, but it was obvious he was having some trouble breathing.

"Are you dizzy or light-headed?"

"Stop pestering me, Hayley! I am not having a heart

attack! This happens all the time when I get upset. I just need to sit down and let it pass," Romeo said, pulling up a chair and plopping down his large frame.

"This is nothing to mess around with," Hayley warned. "If you're having chest pains of any kind, we should get you to the emergency room as soon as possible."

"Forget it! I hate hospitals!" Romeo barked. "Trust me, there is nothing to worry about here, this is just me being Italian, screaming and yelling and getting worked up is just part of our nature! My whole family acts like this!"

Hayley eyed him warily, not quite believing his state of health was no cause for concern.

He sat slumped over in the chair, taking long, deep breaths until his blood pressure seemed to come down a bit, and whatever pain he refused to acknowledge had subsided. He finally glanced up at Hayley and flashed her a grin. "See, I'm feeling better already."

If Romeo was going to ignore whatever it was that just happened, the least she could do was try to get his mind off Vic Spencer, and she had the perfect way to do that. She brought something up on her phone screen and then handed it to Romeo.

"What is this?"

"A sneak peek of my column that will be in tomorrow's paper," Hayley said, smiling.

Romeo read the review on her phone, his lips moving along, and then an elated smile began to creep across his face. "Five stars?"

"I would've given six if there was such a thing," Hayley said with a wink.

Romeo leaped to his feet and grabbed her in a bear hug. "Thank you, Hayley! I could kiss you!"

"Well, since I'm married, that might not be appropriate—"

He ignored her by pursing his lips and going in strong. Hayley managed to duck her head to the side so his lips landed on her cheek instead, then she gently wiggled out of his tight grasp.

"Let's celebrate with some vino!" Romeo roared, hurtling off toward his wine rack.

"It's getting late, and I promised to stop by my brother Randy's bar to say hello. He's feeling lonely lately since his husband—"

"That's too bad," Romeo said, totally uninterested. He uncorked the bottle of Chianti and poured two glasses, handing one to Hayley. They toasted before taking a sip. Hayley hung out with the chef for another forty minutes, mostly to make certain he did not suffer another suspected heart episode. The two bonded over their mutual love of food. Hayley knew she had made a friend for life after her rave review of Romeo's restaurant.

"So you really thought my cannoli was the best you've ever tasted, even when you vacationed in Italy?"

Hayley nodded. "I wouldn't have written it if I didn't believe it."

"What can I say, the lady has impeccable taste!"

"I don't know about that. I just know what I like," she demurred.

Romeo downed the rest of his wine and then laser-focused on Hayley, a dead serious look on his face. "You really should not be wasting your time writing about food."

Hayley arched an eyebrow. "Oh?"

Romeo slammed his wineglass down. "No. You should be sharing your talents with the world! You live in a tourist town. Acadia National Park is one of the most popular vacation spots in the whole country! We get millions of visitors a year! And they all have to eat! If you won't come work in my restaurant, you should open up your own!"

Hayley chuckled. "That's very sweet of you to say, but I'm not sure I'm really cut out to run my own restaurant."

"Why not? You're a smart cookie. You could figure it out. Just don't open an Italian place. That's my territory. You can do anything else, just not Italian!"

"Okay, no Italian," Hayley said, humoring him and sipping more wine.

"I see you with a seafood joint, maybe putting a spin on your spaghetti carbonara by adding lobster or shrimp. I got a million ideas. I'd be happy to help you if you ever decide to go for it!" Romeo bellowed. "Let's do a couple of sambuca shots!"

"No, I really shouldn't—"

But Romeo was already on his feet, heading toward his junky cupboards. He stopped suddenly, his back to Hayley. She could see his shoulders moving up and down as if he was having trouble trying to breathe again.

"Romeo?"

He raised a hand. "All good."

But he swayed to the side and had to grab the counter to steady himself.

Hayley sighed. "I really think you should at least go see a doctor."

"He always tells me the same thing. 'You need to lose weight and exercise more!' Forget it! If I did that, it would destroy my image! No one wants to see a scrawny, starving Italian chef! Who would come eat my food if it was clear I wasn't eating it myself? No way! Ain't gonna happen! I love my work too much!"

He wiped the sweat beads off his brow defiantly and threw open the cupboard to retrieve his bottle of sambuca. When he slammed the door shut, the entire row of shelves collapsed, crashing to the floor, dishes and glassware shattering everywhere.

Chef Romeo exploded again and Hayley clutched her phone at her side, fully prepared to call an ambulance if need be. But happily, after another shot of sambuca, Chef Romeo appeared to be back to normal and ranting about the despicable, lowlife Vic Spencer and the multiple ways Romeo planned to exact his revenge, all signs of his ill health dissipated.

# Chapter 5

Hayley sat on the stool at the bar of her brother's local watering hole Drinks Like A Fish, sipping a Diet Coke and staring off into space as Randy emerged from the kitchen with a large plate of fried clams and set it down in front of a scrawny, scraggly gray-bearded fisherman in a Red Sox cap seated at the other end of the bar.

"Enjoy, Cappy. Let me know if you need more tartar sauce," Randy said, wiping his hands with a dishrag. The fisherman grunted a nonsensical reply and started devouring the clams as Randy ambled down to the opposite side of the bar where Hayley was currently lost in her thoughts.

"You sure I can't get you something to eat? Kitchen's open for another thirty minutes," Randy said.

Hayley raised her head, eyes blinking. "I'm sorry—what?"

"Are you hungry?"

"No, thanks, I'm fine. I ate quite a bit of spaghetti carbonara earlier at Chef Romeo's place," Hayley said.

"What about something a little stronger?" Randy asked, pointing to her glass of soda.

"Not after two shots of sambuca," Hayley said. She guzzled the rest of her Diet Coke and handed the empty glass to Randy. "I should be getting home."

"Why? There's no one there waiting for you."

"Tell that to Leroy. I'm sure he would take great offense."

"Leroy's got a doggy door if he needs to get out into the yard and I'm sure a full bowl of Kibbles 'n Bits. Stay. Keep me company. Cappy over there is about four clams away from passing out, so he does me no good, and Michelle is busy in the office counting receipts. I have no one else."

"You lonely at home without Sergio?"

Randy nodded. "When he was leaving, I pretended to be happy for the break. I told him all the projects around the house I was going to get done while he was away. But instead, I stay here late every night because I dread the thought of going home to a big old empty house and staring at the walls with no one to talk to. I've caught myself talking back to people on television. I've actually gotten quite close with Anderson Cooper."

Hayley chuckled. "I know what you mean. I have convinced myself that Leroy is perfectly capable of understanding every word I'm saying to him. This morning I was in the middle of talking about what I was going to make myself for dinner on Wednesday—that's two nights from now—and he literally turned his back on me and walked out of the room. I'm boring my own dog! It's come to that!"

"I honestly thought we would both do a lot better being by ourselves, but it hasn't worked out that way, has it?" Randy laughed.

Hayley slid off the barstool and waved at Cappy, who was droopy-eyed and had some fried crumbs from the clams stuck in his beard. "Good night, Cappy!"

He acknowledged her with a shaky wave of his hand and then slumped over, his eyes shut.

"Wait, don't go," Randy pleaded. "Let's do something fun."

"Like what?"

"I don't know. Mondays are always so slow here. I don't expect to get many more customers and Cappy's about to take a nap. Michelle can cover for me." Randy grabbed a copy of the *Island Times* from underneath the bar and rifled through to the entertainment section.

He suddenly gasped.

Hayley leaned forward, curious. "What?"

"Tonight is camp-tastic movies night at the Criterion Theatre," he blathered, eyes wide with glee.

"Camp-what?"

"It's always dead at the Criterion on Monday nights, so they've been looking for new ways to draw people in. Last month they started camp-tastic movies, which essentially are Hollywood movies so hilariously bad they're really fun to watch and comment on. I missed the first one they did, *Valley of the Dolls*, much to my chagrin, but tonight they're featuring the ultimate camp classic, *Mommie Dearest*!"

"I didn't realize that was a bad movie. I remember

watching it as a little kid on TV and thinking it was really good."

"Of course. To a seven-year-old, it's high-class drama! There are so many deliciously awful scenes, and I can re-cite most of them word-for-word! We have to go!"

Hayley hesitated. "When does it start?"

Randy checked the ad. "Eight o'clock."

"But it's already five minutes past."

"The theatre is right across the street. They usually show fifteen minutes of previews, and I hear they have somebody introduce the movie. We have plenty of time . . . I will buy all the popcorn and candy you want!"

That was all Hayley needed to hear. Although she was still full from carbonara, she was incapable of refusing buttered movie popcorn and peanut M&M's. She turned and headed to the door as Randy bounded back to the of-fice to let Michelle know he was running out for a couple of hours.

After buying tickets at the booth outside, Hayley and Randy loaded up on concessions, each selecting a bucket-ful of popcorn, four different types of candy, and two big-gulp–size sodas. They strolled down the aisle to the fourth row from the screen, Randy's preferred choice of theatre seating. There was a smattering of people in the orchestra, but the balcony upstairs was closed off and empty. Hayley counted about six others besides them-selves.

A coming attraction of next month's camp-tastic clas-sic *Xanadu*, starring Olivia Newton-John post-*Grease*, a silly, bewildering musical with roller skates and leg-endary dancer Gene Kelly from the early 1980s. Randy excitedly leaned in and whispered into Hayley's ear, "We have to come back next month for that!"

Hayley nodded, but was wary about sitting through what looked like a disaster of a film.

A short, pudgy high school kid in a red vest huffed down to the front of the stage and spoke into a wireless microphone, spouting a few tidbits about the film that he seemed to be reading off a napkin, how Anne Bancroft was originally slated to star before Faye Dunaway ultimately took the role, how the film's subject, Joan Crawford, had been a fan of the woman portraying her, how Dunaway called Frank Sinatra for help when she lost her voice screaming "No more wire hangers!"

Hayley was almost through half her bucket of popcorn by the time the kid finally wrapped up, the chandelier lights went down, and the movie began unspooling on the giant screen.

Hayley instantly got into the spirit of the so-bad-it's-good nature of the picture as Joan Crawford scrubbed her arms and face with soap and boiling water and then plunged her entire head into a bowl of witch hazel and ice cubes to close the pores. Hayley leaned in to Randy. "I do this every morning before I leave for work at the *Island Times*."

Randy cracked a half smile but didn't respond. He shifted in his seat as if he was feeling unsettled. Hayley went back to watching the movie, and after a few more minutes, she noticed Randy continuing to squirm in his seat, trying to get himself in a more comfortable position.

"Are you okay?" Hayley whispered.

Randy gave her a half-nod, his eyes still fixed on the big screen. Finally, by the time Joan was throwing her recently adopted daughter Christina a lavish birthday celebration with ponies and carousels at her sprawling Beverly Hills estate, forcing her daughter to choose one gift while the rest would be donated to charity, Randy suddenly put his popcorn bucket down on the floor and hurried up the aisle and out the exit door.

Hayley assumed he was heading to the men's room, and so she stayed where she was, shoveled a fistful of popcorn in her mouth, and kept watching the movie. By the time Louis B. Mayer canceled Joan's contract at MGM after theatre owners labeled her "box office poison" and Joan devolved into a jaw-dropping epic meltdown by hacking down her prized rose garden with a pair of grossly oversized gardening shears and an ax, Hayley was really starting to worry about Randy. He had been gone quite a long time. She set her own popcorn bucket down on the floor, and walked up the aisle and out of the theatre to the concession stand, which was manned by the same pudgy kid who had read the film facts off a napkin prior to the show.

"Excuse me, did you happen to see my brother come out? I was sitting with him down front when you were introducing the movie," Hayley asked.

"Nope," the kid said impassively as he wiped down the glass counter with some Windex and a paper towel. "But I just came back from my break."

Hayley frowned, then marched down a hallway to the men's room. She rapped on the door. "Randy, are you in there? Are you okay?"

There was no answer.

Concerned, Hayley pushed open the door a crack and peered inside. "Randy?"

She heard a soft moan.

Hayley flung open the door all the way to see Randy writhing on the tiled floor next to the sink, his face a ghostly white, in agonizing pain. She raced in and knelt down beside him, gently placing a hand on his sweaty back. "Randy, what is it? What's wrong?"

He couldn't speak. He just winced and sweated, his arms folded over his torso, in obvious distress.

Hayley popped back up to her feet and flew out of the men's room, screaming at the kid behind the concession stand. "Call 911! Hurry!"

"W—what?" he sputtered, thoroughly befuddled.

"Just do it!" Hayley commanded, fearing on a gut level that the situation was critical and time was of the essence as the startled kid scrambled for his phone.

### Island Food & Spirits
BY HAYLEY POWELL

I have always loved pasta from as far back as I remember. I can easily crack open an old photo album and find baby pictures of me at two years old sitting in my high chair covered from head to toe with marinara sauce while shoving fistfuls of spaghetti noodles in my mouth.

For most of my formative years, into my teens in fact, my addiction to pasta was basically confined to mass quantities of boxed mac and cheese or canned Chef Boyardee, or if Mom was especially ambitious, pasta shells with a simple meat sauce. That all changed my sophomore year in high school when I was invited to New York with my best friend Liddy and her mother. Mrs. Crawford, or Celeste as she insisted I call her while in New York so she could feel like one of the girls and not so old, took us to her favorite Italian restaurant downtown in Little Italy for a late-night dinner following my first Broadway show, *Joseph and the Amazing Technicolor Dreamcoat* at the Minskoff Theatre. When people asked me what I thought of the show, I gave an honest answer. "It was nice, but it paled in comparison to the spaghetti carbonara that changed my life that night in Little Italy!"

We arrived at Capri Ristorante on Mulberry Street after eleven o'clock at night, which to me was the most glamorous thing in the world. At home we usually were done eating by five-thirty. As the maître d' led us to a table inside, I swooned at the aroma of garlic and spices that permeated the air. I actually bumped into a table, knocking over a man's wineglass because I was so distracted by waiters passing by, loaded up with plates of antipasto, focaccia bread, and every kind of pasta imaginable. But one dish delivered to a woman at the table next to us as we sat down caught my eye above all the others: Stringy spaghetti piled high on the plate and covered with a thick, rich, decadent, creamy white sauce. It was a work of art and I knew I just had to have it!

The time between pointing it out on the menu for the waiter to write down and him setting it down in front of me was interminable. I had to endure both Celeste and Liddy's maddening indecision on what they should order, the salad course, Celeste sending her white wine back because it tasted "vinegary," but finally, the main courses were delivered to our table, and I could barely contain my excitement as I snatched up my fork and began twirling the noodles around on it. I can recall in exquisite detail that smooth, silky Parmesan sauce with the pieces of crispy pancetta clinging to the noodles as I drew it closer to my wide-open mouth.

It was love at first bite.

And I have been hooked on spaghetti carbonara ever since.

The first thing I did when I got home was set out to re-create that magic that I had discovered in Little Italy. I thought it would be a cinch: Just follow a similar recipe I cut out of *People* magazine, but it turned out to be an ongoing process that required a lot of failures and a tremendous amount of patience.

For months, I remained frustrated that I was unable to produce a batch of spaghetti carbonara that even came close to my experience at Capri Ristorante. Finally, as I was about to run away from home and go to New York so I could personally grill the chef at Capri Ristorante on his secret ingredient, Liddy's mother Celeste suggested the cup of grated Parmesan I was using might possibly be my fatal flaw. A good carbonara doesn't rely on store-bought, processed cheese from a green container. No, fresh blocks of Parmesan you grate yourself was the key! That had to be it! My mother tried convincing me store-bought was just fine; the blocks in the gourmet food section were too expensive and unnecessary. She reminded me that Liddy's mother Celeste never had to worry about money, ever! But I was on a singular mission, so I took the money I made scooping ice cream that summer and bought a huge block of fresh Parmesan that would feed . . . well, our whole block.

That did the trick. Well, it got me closer, anyway. It took a lot of tinkering with my own recipe throughout the years, adding my own little twists along the way, but now I can finally say with confidence, my spaghetti carbonara is pretty darn special.

So special, in fact, it's usually the first dish I prepare whenever I want to impress a date. Of course, now I'm married, and my husband Bruce will eat just about anything I put in front of him, so I don't have to try so hard.

Things were quite different during the years between my first husband Danny and when I finally got it right with Bruce. There was one dinner date a few years back with—Well, I am going to withhold his name for privacy's sake, but let's just say he worked with animals (I can hear you all guessing as I write this!). I invited him over for dinner, hoping to impress him with my culinary skills, specifically my spaghetti carbonara. Of course, I knew food alone would not do the trick, so I also took the time to fix my hair, slap on some makeup, and do my nails.

The way he lit up when I answered the door immediately built up my confidence, and things just got better from there. The Manhattan cocktails also certainly helped, and he appeared quite happy as I led him out to the candlelit table on my outdoor deck. He excitedly tore into my homemade focaccia bread, moaning with pleasure as he dunked it in the plate of olive oil and balsamic vinegar in front of him and continued sipping his Manhattan.

Enough of the preshow. It was time for the main attraction. With great fanfare, I breezed outside from the kitchen and presented him with Hayley's Famous Spaghetti Carbonara.

He dug in with gusto, and I could tell from his euphoric expression, he was not disappointed. As I sat back to enjoy my resounding victory, silently raising my Manhattan to toast myself for a job well done, that's when things took a dark turn. He was on his third or fourth bite, shoveling it in so fast it was as if he had just been plucked from a desert island, half-starved, when I heard a loud crunching sound. That was followed by another in quick succession. My date sat back in his chair, a confused look on his face. He placed his napkin up close to his mouth and spit out something that looked plastic. He looked down at his napkin, dumbfounded, then back up at me.

"Are you missing something?" he asked.

"No, I don't think so. What do you mean?" I replied.

That's when he held his hand out and I could see one of my press-on nails in the middle of his palm. Oh no! I had been so focused on my cooking I didn't have time to visit the salon and have my nails done professionally that day, so at the last minute as I was preparing dinner, while hurrying to get ready, I went with my fallback position of just slipping on some press-ons. I looked down at my right hand. Three of them were now missing! Were they *all* in the pasta? I wasn't about to take any chances. I jumped up, grabbed his plate off the table, ran inside to the kitchen, and scraped the rest of his carbonara into the trash. Then I grabbed the pan off the stove and emptied what was left into the trash can as well.

I will admit, he was remarkably under-
standing, and he did hang in there with me
for quite some time after that ill-fated evening, although eventually we mutually agreed
that we were better off as just friends. I also
learned a valuable lesson. Never wear press-
on nails when cooking for a date. It sounds
like common sense, but I learned that one
the hard way.

Today, I'm sharing my nail-free spaghetti
carbonara recipe with you so you can impress
a loved one too with a memorable meal, as
well as one of my favorite cocktail recipes,
which will add pep to any special date night.

## HAYLEY'S SPAGHETTI CARBONARA

**INGREDIENTS**
1 pound of thin spaghetti
8 ounces pancetta or bacon, chopped
2 cloves garlic, minced
3 eggs
1 cup fresh grated Parmesan cheese
Fresh ground black pepper
Pinch of red pepper flakes (optional)

Whisk the eggs, Parmesan, and black pepper in a bowl and set aside.

In a large pan, cook your pancetta over medium heat until crisp, then remove from pan and add your minced garlic and red pepper flakes, if using. Cook for one minute. Add back pancetta.

Meanwhile, cook the pasta in salted water until al dente. Reserve 1 cup of the pasta water, then drain the pasta and add it to the pan with the pancetta and garlic using your tongs to combine. Remove pasta from heat and add the egg mixture. Mix well with tongs, adding your pasta water as needed.

Plate and add extra Parmesan if you like, then dive in and be prepared to pat yourself on the back for a job well done.

As you know by now, when I eat spaghetti carbonara, I always crave a Manhattan cocktail. I find it the perfect accompaniment to a hearty pasta meal. And Manhattan is also where I had my first taste of spaghetti carbonara that would change my life!

## MANHATTAN COCKTAIL

**INGREDIENTS:**
2 ounces bourbon (your choice)
1 ounce sweet vermouth
2 dashes aromatic bitters
Cherry for garnish

Combine your ingredients over ice in a shaker.
Shake and strain into a cocktail glass over ice, or
no ice if you prefer. Garnish with the cherry and
enjoy!

# Chapter 6

Hayley restlessly paced back and forth in the Bar Harbor Hospital waiting room, worried and not sure what she should do. Two paramedics had arrived at the Criterion Theatre within minutes, and carefully lifted Randy, who was moaning and in obvious pain, onto the gurney and into the back of the ambulance before whisking him off to the hospital. Hayley had followed closely behind them in her own car.

Once they wheeled him into the emergency room, the admitting nurse had to only take one brief look at him to assess the severity of his condition, and quickly got on the phone to call a doctor, which managed to send Hayley into even more of a state of panic. After what felt like an eternity, a doctor finally appeared, Dr. Robert Cormack, whom Hayley had met socially a few times. He was handsome, with dark hair that was graying at the temples, and kind eyes behind a pair of wire-rimmed glasses. He asked Randy a few questions, none of which Hayley could hear, and then he instructed a couple of orderlies to take him to exam room one pronto.

The orderlies rushed him through some swinging doors and he was gone from Hayley's view.

She decided against accosting Dr. Cormack for information because she didn't want to distract him from taking care of Randy. After a few seconds conferring with the admitting nurse, he too disappeared through the swinging doors. The waiting room at the hospital was typically quiet on this Monday night, one elderly man sitting in the corner, flipping through a *Game & Fish* magazine. Hayley tried to sit and wait, but she was a fidgety mess, worried about what was wrong with her brother. She decided to wander down to the cafeteria for a snack, but it was closed, so she got some coffee from a vending machine and continued her nervous pacing.

During her interminable wait for any news of his condition, she considered calling Sergio down in Brazil, but opted to at least hold off until she had something concrete to tell him, besides the fact that there was something seriously wrong with him. She knew Bruce was probably back in his hotel room in New York City after a long day covering the trial, but again, he would also want a medical update as to what was happening, and she had nothing to tell yet. So she took a deep breath and kept walking back and forth, back and forth, compiling a number of worst-case scenarios in her mind that only made the worry lines on her face deepen. Even the elderly man perusing his outdoor magazine glanced up a few times, annoyed by her constant pacing. But he chose not to complain about it and just tried to concentrate on the article he was reading.

Finally, Dr. Cormack emerged through the swinging doors and approached Hayley.

"Hi, Hayley, I'm Robert Cormack."

"Yes, Doctor. We've met. My husband Bruce and I sat next to you and your wife at the Woodworth-Gabbard wedding reception at the Harborside last summer."

"Of course," Dr. Cormack said with a knowing smile.

"How's my brother?"

"It's his gallbladder."

A wave of relief washed over Hayley. "Oh, thank God. That's not too serious, right? I mean, there is a simple operation to take care of that. I know lots of people who had gallbladder attacks and were back to work within a week."

"Normally, yes. But your brother's situation is a bit more complicated, so we cannot proceed with a typical laparoscopic surgery to remove it."

Hayley swallowed hard. "What do you mean by *complicated*?"

"Not only is he suffering from an inflamed gallbladder, but unfortunately he has also developed gallstone pancreatitis."

"Oh no . . ." she whispered.

"It's a bit like the age-old question: Which came first, the chicken or the egg? I am not sure if the inflammation of the gallbladder was caused by the pancreatitis, or vice versa. But they're both aggravating the other. All I know is we cannot operate until we get his pancreatitis under control."

"But he's going to be all right?"

"I'm not going to lie to you. It's a very dangerous time, and we are doing everything we can to curb the inflammation, but I'm optimistic he will come out the other side of this as good as new. In the meantime, we're giving him morphine to take care of the pain and keeping a close watch over him."

"Can I see him?"

Dr. Cormack shook his head. "He's out like a light right now, but I will tell the nurse to come and get you when he wakes up, okay?"

Hayley nodded, fighting to keep herself from dissolving into a puddle of tears. "Thank you, Doctor."

Dr. Cormack gave her a reassuring smile and then turned and disappeared back through the swinging doors.

Hayley felt so alone. The admitting nurse at the desk was on her computer, tapping her keys, oblivious to her presence, and when Hayley turned around to the elderly man in the corner who was watching her, he immediately averted his eyes back to his magazine article.

Hayley rummaged through her bag for her phone and tried calling Sergio. She expected to get his voice mail since he was all the way down in South America. She had no clue what the time difference was. To her surprise, a woman answered the phone.

"*Ola?*"

"Hello, hello, who is this?"

"*O que?*"

Hayley sighed, frustrated, not knowing any words in Brazilian Portuguese. "I need to speak to Sergio!"

The woman spoke rapidly in her native tongue, but it was all gibberish to Hayley.

Hayley spoke louder, as if increasing her volume

would make the woman understand what she was saying. "This is Sergio's sister-in-law, Hayley!"

"Hayley?"

Finally she was getting somewhere.

"I'm calling from the United States."

"Hayley?"

"Yes, Hayley!"

"*Esperar*," the woman said.

Hayley strongly suspected she was talking to Sergio's mother, with whom he was visiting.

There was a long pause and then another woman, who sounded much younger, got on the phone.

"Is this Hayley?"

"Yes, Randy's sister!"

"Hello! This is Fernanda, Sergio's cousin. We have all heard so many nice things about you."

"Thank you! Same here!" Hayley gushed, relieved to be communicating with someone who spoke English. "Fernanda, I need to speak to Sergio. Is he there?"

"No, I am sorry, he is scuba diving in Fernando de Noronha with his brother. He will be back *quarta-feira* . . . Wednesday."

Hayley's heart sank.

Wednesday seemed so far off.

"And there is no way to reach him? It's an emergency."

"No, there is no service where they went, that is why he did not bother to take his phone. He was afraid he might lose it. Hayley, what is wrong?"

Hayley debated whether or not she should say anything until she spoke to Sergio personally, but she had already worried his family with her call, and so she felt it was better to just be open and honest. After quickly filling in Fernanda on what Randy's doctor had told her, Fernanda promised to get word to Sergio just as soon as she possibly could. Hayley thanked her and hung up, and then went back to doing something she had always been terrible at.

Patiently waiting.

Whoever said patience was a virtue did not have a clue as to what he or she was talking about.

# Chapter 7

"I'm so sorry, Hayley, we did everything we could."

Hayley stared numbly at Dr. Cormack, confused.

"What did you say?"

"I'm afraid he's gone."

"Gone? What do you mean, gone? You said earlier he had a pretty good chance of getting on the other side of this." Tears began pouring down her cheeks. There was a lump in her throat and a knot in her stomach. This could not be happening.

"Excuse me, Mrs. Powell?"

She looked up at Dr. Cormack. She had heard him speak but didn't see his lips moving. He simply stared at her grimly, mustering up a sympathetic look on his face even though she could see in his eyes that having delivered the bad news, he was anxious to get back to his other patients, ones still living.

"Yes, Doctor?"

She waited for him to speak again but he just stood there.

"Excuse me, Mrs. Powell?"

The doctor's lips still had not moved.

Where was this disembodied voice coming from?

Hayley glanced around, but there was no one else in the waiting room. Not even the old man with the fishing magazine. She turned back to the doctor and was struck by how transparent he suddenly appeared, slowly dissolving, as if his whole being was suddenly vanishing from earth, like half the world's superheroes in that big *Avengers* movie.

"Mrs. Powell?"

Hayley's eyes popped open.

She had fallen asleep in a chair and was dreaming.

Leaning down in front of her was a young, dark-skinned man with black wavy hair in sea-foam green hospital scrubs. He had a hand gently placed on Hayley's right arm.

"I was told to come get you when your brother was awake," he said softly.

Hayley found his voice oddly soothing.

Maybe it was because he was telling her Randy was thankfully still alive.

Hayley fumbled for her bag on the floor and struggled to her feet. "Yes, thank you. Can you take me to him?"

"Of course," he said. "I'm Fredy, by the way. I've been looking after your brother."

"I appreciate it, Fredy. This all came so out of the blue. Randy has always been so healthy and full of vigor, I was just so shocked and scared when I walked into that bathroom at the movie theatre and saw him—"

"I understand. These things can creep up on you with no warning, and then your whole life can change. But from what I have heard, your brother's a fighter. I'm sure he's going to be just fine," Fredy said, smiling.

He had a beautiful smile.

It seemed to light up the already harsh hospital lighting in the hallway even more.

Fredy escorted Hayley down toward the last room on the left at the end of the hallway. She was not sure how she felt about Randy's room being so far away from the nurses' station, but trusted Fredy to keep an eye on him.

"I've never seen you around town before," Hayley commented.

"I'm relatively new to Bar Harbor. I showed up about a year ago."

"From where?"

"Honduras."

"Oh, that far! I thought you were going to say Bucksport or Belfast."

Fredy chuckled. "Actually, Honduras was where I was born and where most of my family still lives. But I've been in the States for about ten years, staying with relatives in North Carolina while I worked to get my nursing degree."

"What brought you all the way up here?"

"The weather."

Hayley laughed. Maine was hardly known as a tropical climate hotspot.

"What can I say? I like cold weather. Maybe it's because I grew up in Honduras with scorching temperatures, and wanted something different. I actually cried with joy when I experienced my first snowfall. It was magical."

"Well, then you're in the right place! You'll be in heaven come January when the snow gods dump twelve feet of it. Believe me, you won't be the only one crying!"

Fredy chuckled and led Hayley into the semiprivate room. Randy was in the bed on the far end next to the window. There was no curtain dividing the two beds, because the one closer to the door was currently empty.

Hayley was taken aback by the sight of Randy lying flat underneath a white sheet, hooked up to a morphine drip, his vitals refreshing on a digital monitor. It was disconcerting to see him like this, but at least he appeared stable. She clutched her bag and walked across the room. She hovered over him a moment before taking his hand that had a white patient ID bracelet on his wrist, and squeezed it until he opened his eyes and smiled up at her.

"How are you feeling?" Hayley gently asked.

"Happy . . ." he slurred, a big, goofy grin on his face as his eyes slowly glazed over.

At least the morphine was working.

She knew that under the heavy influence of drugs, he would not be feeling any serious kind of pain or be worried about his upcoming surgery.

Randy tried raising his head off the pillow in an effort to sit up, but he was just too weak and dropped it back down again.

Hayley asked, "Can I get you anything?"

"How about my nurse's phone number?" Randy drunkenly joked, trying to wink at her but only managing to blink both eyes at the same time.

Hayley stepped aside so Randy had a clear view of Nurse Fredy standing right behind her, his hands clasped behind his back, a knowing smirk on his face.

"Oh, hi," Randy cooed, lifting an arm up to give a little wave. "I didn't know you were still here."

"I am always watching," Fredy said with a playful wink.

Fredy managed to get his wink right. But to be fair, Nurse Fredy was sober and on duty, not pumped full of morphine and prone to unintelligible babbling.

"Hey, Hayley, come here," Randy garbled, motioning for Hayley to come closer. She leaned down close enough so he could whisper something in her ear.

"My nurse is, like, really cute, don't you think?" Randy announced so loudly Hayley had to withdraw from him before she busted an eardrum.

"A real stud-muffin," Hayley agreed, turning to smile at Nurse Fredy, who didn't seem at all embarrassed.

Randy gasped. "Muffin . . . Can you bring me a blueberry muffin from Jordan's for my breakfast?"

"Anything you want," Hayley promised.

"It did not take long for me to get tossed aside in favor of baked goods. What a harsh blow," Fredy joked.

Randy smiled vacantly at Fredy, not really comprehending what he was saying, and then looked up at Hayley with pleading eyes. "Ask him if he's single."

"We'll save that for next time, maybe after I have talked to your *husband* Sergio Alvares, Bar Harbor's chief of police. You remember him, don't you?"

"Who?" Randy asked with wide eyes before chortling, "I'm joking . . ."

"I haven't been able to reach him, but I left word with his family in Brazil to have him call me as soon as he possibly can."

"That's nice . . ." Randy mumbled before slowly drifting back to sleep.

"Randy?" Hayley asked, leaning closer.

He began to lightly snore.

Fredy stepped forward. "I think that's all you're going to get out of him tonight."

"Probably so," Hayley said. "Thank you for taking such good care of him, Fredy. I have such respect and admiration for what all you nurses do."

"Thank you, Hayley," Fredy said with a warm, genuine smile.

"How long will you be on duty tonight?"

"My shift ends at seven AM."

"Good, I'll be back before then. Do you like blueberry muffins? They also make a mouthwatering cinnamon apple, and the cranberry orange is pretty tasty too."

"You don't have to . . ."

"You're taking care of my brother. It's the least I can do."

"Cinnamon apple sounds pretty good."

"Done. Have a good night."

"You too."

He flashed that winning smile again.

It was spellbinding.

In fact, she noticed for the first time just how good-looking he was all around. The eyes, the smile, the obviously worked-out physique underneath those scrubs.

The scrubs just added to his attractiveness. She had always been a sucker for a man in uniform.

How could he have been in town for a whole year and she had not have heard about him from someone?

Was this guy devastatingly handsome, or was she imagining it because she was missing her own good-looking husband?

She sized up Nurse Fredy one more time before turning to leave.

No, he was definitely a ten.

Hayley hurried down the hall and saw that Nurse Tilly, the epitome of perky sweetness, had come on duty and was manning the nurses' station. She instantly noticed that Tilly's reliably friendly and kindhearted nature was nowhere to be seen as she approached, and it didn't take Hayley long to figure out why. Nurse Tilly was engaged in a heated exchange with Andrea Cho.

Andrea Cho was the bombastic, wildly outspoken sports reporter at the *Island Times*. Her husband Leonard was much more low-key, mild-mannered and soft-spoken, which bolstered the theory that opposites must surely attract. Hayley had tried to engage with them socially a few times after they first moved to Bar Harbor, but her efforts were rebuffed and so she simply stopped trying. When Hayley's boss Sal, editor-in-chief at the *Times*, hired Andrea to write the paper's sports column, Hayley was then forced to work with her, but much to her surprise, she actually grew to like Andrea over time.

As they got closer, Andrea had admitted to Hayley that she was always a shy person at first, at least until she got to know someone, a claim Hayley found totally unbelievable. But it appeared to be true, since they ultimately did become good friends. But Hayley had no illusions about Andrea's prickly personality, which at the moment was on full display at the second-floor nurses' station.

"The time you took to get my husband checked in was *unconscionable*," Andrea seethed.

"We are a little understaffed tonight," Nurse Tilly tried to explain, her face flushed. "And so I apologize—"

"An apology just won't cut it if my husband's condition worsens because of your incompetence," Andrea sniffed.

Nurse Tilly was on the verge of tears, but managed to hold it together. Her desk phone rang and she gratefully answered it. "Excuse me."

Andrea looked up and noticed Hayley. "Finally! Someone I actually I *like*!" Andrea marched around the nurses' station to give Hayley a brief hug. "Hayley, what are you doing here?"

"My brother has a gallbladder thing," Hayley said.

"Oh, that's nothing! He'll be fine!" Andrea pronounced confidently.

She decided not to fill Andrea in on the more serious complications, the pancreatitis, for fear she would burst out crying, like Nurse Tilly was trying so hard not to do at the moment as she sniffled while talking to someone on the phone.

Hayley directed her attention back to Andrea. "And you?"

"Oh, it's just Leonard again!" Andrea scoffed. "He's having another one of his spells!" She waved it off dismissively.

"What kind of spell?"

"Sometimes he gets light-headed and dizzy and stumbles around like some doddering old fool. The man is only forty-four years old, mind you. It's obviously all in his head! We went through this two months ago. I rushed him here and it turned out to be just an anxiety attack. I'm the one with the high-pressure job! I should be the one having anxiety attacks, not *him*!"

Hayley had never thought of covering high school football games as especially high-pressure.

"Is Bruce a hypochondriac like Leonard? I would guess so," Andrea said in all seriousness.

"Um, no, I don't think so," Hayley said.

"Well, you're lucky! It's so embarrassing to be married to someone who has anxiety attacks! Get a grip, be a man, I tell him, but when has he ever listened to what I say?" Andrea huffed. Her eyes flicked away from Hayley. "Wait, there's his doctor. I better go talk to her." Andrea turned to Nurse Tilly, who was just hanging up the phone, and pointed a finger at her, glowering. "I am not through with you."

Nurse Tilly's whole body seemed to spasm as Andrea stalked off toward the doctor, Dr. Webber, a pleasant woman in her late thirties with two little adorable twin boys who were in the third grade at Emerson Conners School.

"Have you figured out what's wrong with him, if anything?" Andrea mocked.

"Not yet. His blood pressure and heart rate are both disturbingly high, so I want to keep him overnight for some tests and to monitor him."

Andrea's mouth dropped open in surprise. "You mean he's not faking it?"

Dr. Webber shook her head. "No, give us some time and we will figure out what's going on with him. We'll know more in the morning."

Dr. Webber then moved on to the old man with the fishing magazine, who had unobtrusively reappeared in the waiting room. Apparently, she was also his wife's doctor. She knelt down and spoke to him in a low voice as Andrea spun back around and marched over to Hayley.

"High blood pressure? What could possibly cause Leonard to have high blood pressure?" she wondered out loud.

Hayley bit her tongue, fighting the urge to point out perhaps the root of the problem was an overbearing, exhausting wife.

No, best not to start a war this late at night.

# Chapter 8

"I'm starting to feel a tickle in my throat already!" Mona wailed as she rode up on the elevator to the second floor of Bar Harbor Hospital with Hayley and Liddy.

Liddy rolled her eyes. "Oh, Mona, relax. You're not going to catch something. Please. You've raised more kids than you'll find at Disney World. If that hasn't built up your immune system, nothing will!"

"I can almost see the germs in the air," Mona snapped, eyes blinking as if she was actually trying to spot them. "Hospitals are crawling with all kinds of diseases. I've known more than a few people who came in here for a simple run-of-the-mill procedure, like a bunion removal, and never left. They were just shipped straight to the morgue."

"Well, I'm sure Randy will appreciate you braving it to come see him this morning."

"He's always treated me right; keeps my beer mug full at his bar. I guess it's worth the risk," Mona sighed. "I haven't got much going on this morning anyway, since my sons are out hauling my lobster traps today. They insisted I take a personal day, maybe get my nails done."

Liddy erupted in laughter.

Mona waved her off. "I know, I know, that was their idea, not mine."

"What a waste of money. Honestly, have they seen how you gnaw at your fingers like a chipmunk on an acorn?" Liddy said.

The elevator dinged and the doors opened.

The floor was quiet.

Nurse Tilly was the lone person at the nurses' station and was busy at her computer. She didn't even look up as Hayley, Liddy, and Mona breezed past her and proceeded down the hall to Randy's hospital room.

The curtains were still drawn, but Randy seemed to be awake. His eyes were open and he was staring up at Gayle King delivering the early headlines on *CBS This Morning*.

"How are you feeling today?" Hayley asked, leaning over his bed and kissing him on the forehead.

Randy shrugged. "Fine . . ."

He mustered a smile but his eyes were glassy and unfocused. He swallowed a couple of times as if he was dehydrated.

"Do you need some water?" Hayley asked, picking up the plastic pitcher from the Formica table next to the bed.

Randy shook his head. Then noticed Mona and Liddy hovering in the doorway and smiled.

They both waved at him.

"Mona, you look like you're going to be sick," Randy said.

"No, I'm fine. I'm here to show you my support. I'm sure someone didn't breathe on me and give me some life-threatening disease when we first walked in that's getting worse by the minute," Mona moaned.

Hayley threw her a look and then turned back to Randy, setting the bag of muffins she had brought from Jordan's on the side table. "Has the doctor told you when they might be able to schedule your gallbladder surgery?"

He shook his head again.

"Has he been in here yet this morning?" Hayley asked.

"No, they did a bunch more tests earlier, like around six o'clock, so we're still waiting on the results," Randy said, shifting uncomfortably in his bed.

Unexpectedly, two orderlies wheeled someone in on a gurney and began preparing the free bed across from Randy.

"Looks like you're getting a roommate," Liddy said.

Nurse Fredy followed behind the orderlies, one of whom was turning down the bed as the other spoke softly to the large man lying prone on the gurney. Fredy smiled at all of them and was about to close the drape to give them some privacy when Hayley suddenly saw who it was the two orderlies were lifting up and lowering down on the bed.

"Chef Romeo?" Hayley gasped.

Romeo turned on his side toward Hayley as the orderlies got him settled, propping up his pillows and pulling the sheets up over his big belly. "Well, good morning, Hayley! What brings you here!"

"My brother Randy. Looks like you two will be sharing this room. What happened?"

"Oh, it's nothing!" Romeo scoffed.

Hayley noticed Nurse Fredy grimacing.

It was obviously not nothing.

Nurse Fredy bit his tongue as he pretended to be busy perusing Chef Romeo's chart.

The two orderlies finished and departed the room as Nurse Fredy took Romeo's blood pressure. "It's still a little high. I'll make sure the doctor gets you on something to bring it down some more."

Romeo shrugged. "Don't bother. I'll be out of here by lunchtime. I need to shop for some ingredients for tonight's special, osso buco à la Milanese. Yes, it will be as scrumptious as it sounds!"

Fredy smiled skeptically at Romeo.

Hayley could tell that Fredy knew Romeo would not be going anywhere, but chose the path of least resistance and refrained from arguing with him.

"Get some rest," Nurse Fredy ordered before turning to Randy and lighting up with a warm smile. "I'll be around with your breakfast soon, Randy."

"You're too good to me, Fredy," Randy cooed with a blast of renewed energy, blowing him a kiss.

Nurse Fredy chuckled and headed out.

"Would you stop flirting with your nurse?" Hayley sighed.

"It's the morphine . . . It's causing me to lose my inhibitions," Randy slurred.

"Oh, is that it?" Hayley asked dubiously, chuckling. "Remind me when he comes back to give him his muffin."

Romeo grabbed the TV remote from his bedside table. "Hey, do you mind if I switch over to the *Today Show*? I got a big crush on Savannah Guthrie."

"Knock yourself out," Randy said.

Romeo changed the TV channel, and then settled back in his bed as Hayley wandered over and folded her arms. "So are you going to tell me why you're here?"

Romeo frowned, not eager to discuss it, but it was obvious Hayley was going to pester him until he spilled the details. "Like I said, it's nothing. After you left yesterday, I started to feel some dull chest pains. I figured I was just still upset over Vic Spencer and his goon showing up and making threats the way they did. But the pains lasted through the night. I thought it was just indigestion, but early this morning, the pains got sharper and I felt a tightening in my chest . . ."

"You had a heart attack," Hayley gasped.

"A mild one. Nothing to worry about. I feel fine now, so if they think they're going to keep me here for longer than an hour or so, they're going to be in for a big surprise."

"You really should take this more seriously, Romeo," Hayley warned.

"Don't you worry your pretty little head about me, Hayley, I've had heart attacks before."

"Heart *attacks*? You mean you've had more than one?"

"Three, I think. Wait—no, four. I forgot about the one I had when I was in Sicily visiting relatives two summers ago."

"Romeo, you really should listen to your doctor. This mild attack could be a warning for a much bigger one ahead if you don't take care of yourself," Hayley said solemnly.

Romeo shrugged, unconcerned. Suddenly his face

flushed red and he slammed a meaty fist down on his over bed table. "Oh no! You have got to be kidding me!"

"What?" Hayley asked, staring up at the TV.

"Savannah's off today. I hate when she's not there. We might as well turn back to Gayle King!"

"Calm down. I can literally see your blood pressure rising on the monitor over there."

Fredy returned with Randy's breakfast tray. Soupy scrambled eggs. A packaged plain bagel. A box of Rice Krispies and a carton of low-fat milk. Of course, Randy acted as if Fredy was presenting him with a meal personally prepared by Chef Bobby Flay.

Once Fredy took the muffin Hayley had brought him and left, Romeo reached over and pulled back the dividing curtain just as Randy scooped up a generous forkful of eggs and took a bite.

"Don't bother eating that crap, it'll just make you sicker," Romeo cautioned. Then he grabbed the phone next to his bed and called the operator. "How the hell do I get an outside line? This is an emergency!"

Hayley, Liddy, Mona, and a loopy Randy all stared at him, curious to know what he was planning to do.

"I have muffins from Jordan's," Hayley offered, pointing to the bag on the side table.

"That won't cut it!" Chef Romeo scoffed as someone came on the line. "Betty, it's me. I want you to cook up some menu items: spaghetti and meatballs, some eggplant parm, a couple of pizzas. Make sure you include lots of garlic bread and get it over here to the hospital just as soon as you can!"

Mona perked up.

"I don't know, a lot! There are one, two, three, four, five of us—wait, bring enough food for the hospital staff too. Hell, bring enough for the whole floor. There are a lot of starving people in dire need of some decent food around here! Okay, hurry!"

Romeo slammed down the phone.

"I'm not sure that's going to go over well with the hospital administrators. They have certain rules," Hayley reminded him.

"Rules are made to broken," Romeo roared. "Trust me, they won't be complaining once they taste it!"

"Well, we should be going," Hayley said. "I have to get to the office."

"We'll be back later, Randy," Liddy said.

"Thank you for stopping by," Randy said softly.

As they walked toward the door, Hayley noticed that Mona had remained behind, still standing next to Randy's bed.

"You coming, Mona?"

"I think I'll stick around for a few more minutes," Mona said.

Liddy threw her hands up in the air. "But you hate hospitals. You just said—"

"I'm staying until the eggplant parm gets here. I love eggplant parm. You got a problem with that?" Mona growled.

Liddy turned to Hayley. "She has a point. Chef Romeo's meatballs are to die for."

Hayley sighed, then rummaged through her bag for her phone and made a quick call. "Hi, Sal, I'm going to be a little late this morning."

# Chapter 9

Mona moaned with blissful pleasure as she scarfed down Chef Romeo's eggplant Parmesan, eating out of a Styrofoam container with a plastic fork. Hayley enjoyed a couple of large, tasty meatballs on top of a pile of spaghetti and Romeo sat up in his bed with a folded-up slice of pizza in his hand and some tomato sauce dripping down his beard. Liddy had left to go pick up some beverages for them in the cafeteria and Randy, the only one not to partake in the feast, was having trouble keeping his eyes open as his morning dose of morphine pumped through his veins, sending him into a state of heavy sedation. Hayley thought that it was just as well. He shouldn't be eating Italian food in his condition anyway, and neither should Romeo, but there was no talking him out of it.

Liddy suddenly scooted back into the room with a tray of coffees in her hand and a plastic bag with a few cans of soda looped around her wrist. "Quick, hide the food! The doctor's coming right behind me!"

They all hurriedly closed the containers and shoved them back into the grocery bags that Romeo's head wait-ress Betty had delivered to them in, and looked around for some place to hide them.

"What do we do with them?" Hayley asked, panicked.

"Under the bed!" Romeo suggested.

Hayley and Mona dropped to their knees, sliding the bags of food under Chef Romeo's hospital bed, then sprang back up to their feet just as Dr. Cormack entered the room wearing a white coat and reading some numbers on his iPad. He was followed closely behind by Nurse Fredy.

The doctor stopped, looked up, surprised, and sniffed the air. "Why am I suddenly reminded of the time my wife and I took a second honeymoon to Italy and were enjoying an espresso in a charming piazza in Florence?"

No one dared to answer.

Nurse Fredy glanced around the room suspiciously. "I don't remember Italian being on today's lunch menu. I thought we were serving meat loaf."

Again, everyone kept their mouths firmly shut.

Dr. Cormack seemed to decide to let it go, and turned to address Randy. "I have some good news. Your inflam-mation of the pancreas has come down enough so we can prep you for surgery tomorrow morning."

Randy attempted a smile, which drooped, and nodded his head. He was still clearly out of it.

"Oh, what a relief," Hayley sighed.

"I suggest your visitors leave so you can get plenty of rest before tomorrow," Dr. Cormack said.

"Of course, Dr. Cormack, thank you," Hayley gushed,

so happy that they were finally moving ahead after such a touch-and-go period of helplessness.

"Don't you worry, Randy, I'll be leaving soon so I won't be here blathering on and keeping you awake," Romeo said. "You'll have the whole place to yourself."

Dr. Cormack turned to Romeo. "Where are you going?"

"I got a restaurant to run, doc," Romeo explained. "I'm just waiting for some tests to come back so you can release me and I can get on with my day."

"The tests did come back, and I'm afraid you're not going anywhere."

"Oh come on, doc, it was a mild heart attack!" Romeo roared.

"There was nothing mild about it. Your coronary artery was almost completely blocked. We're still assessing the damage to your heart, but it's already quite significant given your past history. I'm consulting with Dr. Grant, our heart surgeon, later on how to proceed, but you're probably looking at triple bypass surgery."

"You must be joking!" Romeo gasped, eyes bulging. "How long is that going to take?"

"We can operate in the next day or two, but you're looking at a week's recovery at a minimum, and even that may be overly optimistic."

"I just had my grand opening! This is a very critical time for any new business! I can't be out of commission for that long!" Romeo roared.

Dr. Cormack gave Romeo a stern look. "You can, if you want to live. You need to take this seriously, otherwise you may not be around to run your restaurant at all."

Dr. Cormack stepped forward to Randy's bed and smiled down at him. Randy drowsily smiled back. "Dr.

Kendall will be performing your laparoscopic surgery, Randy. He is going to stop by this afternoon to see you, okay?"

Randy nodded again, still grinning.

Hayley noticed her brother was looking past the doctor and his droopy eyes were more focused on the handsome Nurse Fredy hovering behind him.

"Don't worry, we'll be leaving now, Dr. Cormack," Hayley promised. "We're just going to say goodbye."

"Fine," Dr. Cormack said brusquely before turning around and marching out the door.

Nurse Fredy waited for him to be gone before turning and practically panting, "I smell garlic bread. That's my biggest weakness. Where is it?"

"Under the bed." Liddy pointed.

"Do you mind if I have a piece?" Fredy asked.

"No, no, help yourself," Romeo groaned, his mood souring. "This is a disaster. What am I going to do?"

"Don't worry, Romeo," Hayley said. "Your restaurant will survive. The important thing is for you to follow the doctor's orders and get better so you'll be as good as new."

"But you heard him. It might be weeks before I can go back to work. Who's going to run the place while I'm laid up? I'd put Betty in charge—she can handle the reservations and take care of the books and pop open a wine bottle—but she's a lousy cook! The poor girl can barely boil water!"

Fredy was foraging underneath Romeo's bed, finally locating the bag stuffed with buttery garlic bread. He grabbed a hunk and took a bite, closing his eyes and happily chewing.

"Hey, can you find the eggplant parm under there? I

want to take it with me and finish it later," Mona said, leaning down.

"Sure," Nurse Fredy answered as he pulled bags of food out.

Chef Romeo suddenly bolted up in his bed and pointed at Hayley. "How about you?"

"How about me what?"

"You can run the restaurant!"

Hayley burst out laughing.

"I'm dead serious, Hayley! You proved to me yesterday you're an excellent chef with your spaghetti carbonara. You can do this! I have complete faith in you!"

Hayley paused. "What do I know about running a restaurant?"

"Betty can help you. She can deal with the staff and the customers. You just oversee the orders in the kitchen."

"But I have a full-time job at the *Island Times*," Hayley said.

"Which you can do in your sleep!" Liddy piped in.

Hayley threw her an irritated look.

"I'll have Betty do all the shopping and ordering and prepping. You just have to show up right before we open and make sure the food gets out to the tables."

"I'm sorry, Romeo, I would really like to help you out, but I just don't have any experience—"

"You do, you just don't know it. This isn't rocket science. You know your way around a kitchen and can read a recipe. I'm begging you, Hayley, please, help me out here—"

"Oh, Hayley, I always thought you would be so good at something like this," Liddy cooed. "And you were just saying you were searching for a new challenge."

Hayley wanted to resist some more, but she knew the larger-than-life Chef Romeo would not stop putting pressure on her until she finally agreed.

"We can keep the restaurant closed a few days, just to give you a chance to get up to speed with Betty, and then you can reopen on Friday for the weekend rush."

They were all staring expectantly at Hayley, even Fredy, who was still devouring his big hunk of garlic bread.

A slight, almost inadvertent nod of her head sent Romeo whooping and hollering with relief and joy. He followed up with heartfelt thanks and promises that she would enjoy her new stint as his head chef, albeit temporarily.

And at least now she would not be spending the weekend at home feeling lonely without Bruce. That was a plus. Still, there was a nervous, gnawing feeling in the deep pit of her stomach. Would she rise to the challenge or would she spectacularly crash and burn?

Only time would tell.

# Chapter 10

Hayley suddenly stopped short in the doorway of the hospital room the following morning, startled to find Randy's bed empty. She glanced over at Romeo, who was sitting up in his own bed, pillows propped up behind him, casually staring at his phone in his hand.

"Where is he?"

Romeo looked up at her, befuddled. "Who?"

"My brother. Where did he go?"

"Oh, they came in about an hour ago and took him away."

"Who took him?"

Romeo shrugged. "I don't know, a couple of order-lies."

Hayley checked her watch. "But it's only eight-thirty. His surgery isn't scheduled until ten."

Romeo shrugged again. "What can I tell you?"

"Did he look like he was in any kind of distress when he left?"

Romeo, who by now was finally picking up on Hayley's rising anxiety, set his phone down on the over table and tried thinking back so he could tell her something to calm her down. "I actually wasn't paying much attention. I was watching Savannah Guthrie on the *Today Show*, who is back, thank God. He didn't seem upset or anything, just . . . you know, kind of out of it."

Hayley spun around to leave.

"Hey, can you spare a few minutes? I'd like to discuss a twist for my chicken piccata recipe you could roll out as a Friday night special."

"Not now," Hayley said brusquely as she marched back down the hall to the nurses' station where Tilly was manning the phones while Fredy was at a computer filling out some kind of report. "What happened to Randy? He's not in his room."

"He's in surgery," Fredy calmly explained.

Hayley checked her watch again. "The doctor told us ten o'clock. It's not even nine."

"There was an earlier opening in the operating room, and Dr. Kendall decided to take it. I'm sorry, didn't anyone call you?" Fredy asked, concerned.

"No, nobody called," Hayley said, her lips tightening.

Nurse Tilly gasped. "Oh, Fredy, you left a note for me to call Hayley and I plumb forgot. It's just been such a hectic morning." Then she turned to Hayley with pleading eyes. "Hayley, I'm so sorry, please forgive me."

Hayley knew how hard nurses worked, the stresses they faced on a daily basis, and how little things could easily fall through the cracks, so she was not going to make an issue out of it. But she had hoped to see Randy before he was wheeled off to the operating room, to squeeze his hand and tell him everything was going to be all right, and that she would be waiting for him when he got out.

But now those hopes had been dashed.

"It's okay, Tilly," she whispered.

She could tell by Tilly's gloomy face that she had not been convincing with her reassurance. But Hayley feared that if something went wrong, some unexpected complication developed, if for some reason he didn't make it as had happened during many routine surgeries, she had missed her chance to see her brother one last time. The possibility was admittedly remote, but it hung over her like a dark cloud.

Fredy circled around the nurses' station and put a comforting hand on Hayley's shoulder. "Why don't you head down to the cafeteria and get some coffee? It's going to be a while. But I promise I will let you know the minute it's over, so you can talk to the doctor."

"Thank you, Fredy," Hayley said.

His calm, soothing voice was doing wonders for her jangling nerves. She gratefully patted his hand that was still resting on her shoulder. Hayley then nodded at Tilly, who was on the phone but mouthed the words, "I'm so sorry," before wandering down to the cafeteria to buy a cup of coffee. Then she made her way back toward Randy's room, but as she approached, she decided she just was not up to the task of spending an extended period of time listening to Chef Romeo's bountiful ideas on how she should run his restaurant when it reopened on Friday, so instead she decided to wait out the surgery in the hospital waiting area. Just as she turned to head off in the opposite direction, she heard Romeo shouting.

Curious, Hayley made a beeline back to the room and walked in to find Romeo still sitting up in his bed as a middle-aged woman with big, teased-out black hair, too much makeup, and the longest ruby-red nails Hayley had ever seen, standing at the foot of the bed, wagging a finger at Romeo.

"You cannot talk to me like that! I will not allow it!" the woman snapped.

"All I said was I'm too tired to deal with you. Don't get your panties all in a twist," he screamed, waving his hand as if dismissing her.

"I hope I'm not interrupting," Hayley said quietly.

The woman huffily spun around and sized Hayley up with her big, brown angry eyes. "And who is *this*?"

"The gal who is going to save my business!" Romeo barked. "Hayley, this is Connie, a friend of mine."

"A *friend*? That's what you're going to go with? You can be so insulting and infuriating," Connie roared before whirling back toward Hayley and loudly announcing, "I'm Romeo's girlfriend! He just has a hard time *saying* it!"

Romeo winced.

Hayley was suddenly distracted by the amount of cleavage that was spilling out of Connie's tight pink blouse, a startling sight even for Hooters, let alone a small-town hospital.

Connie instantly noticed. "Jealous?"

"No . . . I—I was just—" Hayley fumbled.

"Connie, don't start!" Romeo yelled. "Now stop harassing everybody and get the hell out of here before you give me another heart attack!"

Connie bristled and glared at Hayley. "Why does she get to stay and I have to leave?"

"Because she's not here for me, she's here for her brother!" Romeo sighed.

Nurse Fredy appeared in the doorway. "Excuse me, could you please keep it down in here? We can hear you all the way down the hall and you're disturbing other patients who need to get their rest."

"What is this, a Nazi-run hospital? How dare you order me around like that!" Connie shrieked. She turned to Romeo. "I will be back when you're not so grumpy!"

And then she huffily pushed past Fredy and stormed out of the room.

Once she was gone and out of earshot, Fredy grinned slightly. "She seems like such a breath of fresh air."

And then he ambled off back down the hall to the nurses' station.

Romeo sighed heavily, covering his face with his meaty hands. "She can be so exasperating!"

"No relationship is perfect," Hayley observed.

Romeo quickly dropped his hands from his face. "Let me be clear. We are *not* a couple. She likes to think of herself as my girlfriend, but she's not. Not even close."

"Does she live in Bar Harbor?"

"She's just here for the summer from New York. When I moved here and decided to open my restaurant, she offered to be an investor. I needed capital for start-up costs so I happily accepted. But now the woman thinks she owns me! And I don't know how she got the misguided impression that I am even remotely interested in her as anything other than a strictly platonic business partner!"

Hayley eyed Romeo suspiciously.

She knew there was probably more to the story.

Romeo could see the skepticism on her face. "Okay, okay, so maybe I played up a little romantic interest in the beginning in order to secure the deal. But she's gotten way out of hand. She's become obsessed with me, like in that Glenn Close movie from the eighties. Seriously, I'm scared once they release me from the hospital I'll go home and find a bunny rabbit boiling on my stovetop!"

"She does appear slightly unhinged," Hayley said.

"I swear, if I had known she was going to be this possessive and clingy, I never would have taken her money!"

"Is she going to be around when I reopen your restaurant on Friday?" Hayley asked.

Romeo vigorously shook his head. "No, I promise. I will talk to her and make sure she doesn't try to stir up any kind of trouble while you're running things. Have you gotten in contact with Betty yet? She's waiting for your call."

"No, I am not doing anything until I am certain Randy is out of the woods and on the mend," Hayley said, nervously checking her watch one more time.

"I understand," Romeo said, finally lowering his voice and oozing a little care and compassion. "Family comes first."

# Chapter 11

Hayley jumped out of the shower, quickly dried off with a fresh white towel, then dashed naked down the hall to her bedroom to throw on some clothes that she had laid out on a chair the night before. She hurriedly buttoned up her blouse, shimmied into some panties and a pair of loose slacks, since she was still feeling full from gorging on some homemade pizza the night before, leaned down for a quick glance in her makeup mirror on her dresser before applying some light lipstick and rouge, and then fussed with her matted hair, hoping when it dried it wouldn't be too frizzy. After slipping on a pair of comfortable shoes and snatching up her phone and car keys, Hayley flew down the stairs.

As usual, she was running late.

Leroy, who had been snoozing on the couch, was instantly alerted by the pounding on the stairs and took a flying leap off the cushion, scampering ahead of Hayley to the kitchen, anticipating his long-awaited breakfast.

Hayley glanced up at the clock on the wall.

Seven-thirty-seven AM.

Her boss Sal knew she had planned to stop by the hospital to check on Randy before work, but he still had expected her to be at the office promptly at eight. She knew in her gut she was never going to make it in time.

After pouring some Kibbles 'n Bits for Leroy in one bowl and splashing a glass of water into the other, promising the panting, happy dog a heartier meal when she got home after work, Hayley was halfway out the door when her phone started buzzing.

It was Bruce calling on FaceTime.

"Oh no," Hayley moaned.

Bruce.

She had completely forgotten to call him last night before bed because she had been so exhausted. She tapped her phone and Bruce appeared. He was holding the phone close to his face, but she could still see lots of people milling about in a long corridor behind him.

"Bruce, I'm so sorry, I passed out last night before I had a chance to call—"

"No worries, babe. The judge just called a thirty-minute recess, so I've got some free time. How's Randy?"

"The surgery was successful," Hayley said, smiling.

"That's great," Bruce said, a palpable relief in his voice.

"I stayed late at the hospital waiting for him to wake up so I could see him, but the surgeon, Dr. Kendall, said he would be unconscious for a while and it would probably be best if I just came back this morning."

"Give him my best," Bruce said.

"I will. How's the trial going?"

"It's not looking too good for the defendant. The prosecution has dumped a mountain of evidence that's going to be pretty tough to argue against, but she's lawyered up with some very expensive sharks who are paid to muddy the waters, so there's reasonable doubt. So we shall see, I guess. But more importantly, do you miss me?"

"Every waking moment."

"What about when you're sleeping? Do you dream about me being next to you?"

"Sometimes. But not last night. Last night you were replaced by Chris Hemsworth," Hayley cracked.

"You could've just fibbed and told me *yes*."

"But then our marriage wouldn't be based on honesty."

"Okay, then, last night I dreamed I was in bed with Beyoncé!"

"Seriously?"

"No, actually I dreamed I was with you, but Beyoncé was playing in the background while we made out. I just wanted to get back at you for the Chris Hemsworth crack."

"Listen, I still have to get to the hospital, and Sal is going to blow a gasket if I show up too late for work."

"Go. I'll call again tonight when I get back to the hotel."

"Love you," Hayley said.

"Love you too, babe."

She ended the call, pocketed the phone, and scooted out the back door as Leroy noisily scarfed down his dry food, ignoring her harried departure.

Hayley was pulling into the hospital parking lot within five minutes, and racing up the elevator to the second floor, wheezing from all the frantic rushing around. The elevator dinged, the doors opened, and Hayley stepped out onto the second floor to discover absolute chaos. Lots of nurses and orderlies running around, phones ringing, a crippling tension in the air.

What on earth was happening?

There was no one manning the nurses' station she could ask, so she hastily marched down the hall toward Randy's room. She stopped dead in her tracks as she realized the center of whatever crisis was unfolding at the moment was inside his room!

Hayley's heart began pounding against her chest.

Her head was spinning and she was suddenly feeling light-headed.

A doctor, not one she recognized, emerged from the room conferring with two nurses Hayley had never seen before.

Where were Nurse Tilly and Nurse Fredy?

Hayley collected herself and began walking toward the doctor to ask what was going on when two orderlies wheeled a gurney out of the room.

A white sheet fully covered a body from head to toe.

Hayley thought in that instant she might faint and collapse to the floor. As they pushed the body on the gurney toward her, Hayley stepped into the middle of the hall, blocking their path, and cried, "What happened? What happened to Randy?"

The orderlies stared at her blankly.

Someone touched her arm.

She spun around to find Nurse Tilly.

Finally, someone she knew.

"It's not Randy," Tilly said reassuringly.

Her head was still spinning and she practically fell into Tilly's arms, surprising her. "Oh, thank God!"

Tilly gently pulled Hayley to the side of the hall so the orderlies could get by and whisk the body away.

Hayley steadied herself. "Then who is it?"

Tilly bowed her head solemnly. "Chef Romeo."

"*What?*" Hayley gasped.

Tilly nodded with deep, sorrowful eyes. "He died earlier this morning. Complications from his heart attack, according to the doctors."

"I can't believe it," Hayley whispered.

But deep down she could.

Romeo had been a ticking time bomb.

Especially with his bad eating habits and lack of exercise and sky-high blood pressure.

But still, it was a shock.

"Where's Randy?" Hayley asked.

"He's in there. A little groggy, but fine," Tilly promised.

"Thank you, Tilly."

Hayley abruptly turned and hustled into the room. Chef Romeo's bed had already been stripped and the dividing curtain was drawn so Randy didn't have to see them moving the body.

Hayley stepped around the curtain, a wave of relief washing over her as her eyes fell upon her brother, apparently sleeping, but thankfully alive and breathing.

As she made a move closer to his bed, he seemed to sense her presence and his eyes slowly opened.

Hayley touched his shoulder with her hand. "How are you doing, little brother?"

Randy slowly shook his head.

It seemed to take every ounce of strength he had.

That's when she noticed his eyes.

They were full of fear.

And his hands that were by his sides trembled.

"Randy, what's wrong?"

He opened his mouth to speak, but no words came out. His lips were dried and cracked.

Hayley poured him some water and held the plastic cup to his mouth. He took a few sips and then moistened his lips with his tongue.

Hayley set the water down and waited.

Finally, Randy, who was dopey from the morphine, managed to get some words out. "He—He—"

"He what?"

"He . . . *killed* him," Randy whispered, barely audible.

Hayley's mouth dropped open in shock. "Who?"

"A man. I—I saw a man kill Chef Romeo."

### Island Food & Spirits
BY HAYLEY POWELL

From the moment I first tasted spaghetti carbonara when I was a young girl, I quickly became convinced that I had to be born with deep roots in Italian heritage. My brother had a spinning globe in his bedroom, and I would spend hours studying all the cities in Italy where my ancestors might have hailed from, perhaps in the hustle and bustle of a major city like Rome or Milan, or a quiet fishing village like Portofino, or a Renaissance city such as Venice or Florence. Okay, maybe I didn't have the smooth olive skin of a true Mediterranean native, since my lily-white skin always burned something awful at the beach during the summer, but that didn't mean I wasn't a fiery Italian woman!

Actually, it did when I sent in a DNA sample to one of those genealogy sites and they dashed my hopes by sending me a report that clearly stated my ancestors were nearly 100 percent from England, Wales, and northwestern Europe, with a tiny smattering of Irish and Scottish. So much for me being the next Sophia Loren! Still, I was not about to ignore my connection to my favorite country, and so I embraced everything and anything Italian, especially the food.

Oh, the food . . .

I had decided at the age of sixteen that I was mature enough to travel abroad on my own and visit my adopted homeland for a whole summer. I wanted to live among the locals, learn the language and customs, and especially take a cooking class so I could improve my skills at making a wide array of scrumptious Italian dishes. Ever since that first bite of spaghetti carbonara in New York's Little Italy, I had been experimenting in our kitchen to decidedly mixed results. My dishes certainly wouldn't pass muster on the menu at a five-star restaurant, but my mother and brother liked them well enough, so I knew at least I didn't completely stink as an Italian chef.

Our high school did not have a summer student exchange program and the only foreign language classes they offered were French and German, so I knew I had to go big or go home. I had to go on a trip to Italy!

When I told my mother of my exciting plans, her first question was, "How are you going to pay for it?"

I had assumed my mother would jump at the chance to finance this once-in-a-lifetime educational opportunity to expand my horizons, but when I quietly suggested that, she didn't stop laughing for a full ten minutes.

I knew I probably had to come up with another solution.

That's where my BFFs, Liddy and Mona, came in.

It was Christmastime, mid-December, a full seven months before summer vacation, so I still had time to formulate a plan. After listening to me rant and rave about my mother so cruelly crushing my dreams of becoming a worldly, interesting person, a light bulb seemed to pop on over Liddy's head. Her latest beef with living in Bar Harbor during the winter was that there was no decent place to go to dinner on a date. Every restaurant in Bar Harbor was boarded up during the off-season, and if you drove twenty minutes off the island to Ellsworth . . . well, your best option was the takeout at Pizza Hut or the drive-through at McDonald's. How could a girl enjoy a romantic dinner with her boyfriend over a double cheeseburger and fries? That's when Mona came up with a perfect solution.

Since I was already practicing to be an Italian chef, Mona suggested we host a dinner and charge money just like the churches did almost every week with their baked bean suppers. We could invite high school couples to come and pay for a romantic, mouthwatering three-course Italian meal. Each course could be something I had been practicing on—simple Italian minestrone soup, antipasto tortellini salad, baked rigatoni with red sauce. All very filling and best of all, easy on the pocketbook.

The three of us were suddenly very excited about this new, exciting, out-of-the-box, money-making venture. If we limited our dinner to fifteen couples, thirty kids in all, and charged twenty dollars per couple, we could haul in an astronomical (for us, anyway) three hundred dollars! Almost the price of a coach fare abroad!

Liddy was assigned the task of selling tickets to prospective couples at school. Once a reservation was made and the money was paid, she would give them the instructions on what time to show up, and most importantly, she would swear them to total secrecy. Liddy devoured a lot of romance novels so she knew keeping everything top secret would make the lucky couples feel extra-special. Mona then brought up the one stumbling block none of us had thought about. Where would we host the event?

I should have kept my mouth shut, but of course when has that ever happened? I immediately volunteered my house. I knew my mother was going out of town the following weekend with Liddy's mom, Celeste, and Mona's mom, Jane. Every last week in December, they headed to the Portland Mall to do some after Christmas-sale shopping. They always left on a Friday and came back on Sunday morning. So Saturday was perfect for our Italian dinner! We jumped up and down excitedly. I was already picturing myself in a gondola, kissing a cute Italian boy I met while wandering around a museum, taking in the Renaissance paintings or that big, sexy statue of David.

The next week flew by. Liddy sold out in her first study hall. There were dozens more kids clamoring for tickets, but she was forced to shut it down once she reached capacity.

There were a lot of disappointed kids, but Liddy promised that if the night was a success, we would do it again the next time our parents left town!

After our mothers thankfully drove out of town early Friday morning and my brother Randy left for his friend Jerry's house for the weekend, Liddy and Mona got to work setting up extra card tables in the dining room and living room. I was busy in the kitchen, pulling out of the oven pan after pan of my cheesy, saucy baked rigatoni, along with foil-wrapped loaves of warmed garlic bread. By the time I finished preparing the soup and salad, the clock struck six, the appointed time Liddy had told our guests to arrive. We planned to have everyone out the door by eight so we could clean up and watch a movie on the VCR to celebrate a job well done.

Unfortunately, we had forgotten one inescapable fact about teenagers. When you tell one to keep a secret, by the end of the day, the whole school knows.

And that's exactly what happened.

Kids poured into my house, not thirty, but forty, fifty, sixty kids! Cars jammed the streets. I was terrified the neighbors would call the police to report an out-of-control party. Liddy had carelessly not written down the names of the kids who paid for dinner, so we had no idea who belonged and who was crashing. It was an unmitigated disaster! All the food was gone before we even finished serving the soup course, because kids didn't wait and just helped themselves. Somebody found paper plates in the cupboard and they formed a buffet line that started in the kitchen and stretched out the front door and down the street. Some kids plopped down on the floor and ate because there were no seats left. Others chowed down outside in the cold on the front lawn.

We had no control over the situation, and I thought to myself, *Could this get any worse?*

Well, as life has taught me, it can *always* get worse.

It was right about that time when I heard someone behind me say, "Reservation for three, please."

We froze in place because we all recognized that stern voice.

It was my mother.

And she wasn't alone.

She was flanked by Celeste and Jane.

Liddy and Mona both ran out the door in a panic, leaving me to deal with the aftermath.

I had nowhere to go.

I was already home.

The only thing I could think to do was slap a silly smile on my face and say in a bright, cheery voice, "Oh, you're home early! Would you like some rigatoni with red sauce?"

My mother quietly explained that a snow-storm was in the forecast, and so they had cut their trip short to get home safely.

It didn't take long for the crowd to clear out. Everybody could see my mother's face reddening, ready to explode. Celeste and Jane set off to track down their own delinquent daughters and I was left to explain myself.

Suffice it to say, we were ordered to return

all the money, which left us in the hole for a hundred bucks for all the food we bought, which we were told we would pay back with hard labor over the next few months, starting with me helping my uncle insulate our attic on the night of our winter formal.

There was somewhat of a happy ending.

After everyone left that night and my mother ordered me to my room, I snuck out later to go to the bathroom and could hear my mother downstairs talking on the phone with Jane. She had stumbled across a little tortellini pasta salad and some rigatoni that had not been devoured by the starving kids and ate it as a late-night snack. She was raving about how delicious it tasted, what an impressive cook I was, and how I might have a promising future as a real Italian chef. I knew it wasn't just her favorite brandy coffee she was washing it down with—I knew she really meant it. My mother was proud of me.

But that still didn't get me out of helping my uncle insulate the attic.

## Mom's Favorite Brandy Coffee

**Ingredients:**
1 ounce crème de cacao
1 ounce brandy
1 ounce freshly brewed espresso
1 ounce cream
1 cup crushed ice

Place all your ingredients in a shaker and shake until well mixed, strain in a cocktail glass and serve.


My antipasto tortellini salad is insanely delicious and absolutely customizable to your own taste. I have been making it since I was sixteen years old, and I have made it with every kind of cheese and meats imaginable. I love them all, but this is one of my favorite combinations. By all means, feel free to add other ingredients or take away any of these depending on you and your family's tastes and preferences. This is really a great salad to make and call it your own!

### ANTIPASTO TORTELLINI SALAD

**INGREDIENTS:**
16 ounces fresh or frozen cheese tortellini
1 pint grape tomatoes halved
2 cups cubed hard salami
2 cups cubed provolone cheese
1 cup chopped red onions
½ cup green/black olives
1 cup peperoncini peppers
1 cup mozzarella pearls

### ITALIAN DRESSING

**INGREDIENTS:**
½ cup olive oil
¼ cup red wine vinegar
2 cloves garlic, minced
1 teaspoon Italian seasoning
Pinch of red pepper flakes
Kosher salt to taste

Add all of your dressing ingredients in a mason jar and shake, shake, shake until well blended. Pour over your salad, mix gently to combine all of the ingredients and refrigerate until ready to wow your guests!

# Chapter 12

Sergeant Vanessa Herrold certainly knew how to command a room, even a small semiprivate one at Bar Harbor Hospital. When she had first arrived, Hayley was out by the nurses' station and had witnessed the orderlies and nurses almost snap to attention as the stone-faced, dead serious sergeant marched with military precision down the hall after getting off the elevator, trailed by Officer Donnie, who almost had to jog to keep up with her.

She stopped to address Tilly, who was back manning the phones. "Who called 911?"

Hayley raised her hand. "I did."

Officer Donnie snickered and Herrold spun around to glare at him. "What's so funny?"

Donnie suddenly felt awkward and self-conscious and sputtered, "N-Nothing . . . It's just that Hayley has a long history of getting involved when there has been a purported crime . . ." He cleared his throat and glanced over at Hayley with pleading eyes. "Isn't that right, Hayley?"

Hayley had no intention of helping him out with his temporary commanding officer.

Sergeant Herrold's eyes narrowed. "And you find interfering with law enforcement amusing, do you?"

Donnie vigorously shook his head. "No, I was just trying to explain—"

Herrold whipped back around, ignoring him and focused her big, dead-serious brown eyes directly on Hayley. "You say you saw someone murdered?"

"No, not me," Hayley said. "My brother."

"Where is he?"

"Down the hall."

"Well, what are we standing around here for? Let's go hear what he has to say. Come on, Donnie," Herrold ordered as she took off down the hall with Officer Donnie scampering after her like a loyal lapdog.

Tilly snorted. "Rumor has it from a few well-placed sources at the police department that Sergeant Herrold is not what you would call, warm and fuzzy."

"It's not just a rumor. We have the proof right here in front of us," Hayley lamented before scurrying after them.

Randy had told her that Sergio recently hired a new sergeant out of New Hampshire. She had a reputation of being tough and no-nonsense, her record was impeccable, and the Manchester police chief had written an effusive, glowing recommendation. She was just out of a bad marriage and wanted a fresh start, so she applied for a new position in Sergio's department when she read online about an opening.

Randy had not been impressed by her cold demeanor

and distant personality when Sergio invited her over to dinner on her first night in town before starting work the following morning. But Sergio appeared to be impressed by her strictly by-the-book way of doing things. He even had the confidence in her to put her in charge when he left for Brazil.

Officer Donnie, who was the usual pick to run things when Sergio was out of town, didn't seem to mind too much that he was tossed aside for the more imposing Sergeant Herrold. In fact, Hayley observed when she entered the room, Officer Donnie seemed downright infatuated with his new immediate superior. He stared at her with adoring eyes and seemed to hang on her every word. Hayley could understand why. Even in a loose-fitting police uniform, she could see Herrold was physically fit, like one of those celebrity trainers such as Jackie Warner, who Hayley used to watch working out on TV while eating a box of Girl Scout cookies. Herrold's silky, raven hair was pulled back into a bun, accentuating her pretty oval-shaped face. Her olive skin suggested she might be Greek or Italian. But there was no makeup, no will or desire to gussy herself up, which she probably considered unprofessional.

Herrold stood by Randy's bedside with Donnie shadowing her, practically on top of her. She stared down at Randy and offered him a tight but friendly smile, saying sweetly, "So tell me what happened, Randy."

The smile struck Hayley as decidedly uncharacteristic and forced, but then again, Sergeant Herrold was certainly aware she was talking to her boss's husband.

"Last night I woke up, and I saw a man standing over Chef Romeo's bed, and he was injecting something into one of the tubes Romeo was hooked up to," Randy explained, a little more clear-eyed now than when Hayley had first arrived at the hospital.

"What time was this?" Herrold asked, scribbling notes down on a pad of paper with a pen.

Randy shrugged. "I don't know . . . Maybe three or four in the morning . . . I can't be sure . . . I was still pretty much out of it from my operation."

Herrold frowned. "I see. Did you know this man? Had you ever seen him here before?"

"I really couldn't see his face. He was wearing one of those medical masks," Randy said softly.

Herrold cocked an eyebrow. "Are you sure it wasn't just a nurse administering some pain medication?"

Randy shook his head. "No. I know all the nurses on this floor who are on duty during the night shift. This guy wasn't one of them."

"But you said you couldn't see his face because of the mask," Herrold said.

"Yes, but there is only one male nurse on this floor, Fredy, and it definitely was *not* him. This guy was much taller and beefier."

Herrold glanced at Officer Donnie skeptically. "I see." She was trying to be careful not to be dismissive of Randy's story, but she was obviously finding that a challenge.

"Wait, there's more," Randy said, struggling to sit up in bed, but still too weak. He laid his head back down on the pillow. "While the guy was using the syringe to inject something in the tube, Chef Romeo suddenly woke up and asked what he was doing. The guy stopped what he was doing and clamped a hand over his mouth, and held him down until whatever he put in the tube took effect and Romeo stopped struggling."

"Did you try and call for help?" Herrold asked.

"Yes. But I had cotton mouth and was having trouble speaking, and I was feeling so weak. I tried to reach for the call button to get someone to come to the room, but I couldn't reach it. I remember falling out of bed, then all these bells and whistles started going off because Romeo was going into cardiac arrest and the guy took off. I must have passed out again, because the next thing I knew, I was back in bed and they were rolling Romeo out with a white sheet covering him."

Herrold stopped writing on her pad and tapped the top of her pen against her chin a few times. "You were under heavy sedation. Is it possible all this might have just been a bad dream?"

"Yes, I'm sure that's it," Officer Donnie agreed. "I remember my dreams all the time. In fact, it's a funny thing, last night I dreamed about you, Vanessa—"

"Not now, Donnie," Herrold snapped. "And can you please stop crowding me?"

"Oh, of course," Donnie said, looking wounded as he took a giant step back, away from her.

"I know what I saw," Randy said firmly. "It was *not* a dream."

"I want you to know, Randy, that I will take this seriously," Herrold assured him.

Her words sounded right, but Hayley didn't hear much conviction in them. It was almost as if Herrold was just humoring him, already convinced that he had been hallucinating the whole event.

"Now you get some rest. I'll talk to the doctor, see what he says about the cause of death, if Romeo's heart just gave out, or if there's something more sinister going on, and we'll take it from there, okay?"

Randy nodded, a dubious look on his face.

"What a shame. Chef Romeo opens a brand-new restaurant in town, and then he dies before he even has the chance to get it off the ground," Herrold remarked.

"He was doing great business right out of the gate. His food is delicious," Hayley piped in.

Herrold gazed over at Hayley as if noticing her in the room for the first time. "Huh. Well, I probably was never going to dine there because I can't stand Italian food."

How odd, because despite her name, she looked so Mediterranean, as if she had just stepped off a fishing boat in Portofino.

"You know, I hate Italian food too," Donnie blurted out. "It's probably because the only thing my ex-girlfriend could make was spaghetti and meatballs, which tasted awful, by the way. How do you screw up spaghetti and meatballs? Still, what a coincidence we both don't like Italian food!"

Herrold rolled her eyes, annoyed by Donnie's fumbled attempts to prove the two of them were somehow meant for each other. "Come on, Donnie."

Herrold turned to go. Donnie raced to catch up with her, and got so close he walked right up on the back of her shoe, causing it to come off her foot, giving her a flat tire. She stopped in the doorway, bent down to slip her shoe back on, then sprang back up, eyes leveled at Donnie. "Let's pretend we still have to socially distance and you stay six feet away from me!"

She stormed out.

Donnie tried not to look too devastated as he hastily followed behind her.

Randy slowly turned his head toward Hayley. "She doesn't believe me. She's not going to do anything."

"Let's just wait and see," Hayley said, moving closer to the bed. "It's her job."

"I wish Sergio was here," Randy lamented. He then reached out and grabbed Hayley's hand and squeezed it. "Will you do it?"

"Will I do what?"

"Find out who came in here last night and killed Chef Romeo! I did not dream this, Hayley! He was murdered!"

She could see him starting to stress out.

His blood pressure and heart rate began rising on the digital monitor next to the bed.

She just needed to calm her brother down, and she knew there was only one way to do that.

"Yes, Randy, I will find whoever did this. I promise."

She just hoped it was a promise she could keep.

# Chapter 13

"He said what?" Sal hollered through the phone after Hayley had stepped outside Randy's room to call her boss and let him know what was happening, and why she would be late to the office.

"He says he saw a man hold Chef Romeo down and inject something into one of his tubes right before he suffered a fatal heart attack."

"What do the doctors say?"

"Well, obviously the coroner is going to have to conduct an autopsy to determine the cause of death, but Randy has already reported what he saw to the police."

"Of course Bruce would have to be out of town when something like this comes up! Okay, Hayley, don't worry about coming in today. I want you to stick around the hospital and see what you can find out. You're always butting into police business all the time anyway, you might as well be the one to fill in for Bruce and cover this story while he's gone."

She opened her mouth to protest his assessment that she was always butting in, but realized that he was, for the most part, 100 percent correct, so she declined further comment. "Okay, Sal."

"One more thing," Sal said. "There is a rumor running around town that you're taking over Chef Romeo's restaurant. How the hell are you going to juggle your full-time job here at the *Times* and run a restaurant?"

"I'm not," Hayley explained. "I only agreed to help Romeo out when he was on the mend from his heart attack. Now that he's sadly passed, there is no point in me even taking over temporarily. I'm sure there will be some provision in his will as to what to do with his business."

"Okay, good. I don't want you stretched too thin. You have very important responsibilities here at the paper that need to be taken care of," Sal warned. "By the way, if you do swing by here at some point today, could you bring me a half dozen of those cream-filled glazed doughnuts from the Cookie Crumble Bakery?"

Somehow tending to her boss's insatiable sweet tooth did not strike her as a serious responsibility.

But as usual, Hayley bit her tongue and replied, "Of course, Sal."

Hayley ended the call, stuffed her phone in her bag, and wandered down to the nurses' station where Nurse Tilly was on her feet, phone clamped to her ear, in obvious distress. "Well, I don't know what to tell you, but I can't cover this whole floor all by myself. Can you please spare one person to come up here and help me?" Tilly wailed. "I told you, I don't know where he is! I've got three call buttons buzzing right now and nobody up here but me to answer them!"

Tilly slammed down the phone, rushed out from behind the circular desk in a state of panic, nearly mowing down Hayley as she raced to see what all the patients needed.

Hayley headed in the opposite direction toward the bank of elevators. She was starving and planned on buying a Danish and coffee down in the cafeteria. When she returned about ten minutes later, the Danish already eaten and carrying her second cup of black coffee, Tilly had returned to her station and appeared a little less frazzled, although still slightly annoyed.

"Busy morning, I see," Hayley said, sipping her coffee.

"It's been nonstop since last night, one thing after another, and one of our nurses decides to pull a disappearing act, leaving me here all by myself! Anyone who knows me can tell you, I have *never* dealt well with too much pressure!"

If that was true, entering the nursing profession seemed an odd career path, in Hayley's opinion, which she kept to herself.

"Who disappeared?" Hayley asked.

"The new guy, the good-looking one," Tilly said brusquely as she shuffled some papers at her desk.

"Fredy?"

"Yes," Tilly sighed.

"Could he just be taking his break?"

"No, he started at midnight and would have taken his break long before this. His shift is scheduled to be over in less than an hour. I have no clue what could have happened to him!"

The elevator dinged and the doors opened. A nurse, short and stout, late fifties, no-nonsense, hustled out, shaking her head as she approached the nurses' station. "I searched the whole hospital. I can't find him anywhere."

"I've been trying his phone," Tilly said. "It keeps going directly to voice mail."

The stout nurse stopped and grabbed the desk to steady herself, out of breath. "I just can't imagine where he went. This is so unlike him. He always seemed so conscientious and responsible."

"And the patients adore him," Tilly said. "Oh, well, I guess you never really know about someone."

"Well, I am not going to waste any more time trying to figure out why he left," the stout nurse snorted. "What can I do to help pick up the slack?"

"The urinary-tract infection in two-thirteen slept through breakfast and they took her tray away and now she's hungry, and the hip replacement in two-nineteen is going to need help with going to the toilet," Nurse Tilly said.

"I'm on it," the stout nurse said before waddling off.

Hayley finished her coffee and held up her paper cup. "Is there a trash can around here?"

Without looking up, Tilly shot out a hand. "I'll take it."

Hayley handed it to her, and Tilly dumped it in a can underneath the desk.

"Thank you," Hayley said.

Tilly didn't respond.

Her eyes were glued to a medical chart.

"Tilly, I know you're crazy busy, but I was just wondering: Were you on duty last night when Chef Romeo died?"

Tilly popped her head up. "What?"

"I was just wondering—"

"I heard the question. Why do you want to know? Are you accusing me of not acting fast enough to save him after he went into cardiac arrest?"

Hayley threw up her hands. "No, of course not!"

"Good, because this is a hospital. Things like that happen all the time," she said, flustered.

Hayley studied Tilly.

She noticed her hands were trembling as she closed the file folder and set it aside.

"Tilly, I'm sorry, I did not mean to upset you."

"I'm not upset."

She was clearly upset.

"Besides, I was not even here when it happened," Tilly said. "Fredy was supposed to be here, but apparently he wasn't. So if they're going to blame anyone, they should blame *him*!"

"Were you on your break?"

The question seemed to startle Tilly.

She paused, not sure how to answer the question.

A very simple question.

And that's when poor Nurse Tilly began to visibly melt down. "It's none of your business what I was doing! Now if you don't mind, I have a job to do, and I don't have time to be hanging around here talking to you!"

Desperate to get away from Hayley, Tilly bolted out from behind the nurses' station and fled down the hall to the break room, violently slamming the door behind her, leaving no one but Hayley standing at the nurses' station, puzzled as to what she had said or done to upset Nurse Tilly so much.

Her erratic and suspicious behavior was suddenly raising a very big red flag.

# Chapter 14

"But we have to open tonight, in honor of Romeo's memory!" Kelton, Romeo's sous-chef, cried, pumping a fist in the air.

The rest of Romeo's staff, consisting of head waitress Betty, another waiter, Devon, who was a student from the College of the Atlantic, and one busboy, Lenny, the big kid who rarely said a word, all murmured in agreement.

When Hayley had gathered the staff at the restaurant, she never in a million years expected the restaurant to open on the same day that its owner had tragically died. She had simply called the meeting to promise that she would try her best to make sure that whoever was executor of Romeo's will would fully pay the staff what they were owed out of the estate, assuming the restaurant would remain closed.

But now she had a potential mutiny on her hands.

Hayley nodded, acknowledging their desire, and spoke slowly and deliberately. "I think it would be a moving tribute to open the doors and invite customers in to celebrate the life and food of Chef Romeo, but I'm not sure practically how we would do that."

"By moving ahead with business as usual," Kelton explained matter-of-factly. "We just do our jobs like it's any other night. I know how to prepare his food. Chef Romeo personally trained me; he had faith in you to run things while he was in the hospital; we have Betty and Devon to serve the customers and Lenny to bus the tables. We can do this."

Kelton had been a fry cook over at Jordan's Restaurant for over a decade, but after years of watching the Food Network, he knew it was time to up his game in the kitchen, exercise some creativity, challenge himself more than just slapping burgers on the grill and frying onion rings every day. Chef Romeo had finally given him that opportunity when he invited Kelton to come work for him.

Hayley certainly understood their passion during this time of grief, but she was hesitant to move forward. "Look, I think it's a great idea, I really do, but I'm not sure tonight is the right time. Maybe after a couple of weeks, once we know who the restaurant now belongs to, if there is even a will, we can plan some kind of memorial here at the restaurant and serve all of Romeo's specialties . . ."

"That may be too late. You know how things go, especially if he didn't write a will. The bank could come in and take over this place, and then we'll never have the chance to do it," Betty argued.

"But is opening tonight even legal, given the circumstances now?" Hayley wondered aloud.

"Who cares? What are they going to do, arrest us? I say we go for it," Devon declared. "Let's give Romeo the befitting send-off that he so richly deserves, one that matches his larger-than-life personality!"

"I don't want to be a Debbie Downer, but we're supposed to open in an hour. How will people even know to come? I'm sure they all heard the news about Romeo by now."

"I checked the reservations. We're fully booked and nobody has called to cancel. We've only gotten a few messages inquiring if we were going to open tonight, given the circumstances. I can call them back and say yes, dinner is still on."

Hayley's mind reeled.

She was not sure what she should do.

Finally, Lenny, the quiet busboy, spoke up, surprising everyone. "It's what Chef Romeo would have wanted."

Hayley knew there was no pushing back on that one, because the kid was right. Chef Romeo desperately wanted his restaurant still open when he was in the hospital recovering from a heart attack, so there was no reason to doubt he would want it open even now in the event of his untimely death.

"Okay . . ." Hayley sighed.

The staff cheered.

"Then let's get to work!" Betty cried.

By the time Hayley opened the doors to the restaurant forty-five minutes later, there was already a crowd of hungry customers milling around outside. They poured in and filled up all the tables, a few stopping to silently mourn for a few moments in front of the portrait of Chef

Romeo Hayley had found in his office and hung over the fireplace in the main dining room before the start of the dinner rush.

More cars pulled into the gravel parking lot, and Hayley knew by five-fifteen she was going to need more help. It was time to call in reinforcements. She phoned Liddy and Mona to hurry over and help. Mona was bored at home alone, so she was easy to convince, but Liddy was a harder sell because she was on her way to a women's-only Yin-restorative yoga class. In the end, Hayley knew they would both show up for her, and they did.

She assigned Liddy the hostess role, in charge of reservations and seating customers. Betty and Devon were overwhelmed, and so Hayley had Mona take a few tables as a waitress. She knew it was a risk. Mona was not what you would call a people person, but Hayley had little choice. Liddy was chipper and friendlier, or at least she could fake it better, so she needed her face to be the first one customers saw as they entered the restaurant.

True to form, Mona had barely been at it for ten minutes before she was flagged down by a man with spaghetti sauce all over his face. "Could I have another napkin, please?"

"Maybe if you ate more like a human being instead of a wild animal, you wouldn't need so much paper to wipe your face! Think of all those poor, wasted trees! Can't you see I'm busy?"

Hayley instantly marched over and pulled Mona aside. "Mona, you cannot talk to the customers like that!"

"What do you mean?"

"You were unnecessarily rude to that gentleman!"

Mona glanced over at him, genuinely confused. "Who? You mean Harry Bunker? Oh, please." She yelled over in the man's direction. "He loves it when I abuse him! Don't you, Harry?"

He smiled and waved at Mona before wiping the marinara sauce off his face with the sleeve of his shirt.

Hayley stared at Mona, dumbfounded.

"Excuse me," said a woman sitting at a table behind them. "Could I get another glass of Merlot?"

Mona folded her arms. "Really, Darla? That'll be your third one already and you haven't even been served your appetizer yet. Are you that anxious to get a second DUI?"

Hayley held her breath.

But Darla just laughed and handed the empty wineglass to Mona, who then turned back to Hayley and barked, "Now if you're done complaining about my obviously winning personality, I have food to serve!"

Mona turned out to be right.

The ruder she got, the more the customers loved it.

It was part of her shtick.

She was a novelty.

A couple of tables even requested her as their server.

And so Hayley left her alone.

She made her way over to the hostess station, where a mob of people crowded the area by the door with dozens more still waiting outside.

On her iPad, Liddy was perusing a diagram of the restaurant with all its tables. She noticed Hayley standing beside her. "We were already overbooked, and now we have a bunch of walk-ins. I told them it was going to be at least an hour and a half on the waiting list, but no one's leaving to go somewhere else."

"I wish Chef Romeo was here to see his restaurant so busy," Hayley said wistfully.

"I'm sure he knows," Liddy said with a sorrowful smile.

The rest of the evening was a blur.

By the time the last customers left around ten-thirty after polishing off their homemade tiramisu, Hayley's feet were throbbing, and she finally plopped down in a chair to catch her breath. Kelton ambled out of the kitchen, Lenny wiped down the last of the tables, Liddy cashed out the register, and Mona popped open a bottle of Chianti as she, Betty, and Devon pooled their tips.

"What a night," Hayley said, declining the glass of wine Mona was trying to hand her, too exhausted to drink. "Chef Romeo would be very proud of all of you."

"Thank you for allowing us to do this tonight," Betty said to Hayley. "We all appreciate it."

"It just goes to show that Chef Romeo was right about this place. It was going to be a huge hit in town," Kelton said, smiling.

"Well, we can't stop now," Liddy said offhandedly as she studied her iPad screen.

"No, this was a onetime thing," Hayley reminded her. "What we did tonight was in honor of Chef Romeo, but I'm afraid the future of his restaurant is out of our hands."

Liddy set her iPad down on a checkered tablecloth. "We are fully booked for tomorrow night. What do we say to all those people who could not get in tonight and want to come and eat and pay their respects tomorrow?"

"Hayley, we made more tips tonight than the last three weeks combined. I have rent due and Devon needs to pay for his tuition. We can't stop now. At least until someone tells us to."

She was hopelessly outnumbered.

Even her BFFs were standing firm with the staff.

Although neither would probably admit it, they had a lot of fun tonight. And why should she be responsible for laying off Kelton, Betty, Devon, and Lenny, devastating their finances as long as there was a way for them to keep making money, at least in the short term?

It was against her better judgment.

But it wouldn't be the first time Hayley bucked her judgment.

And it certainly would not be the last.

"Okay, see you all tomorrow," she sighed.

In celebration, Mona opened another bottle of Chianti from the wine rack.

# Chapter 15

Randy had hoped to be released from the hospital the following morning, but Dr. Cormack wanted to be sure there would be no reoccurrence of the inflammation of the pancreas. Although his gallbladder had been removed and was the suspected cause of the acute pancreatitis, the doctor decided to err on the side of caution and keep Randy another day or two. Needless to say, Randy was not pleased with this decision, and Hayley found him in bed in a foul mood and pouting when she arrived just after eight in the morning, still bone-tired from the night before working at Romeo's and not looking forward to yet another night ahead.

Randy absentmindedly played with a few remnants of scrambled eggs with a plastic fork as she entered the room.

"How are you doing today?" Hayley asked.

"I feel fine, maybe a little weak, but I can rest up at home and be back at a hundred percent in no time," Randy huffed.

"First of all, there will be no going home when you get out of here. Not with Sergio all the way down in Brazil and no one there to look after you. You will be staying at my house, at least for a week or two," she said firmly.

Randy opened his mouth to protest.

Hayley held up a hand. "I have already made up Gemma's room for you, and so I do not want to hear another word about it."

Randy hurled his plastic fork down on the tray. "I'm going stir-crazy here. I can't sleep. What if whoever that was who snuck in here and killed Chef Romeo tries to do the same to me? What if he finds out I saw him? I'm a loose end, a sitting duck!"

Hayley noticed Randy's blood pressure rising rapidly again on the monitor beeping next to the bed. "Okay, you need to calm down. They're not going to let you out of here if your blood pressure is off the charts."

"I just can't get the image out of my head of that man holding poor Romeo down and draining the life out of him with whatever he injected in that tube," Randy said quietly. "It was horrific. I felt so helpless."

"Well, don't worry. The nursing staff is on high alert after what you witnessed. They'll keep a close watch over you."

"All anybody is really talking about is Nurse Fredy. Nobody can figure out what happened to him!"

Hayley paused, wanting to tread carefully. "Do you think it's possible . . . ?"

Randy shook his head. "No, it wasn't Fredy. I'm sure of it. Believe me, I stared long and hard at Fredy with puppy dog eyes, enough to make him feel uncomfortable, so I would recognize him in a heartbeat. This was someone I had never seen before."

Randy threw his head back against his pillow and sighed, exasperated. He stared up at the ceiling for a few moments, then turned back toward Hayley. "Have you come up with anything yet?"

She wanted to tell him that she was too exhausted after working at the restaurant until the wee hours of the morning, and did not have a moment to even think about starting any kind of lone-wolf investigation into what Randy saw. But instead, she just sat down in a chair next to the bed, smiled, and said, "No, but there is no time like the present. Besides this mysterious man wearing the medical mask, did anyone else come into the room to see Romeo that you can remember?"

Randy stared back up at the ceiling again, thinking. "Not that I recall . . . But I was pretty out of it . . . Wait . . ."

Hayley scooted her chair closer to the bed. "What?"

"I was pretty drugged up and in and out of consciousness all day. At the time I thought it was some kind of weird dream . . . But maybe . . . At one point, I heard voices, like they were in my head, they were going back and forth, arguing . . . I couldn't understand what any of it meant."

"Do you remember what the voices were saying?"

Randy struggled with his memory, eyes flickering, a frown on his face. "It was something about . . . a kitchen . . ."

"A kitchen?"

"Yeah, they were yelling at each other about a kitchen."

"Who?"

"Two men. One could have been Romeo, but like I said, I was pretty groggy and I thought I was just dreaming," Randy said.

Something dawned on Hayley and she gasped. "Could one of the voices have been Vic Spencer?"

"The contractor?" Randy asked.

Hayley nodded.

Randy sighed. "I suppose so . . . I mean, I haven't seen Vic in a long time, not since Sergio and I ran into him and his girlfriend at the village green last Fourth of July where we went to watch the fireworks. I can barely remember what his voice sounds like."

"Vic recently renovated Romeo's kitchen at the restaurant. Romeo was not happy with his work, he was refusing to pay Vic the rest of what he owed, and Vic was threatening to sue him."

"I guess it could have been him, but again, I can't say for sure," Randy said, glowering. "I can't even say it wasn't just a dream. I'm sorry. I'm not much help at all."

"No," Hayley said, grabbing his hand and squeezing it. "It's a solid lead. I personally saw Vic making verbal threats against Romeo the day of his heart attack. He is definitely a suspect. Do you think it's possible he could be the man in the medical mask?"

Randy leveled his gaze at Hayley. "Yes." Then there were lines across his forehead as he wavered. "Maybe. I don't know . . ."

Hayley stood up. "Well, get some rest. I promise I will follow up on Vic and keep digging to see who else might have had a motive, okay?"

Randy cracked a smile. "Thanks, sis."

She leaned down and kissed him lightly on the forehead. "I have some errands to run. I'll stop by again later this afternoon to check in on you."

Hayley headed out, passing the nurses' station, where she overheard a few of the staff still discussing what could have happened to Nurse Fredy.

She rode the elevator down to the lobby and walked outside to the parking lot to her car. She unlocked her SUV with the remote and was about to slide up into the passenger's seat when she noticed a glint in the grass nearby. Something was catching the sun, causing it to glimmer. Curious, she wandered over and saw in the grass a metal clasp attached to a laminated card that was face-down. Hayley bent down to pick it up and turned it over.

She let out a gasp.

It was an ID badge.

Fredy Sanchez.

A photo of Nurse Fredy's handsome face smiled up at her.

How did his badge wind up in the grass outside the hospital?

Where was he?

What had happened to him?

# Chapter 16

Clutching Nurse Fredy's ID badge, Hayley marched back inside the hospital and up to the nurses' station on the second floor, where she found Nurse Tilly manning the reception desk while staring into space.

"Look what I found outside, Tilly," Hayley said, slapping the badge down on the counter.

Tilly did not answer her.

She just sat there lost in thought, a troubled look on her face, worry lines stretched across her forehead.

Hayley leaned forward and tried again, louder this time. "*Tilly?*"

That finally did it. Tilly snapped to attention and looked up at Hayley. "Oh, I'm sorry. I guess I'm just not myself today."

"Is anything wrong?"

The question seemed to stump her, as if she wasn't

sure how she should respond, and so her answer was more of a question. "No?"

She was clearly bothered by something, but Hayley knew the typically frazzled nurse didn't want to talk about it, so she shoved the badge closer to Tilly, who reached over to pick it up and examine it.

"What's this?" Tilly asked.

"Fredy Sanchez's hospital ID badge."

Tilly's eyes widened in surprise. "Where did you find it?"

"Outside lying on the grass next to the parking lot."

"How on earth did it get there?"

Hayley shrugged. "Maybe he accidentally dropped it when he left the other night."

Tilly gazed at Fredy's badge photo.

"Or maybe he decided to quit mid-shift for some reason and tossed the badge on his way to his car," Hayley offered.

"That doesn't sound like something Fredy would do. He was always telling us how happy he was working here. I just don't understand it," Tilly said. "Stan, one of the orderlies, stopped by Fredy's apartment after his shift yesterday, and must have rang the bell nine or ten times and got no answer. He even peeked through the windows and said it didn't look like Fredy had been home."

Hayley had no proof, but she strongly suspected Fredy's disappearance must have something to do with what Randy claimed happened to Chef Romeo. However, she had no clue how it was connected. At this point, it was just a simple hunch.

"Should I call the police and tell them we found his badge?" Tilly asked.

Hayley thought about it and nodded. "It can't hurt. Did anyone try to file a missing person report yet?"

"The administrator called the acting chief, Sergeant Herrold, but she's been slow to act. She said we should wait a little while longer to see if he suddenly turns up."

"I'm not surprised," Hayley sniffed. "She doesn't seem to want to believe anyone who tries to report a crime."

Hayley decided against stopping by Randy's room to let him know what she had found, not until she had more information to share. She wanted him to get some rest. So she left the hospital and spent the rest of the morning and early afternoon shopping for food she needed for that night's dinner rush at Chef Romeo's.

When she pulled into the restaurant lot at four-thirty there were already a few cars parked, with people in them patiently waiting for the doors to open. She had a gnawing feeling that it was going to be even busier tonight than the previous evening.

Sure enough, Liddy was behind the hostess station melting down when Hayley entered the restaurant.

"Um, I may have overbooked a smidge for tonight," she squeaked.

"By how much is a smidge?"

"I don't know; a lot. Let me put it this way: There is no way we are going to be able to accommodate everyone."

Hayley sighed. "We'll just do the best we can."

She glanced out the window where more cars were arriving. People were now surging toward the door, getting in line. Hayley hurried into the kitchen, where she found Kelton, the sous-chef, setting up his workstation.

"Kelton, I'm going to need you to take charge tonight

in the kitchen. There is already a crush of people outside, we're going to be insanely busy—"

Kelton flashed her a reassuring smile. "Don't worry. I'll step up. Chef Romeo's been training me. I've been waiting for a night like this. I can handle all the orders coming in. If I fall behind, you can just start handing out appetizers on the house to keep the customers distracted."

"Sounds like a plan," Hayley said. "Thank you."

"I just wish . . ." Kelton's voice trailed off.

"What?"

Kelton shook his head, forlorn. "I just wish Chef Romeo was around to see this, how popular his place has become . . . this is what he worked so hard for."

"He knows," Hayley said. "Let's make him proud."

Minutes later, the clock struck five and the doors opened. Diners poured in and Liddy quickly began seating parties at their reserved tables. Mona, Betty, and Devon began taking orders, and Kelton and Hayley got to work preparing the dishes in the kitchen, while Lenny kept all the water glasses and garlic bread baskets filled. The line of walk-ins stretched all the way across the parking lot and down the street as Liddy took down the names on her waiting list, apologizing to everyone for how long it would take for them to be seated, although silently fearing the possibility that they might not get in at all at this rate.

By nine o'clock there were still no signs of the restaurant slowing down. Since it was a Saturday, nobody was in a big rush to get home. While Hayley and Kelton worked feverishly on fulfilling the orders—Hayley's linguini and clam sauce a particularly popular choice this evening—Liddy burst into the kitchen, armed with her iPad. "People are starting to complain they had a reservation at eight-thirty and now it's past nine! I'm afraid they're going to start a mutiny by the hostess station! I have no idea what to do!"

"I do," Hayley said. "Go to the wine rack, get as many bottles of the cheap house Chianti as you can carry, and start serving free wine as a thank-you for their patience."

"Do you think that is going to work?" Liddy asked skeptically.

Kelton chuckled. "I know when I'm drinking wine and feeling happy, I usually forget what I'm mad about."

"You're probably right," Liddy said before scurrying out, passing Mona, who barged into the kitchen carrying a plate of eggplant Parmesan.

"Kelton, hand me the sharpest knife you've got!" Mona roared.

"Is somebody's steak too tough?" Hayley asked.

"No," Mona barked. "I'm going to stab someone!"

Hayley turned to Kelton. "Don't give her a knife, or anything she can possibly use as a weapon."

Kelton grinned and went back to cooking.

"What's wrong, Mona?" Hayley sighed.

"There is some overgrown, obnoxious jerk out there who keeps sending everything I serve back to the kitchen," Mona spat out, holding up the plate in her hand. "Apparently, there isn't enough breading on his eggplant Parmesan. Before that, there was too much dressing on his salad, and before that, he said his sautéed mushrooms tasted funny. There is no pleasing him, so I might as well just take him out."

Mona reached for a knife lying on the cutting board, but Hayley blocked her with her body. "Mona, there is an old saying: The customer is always right."

"Yeah, I got a saying too, it's two words and the first word starts with an F and the second with a—"

"Mona! Just let Kelton prepare another eggplant Parmesan," Hayley pleaded. "And tell the gentleman we would like to offer him a free dessert, anything he likes."

"You don't reward people for their nasty, rude behavior, Hayley, the way I would handle it—"

"Yes, we all know how you would handle it, Mona. You would gut him like a fish. Give Betty the table, let her deal with him, and you can wait on someone less hostile, okay?"

This seemed to appease Mona for the time being, and within an hour, by ten o'clock, the mad rush seemed to be finally dying down. There were only a handful of tables left, which allowed Hayley to leave Kelton on his own so she could head back to Chef Romeo's tiny office, which was located off the storeroom to search through his files for any information on who she could call about his untimely death. There had to be someone, a family member, or a friend, anyone who might have some idea about a will, or who might be able to come and tend to his affairs, or know of any contingency plans in case of an unexpected event like this.

Hayley sat down in a chair behind the cramped desk and opened the metal drawers. She came across a password scribbled on a Post-it note on top of a stack of files that successfully unlocked his desktop computer.

She clicked through some operating budgets and spreadsheets and found a treasure trove of family recipes he had collected and perfected over the years. There were links to a number of articles written about him in various food and lifestyle magazines, but they were all very recent, none dating back more than a year. There did not seem to be much information on him beyond that, which struck Hayley as odd.

She clicked into his photos. Again, there were very few there. Just some pictures of him standing outside the restaurant in Bar Harbor as a couple of men put up the big Chef Romeo's sign before the grand opening and one of him with his investor Connie, where his smile seemed forced as if he was wishing he was anywhere else.

Hayley then clicked on an album labeled *Family*, hoping this might finally provide the answers she sought. There was only one photo. Romeo had his arm slung around a man, shorter, even heavier than Romeo, balding, maybe a few years older. They were at an outdoor amusement park, a large Ferris wheel looming in the background. Romeo had labeled the photo *Me and Cousin Alonzo, Coney Island, 2018*.

A cousin.

In a relatively recent photo.

Finally, a clue.

It wasn't much to go on, but at least it was a start.

# Chapter 17

Cousin Alonzo.

Hayley knew she had to locate him.

He was the only relative, hopefully still living, of Chef Romeo's that she currently knew about.

She clicked on Romeo's contacts app on his computer and was surprised to discover very few names and numbers listed. There was the restaurant staff, some local business contacts, a few important numbers like the Bar Harbor police and fire departments, but very few personal contacts; only a handful. Connie the investor made the cut, as did Hayley herself, but Romeo had not been in Bar Harbor long enough to develop a wide range of friends and associates. What Hayley found odd upon scrolling down the names alphabetically was that there were literally no family or friends from New York. It was obvious to anyone from his thick accent that Romeo hailed from the great state of New York, and several times he had mentioned his family emigrating from Naples. He spoke of growing up in Brooklyn, where he ran his own restaurant before desiring a change and moving to Maine, so why was he not keeping in touch with anyone from back home? It was as if that part of his life had been wiped clean—on his computer, anyway.

But there was still this one photo of Romeo and his cousin Alonzo at Coney Island. He had kept it, which meant, in Hayley's mind, that this was someone Romeo probably loved and trusted. But there was no contact information. After scrolling down the entire list of mostly local contacts, she almost missed a number at the end. There was not a name or business attached to it, simply the number.

But the area code was 718.

Finally, something that connected Romeo to New York.

But was it Cousin Alonzo, or someone else?

She didn't know whether she should call the number so late in the evening, so instead she decided to send a text to the number and see who eventually responded. After just typing **Hello, I'm a friend of Romeo's** and hitting *send*, she waited a few minutes until someone texted back.

**Who is this?**

Hayley typed back, **Hayley. Who is this?**

There was a long wait, but the answer finally came two minutes later.

**I don't know anyone named Romeo.**

Hayley sighed, exasperated.

What should she do now?

She typed back, **What about Alonzo?**

The wait time for an answer took even longer this time, and Hayley was just about to give up when she received another text.

**This is Alonzo. How did you get my number?**

Bingo.

Hayley typed as fast as she could. **It was in your cousin Romeo's list of contacts.**

This time the reply was immediate. **I told you, I don't have a cousin named Romeo**.

Hayley tapped her phone furiously. **I am looking at a picture of the two of you right now**.

Instant reply. **Send it to me.**

Hayley emailed herself the photo on Romeo's computer and then forwarded it to Alonzo.

Instead of receiving a text, her cell phone lit up.

He was calling her.

She accepted and hit *speaker*. "Hello?"

"Is this Hayley?"

"Yes, Alonzo, thank you for calling me. Did you get the picture of you with Romeo that I sent?"

"Yeah," he shouted in a thick Brooklyn accent. "But the man I'm with is not this Romeo you keep talking about. That's my cousin Luca."

Hayley flopped back in her chair, flabbergasted. "Well, I know him as Romeo Russo."

"Nope. That's not his real name. I grew up with the guy in Bensonhurst, and I'm telling you, his name is Luca Esposito. He's my first cousin on my mother's side."

Why would Romeo change his name when he moved to town?

What was he running from, or hiding from?

"Is he there with you now? Can you put him on the phone?" Alonzo asked.

Hayley's heart sank at the thought of what she was about to have to do. "I'm afraid I have some bad news . . ."

Alonzo listened to Hayley in silence, except for a few sniffles here and there and a clearing of the throat. She had obviously upset and shaken him with the tragic news and when she finished, he did not speak for some time as he processed everything. Hayley had purposely not mentioned Randy's story of seeing someone murder Romeo or Luca—not yet anyway. That was something that would have to wait until she had more answers.

But then, Alonzo blurted out, "Did someone rub him out?"

"Why would you think that?"

"He shut down his restaurant and left Brooklyn pretty quick without saying goodbye to anyone, and you're saying he changed his name to Romeo Russo or whatever, so that tells me he must have been in some kind of serious trouble."

She couldn't argue with cousin Alonzo's logic, because all the evidence she had found so far suggested the same thing.

"All I can say at this point is, that's a definite possibility," Hayley said in a measured tone.

"I wonder if this has anything to do with his house blowing up," Alonzo pondered.

Hayley suddenly snapped to attention. "Excuse me? His house blew up?"

"Yeah, they said it was a combustible gas leak. The explosion was so big it killed the old lady next door, Mrs. Crabtree. They found her wheelchair in the wreckage. The video from a nearby traffic light showed one of the wheels sticking up out of the debris, just spinning round and round. It even made the local news."

What a grisly image, Hayley thought.

"I never believed it was just a sad, tragic accident, because shortly after Luca left town, I started to hear rumors around the neighborhood that the explosion had been deliberately set. Luca can sometimes rub people the wrong way, and word is, he ticked off the wrong person."

"Do you have any idea who might have had it out for him?"

"Nope. But around here, you learn not to ask too many questions, if you know what I mean. I'm just grateful Luca wasn't at home when the place blew up . . . unlike poor Mrs. Crabtree, who wasn't so lucky."

Hayley explained to Alonzo that Romeo, aka Luca, had recently asked her to take over his restaurant while he was incapacitated, but she was now focused on finding out if he had a will or some kind of contingency plan upon his unexpected death.

Alonzo told her that Romeo's parents were dead and his one sibling, an older brother, was back living in Naples with a wife half his age whom he met during a pilgrimage to his homeland, which must have passed by a high school where the girl was a senior at the time. Alonzo claimed he was pretty much Luca's only living relative, in the States anyway.

Hayley promised to keep him apprised of any news in Bar Harbor regarding Luca's death, along with anything else she could find out, before ending the call.

Hayley then immediately called Bruce, who answered groggily, "Hello?"

"Were you sleeping? It's barely after ten."

"It's almost midnight," Bruce grumbled.

Hayley checked the time on her phone.

He was right.

She listened and heard no sounds coming from the dining room. Everyone must have already gone home. She had been so caught up in her investigation, she had completely lost track of time.

Bruce was prattling on about the trial, how the loaded cheeseburger he had ordered from the hotel's room service was probably the best he had ever tasted, how tomorrow was a Sunday so he was going to walk along the Hudson River Greenway on the west side to get some much-needed exercise. She waited until he was finished before breaking the news about Chef Romeo.

Bruce was stunned into silence.

She then filled him in on what Randy had sworn to have witnessed, her conversation with Cousin Alonzo, the explosion in Brooklyn and the sudden identity change. Before she got any further, Bruce interjected, "You want me to look into Romeo's previous incarnation as Luca Esposito and his near-brush with death in the old neighborhood while I'm right here in New York, don't you?"

"That's a wonderful idea," Hayley said brightly, as if this had all been Bruce's idea.

"Sure, why not? It's not like I have a lot to do here, like a major, high-profile trial that could win me the Pulitzer. Why don't I just put that on the back burner and focus on this?"

"I love you, Bruce," Hayley cooed.

"You love me because you know I'll say, 'Yes, Hayley, I will be happy to gather whatever information I can for you during the few spare moments I have.'"

"Yes, and I love you for just being you."

"You can put down the Hallmark card. I already said I'll do it."

"Do you miss me?"

"A little. But I think I'm going to miss the awesome loaded double cheeseburger I had for dinner even more after I leave this hotel."

Hayley chuckled. "I promise to make you one just like it when you get home if you tell me what's in it."

"That's just it, the secret sauce is the magic ingredient. You'll never be able to re-create it."

"I accept the challenge. Now get some sleep."

"Oh, you mean what I was doing before you so rudely called me and woke me up?"

"Goodbye, Bruce."

"Love you too."

## Island Food & Spirits
BY HAYLEY POWELL

A few weeks ago, while at the Shop and Save, I ran into one of Mona's boys. I can't remember his name, there are so many. Anyway, Chet or Digger—I'm pretty sure it was one of them—let me know that he had been out clamming that day, and the Barnes family was fully stocked up, if I was interested. That family knows I am a sucker for fresh clams, especially if they are mixed with a garlicky sauce and topped on a big bed of linguini pasta!

I immediately telephoned Mona as soon as I got home, and told her if she brought over a few pounds of those fresh clams to my house the following evening, I would whip up my famous clams linguini for us. I would also invite Liddy, who could provide her delectable Bellinis, and a fun girls' night in was on the books!

The only hiccup—and truth be told, it was a happy one—was our girls' night in fell by the wayside when my boss Sal's wife, Rosana, called to see if I was free for the evening, because my husband Bruce was going out for a couple of beers and a few games of pool at

Drinks Like A Fish with Sal, so of course I asked Rosana to join us girls for the evening. But when Rosana informed Sal that I was making clams linguine, the pool game was cancelled and Bruce and Sal were suddenly horning in on girls' night. Since we were expanding to a full-blown dinner party, I told Liddy and Mona they might as well bring dates too, so I would be serving dinner for eight.

The evening was a resounding success. Everyone raved about Mona's fresh clams with my garlic linguine, Liddy's Bellinis were a major hit, and with a little prompting, the usual storytelling at the table began with Mona, Sal, and Bruce all trying to one-up each other with their hilarious fishing stories.

That's when Mona looked at Liddy, and asked her if she remembered her first time clamming. Liddy clearly did not want to relive that particular memory, especially in front of her date, so she ignored Mona, which of course, proved to be her undoing. Mona got everyone's attention and launched into the legendary tale, much to poor Liddy's dismay.

It was the summer when we were all sixteen years old. Mona had just gotten her driver's license, and invited Liddy and me to accompany her up to the Trenton campground that her parents' friends owned to go swimming in their pool. Liddy and I instantly jumped at the chance, since it was a scorchingly hot August afternoon. The three of us jumped into Mona's truck (I swear, it is the same beat-up one she still tools around in today) and headed to Trenton.

As we crossed the Trenton Bridge, just minutes from the campground, Mona casually mentioned that she had to get some clams for her mother for supper that night. Liddy's head swiveled around so fast toward Mona that I honestly thought it would fall right off her shoulders.

"What do you mean, get some clams? Don't you mean pick up some clams?"

I groaned, knowing full well that Mona meant she needed to dig for clams out in front of the campground, since it sat just above the ocean, where all the guests would walk down the wooden steps to stroll along the rocky beach at high tide and dip their toes in the icy Atlantic Ocean. However, at low tide, it was an entirely different story. There was always that undeniable stench of the clamflats, and if you drove across the Trenton Bridge with your car windows down, it could be overwhelming. And that's exactly what I smelled as we crossed over and turned into the campground. Mona expected the three of us to dig for clams after a quick swim in the pool. We had been snookered into accompanying her and performing hard labor. I should have been tipped off by the three pairs of waders I had spotted in the back of Mona's flatbed!

Liddy was more concerned with muddying up her expensive designer one-piece bathing suit, which I knew was a lie since I had been with her when she bought it off the rack at JCPenney in Bangor.

Mona grabbed a bag of live lobsters that her mom was giving her friends from the back of the truck, and ran them in to the campground office as Liddy and I got our towels and headed to the pool.

Liddy's mood brightened considerably as soon as we passed through the gates into the pool area and she spotted a trio of cute teenaged boys joking around with each other, clearly on vacation.

For the next hour, we had a blast flirting, splashing, and playing water volleyball with some of the boys, before taskmaster Mona informed us it was time to pay the piper. We needed to head down to the shore and dig the clams before the tide came in. We reluctantly said our goodbyes to the boys and left.

Liddy complained all the way down the wooden steps that Mona had purposely sabotaged her budding romance with the cutest boy of all, Jared, from Massachusetts. He was on the verge of asking Liddy out on a date to the movies at Reel Pizza the following night just as Mona interrupted him. I told Liddy the quicker we finished digging the clams, the sooner we could head back up to the pool so Jared could have another chance to ask for a date.

This got Liddy moving at record speed. She grabbed one of the clam hoes from Mona's basket, and frantically began stabbing at the mud! I think all told, Liddy found about three clams in total. But luckily, Mona and I put more effort into it, and Mona was finally satisfied with her haul. I marveled at how much Mona and I were splattered with mud and how pristine and fresh as a daisy Liddy appeared, not a spot on her JCPenney designer knockoff! Mona cracked that Liddy's loud, complaining voice probably caused all the clams to "clam up!"

As we trudged through the flats back to the beach, Liddy still moaning about how Jared had probably already left and how Mona had ruined her one chance at happiness, I could see Mona resisting the urge to push her face-down in the mud. Finally, when Liddy spun around and yelled for us to pick up the pace, that we were walking too slow, that's when Mona lost it. She dropped her clam basket to the ground, threw down her hoe, and started running toward Liddy. Liddy, realizing she was about to wind up in a mud-wrestling match with Mona, let out a little shriek and started running, but it was slow going in the mud, and then she tripped right over a rock. She waved her arms frantically, trying desperately to regain her balance, but she lost that battle and landed face-first into the muddy clamflats.

Unfortunately for Liddy, it was at that exact moment the boy of her dreams, Jared, had come looking for her with a couple of his buddies, and they all witnessed Liddy's spectacular pratfall into the flats. Boys will be boys, and they all couldn't help busting up laughing, further humiliating poor Liddy.

Mona and I rushed over to help her, but she angrily shook us off, and with her pride stinging, she got up by herself, completely covered in mud, and with as much dignity as she could possibly muster, marched right past the hysterical boys, giving them a withering glare, which did manage to quiet them down.

But once she was past them, inevitably there was more snickering.

Liddy did apologize to Mona and me on the way home for her constant complaining, and she promised never to put a boy ahead of her besties ever again. Of course, that lasted until a few hours later when Jared called and asked her out and she ditched us for the evening. Jared had gotten Mona's phone number from the campground owners, and when he called her, Mona told him how to get in touch with Liddy. Luckily, Jared brought along two friends, dates for me and Mona, and we all ended up going out together. We hung out with the boys for the rest of their vacation, and it gave us girls a fun summer story to tell when we got back to school that fall.

Liddy still sees Jared to this day when he visits the island with his wife and young family, and they stay at the same campground each summer for vacation. And in the biggest surprise of all, Liddy even taught Jared's kids how to dig for clams!

All this talk about clam linguine has, of course, gotten my mouth watering. But first, how about a favorite cocktail of mine to enjoy before dinner?

## Liddy's Strawberry Bellinis

**Ingredients**
3 cups fresh strawberries (green tops cut off)
¼ cup powdered sugar
2 tablespoons brandy
2 cups sparkling strawberry Moscato
4 strawberries for garnish (optional)

In a blender, blend the strawberries, powdered sugar and brandy until smooth. Chill in the refrigerator for at least a half hour.

Divide the strawberry mixture into four champagne flutes, then top each one with a half cup each of Moscato, and garnish with a strawberry, if using.

## Linguini and Clam Sauce

**Ingredients:**
One pound linguini (one box)
6 tablespoons extra-virgin olive oil
6 cloves garlic, minced
½ cup chopped shallots
1 cup dry white wine (I use Pinot Grigio)
Pinch of red pepper flakes (more to taste)
2 pounds littleneck clams, washed and scrubbed
4 tablespoons butter
The zest from one lemon
2 tablespoons fresh lemon juice
Sea salt or Kosher salt

In a large pot fill ¾ water, bring to a boil, and add two tablespoons of salt. Add your linguini and bring back to a boil. Cook as directed for al dente, but take off two minutes. You will finish cooking in the sauce.

In a large saucepan, heat your olive oil over medium-high heat until hot, add the shallots and garlic and sauté for about 30 seconds. Do not let the garlic burn or it will become bitter. Add the wine, red pepper flakes, pinch of salt, clams, and bring to a simmer, then cook covered until the clams open up, around 8 minutes. Throw away any clams that did not open after cooking.

Reserve 1 cup of the pasta water, then drain your linguine and add the pasta to the pan with the clams. Turn your heat to medium and toss the clams and pasta together, letting the pasta absorb the water. You can add some pasta water a little at a time to keep the pasta from getting dried out.

Remove the pasta from the heat and add your lemon zest, lemon juice, butter, and toss to coat. Transfer to a serving platter or individual plates.

Serve to your guests and let the compliments begin!

# Chapter 18

Randy shot up in his hospital bed, eyes widening in surprise. "Murder conspiracy?"

Hayley threw up her hands to slow him down. "Now hold on, I didn't say that. All I said was I uncovered some information that *might* be connected to what you witnessed. I have Bruce looking into it while he's down in New York."

But Randy's mind was already off and running. "So Chef Romeo's real name is Luca something . . ."

"Esposito."

"And somebody blew up his house and sent him fleeing from Brooklyn, and then he randomly showed up here in Bar Harbor under a different name? That has to be it! The guy I saw was probably working as muscle for whoever had it out for Romeo back home in Brooklyn!"

"We can't be sure of anything yet. Not until we hear

back from Bruce. It's Sunday, so he has the day off from the trial. He is going to see what he can find. He is taking the subway to Bensonhurst to meet up with Romeo's—I mean Luca's—cousin Alonzo, and maybe try to talk to a few more people who knew him."

"Finally, I feel totally vindicated," Randy exhaled, relief in his voice.

"We shouldn't get too ahead of ourselves, Randy. It may turn up nothing."

"He changed his name. He was obviously scared of something. It has to be connected. I wonder how they found him."

"We should sit tight until we hear back from Bruce."

"Sit tight? I'm going stir-crazy! I feel like a prisoner in solitary confinement! And I don't even get one hour a day outside in the yard for a little sunlight!"

"I ran into Dr. Cormack at the nurses' station when I arrived. He said you may get released tomorrow morning if your x-rays come back clear of disease in your pancreas."

"I don't know how I will survive another night. Now I know how Mary, Queen of Scots felt after surrendering to the Protestant nobles and getting locked up in that castle."

Hayley laughed. "Don't be such a drama queen. Nobody's going to behead you."

"The movie was on TV last night. I guess being cooped up here made me identify with that Irish actress whose name I can never pronounce, who played Mary," Randy said, chuckling.

"Saoirse Ronan," Hayley said effortlessly and perfectly.

Randy cocked an eyebrow, impressed.

"She was on Stephen Colbert once and she gave a lesson on how to say it, which stuck with me, I guess."

"She'll forever be known to me as Lady Bird."

"Get some rest, and later I want you to think about what kind of food you'd like me to pick up at the Shop and Save, in the event you're able to come home with me tomorrow."

"There is no *if*! I will be leaving this place, even if I have to break out like Stallone and Schwarzenegger in *Escape Plan*!"

Hayley stared at him, smirking. "When was that on?"

"Two nights ago. It's slim pickings around here. It's not like this hospital room comes with a Netflix subscription, which is one more good reason I need to get the hell out of here."

Hayley leaned down and kissed Randy on the forehead. "I'll let you know when I hear back from Bruce."

"Day or night, I don't care what time it is. You call me. I have a good feeling we're on the verge of breaking this case wide open!"

Hayley feared she was getting Randy's hopes up, but the leads, at least so far, were somewhat promising.

She headed back up the hall toward the nurses' station where Nurse Tilly was conversing with a young woman, no more than nineteen or twenty, short, barely over five feet with a curvy figure, straight, long black hair and light brown skin. Her fretful eyes were fixed upon Nurse Tilly as she clutched an ID badge in her hand.

Hayley gingerly approached, overhearing Nurse Tilly calmly explain, "We have reported him missing to the police, but unfortunately we have not heard any news yet on what they think might have happened to him."

The woman's bottom lip began to tremble as her eyes

fell upon the badge she was holding in her hand. "But I do not understand. I just spoke to him on the phone a few days ago. He sounded perfectly fine. Where could he have gone?"

Tilly shrugged, distressed that she did not have any positive news to share. "None of his coworkers can understand either. He was so popular around here, patients were always requesting him. Everyone has come together, working overtime to cover his shifts until he— well, we're all just praying he will turn up soon."

The woman's eyes brimmed with tears and Tilly grabbed a few tissues from a box on her desk. She handed them to the young woman so she could wipe her eyes and blow her nose. Tilly then noticed Hayley hovering behind the woman. "This is Hayley. She was the one who found Fredy's badge in the parking lot."

The woman slowly turned around and tentatively nodded, holding the badge up in her hand. "You found it just lying in the grass outside?"

"Yes, I'm afraid so. I'm Hayley Powell," she said.

The woman sniffed and tried to smile, dabbing at her tear-streaked cheeks with the wadded up tissue. "Hello. I'm Fredy's niece, Christy. I'm sorry, I'm just a little emotional right now. I don't mean to cause a scene."

"Please, let's go sit down over there," Hayley suggested, gently guiding her by the arm to the waiting area, which was empty at the moment.

Nurse Tilly gave her a grateful smile, and then went back to her work.

Hayley and Christy sat down next to each other in a couple of gray vinyl chairs.

"Can I get you some coffee?" Hayley quietly asked.

She shook her head. "No, thank you."

"Do you live here in town?"

She shook her head again. "No, I just arrived last night. I'm from Honduras, the same village where Fredy grew up, near the Mosquito Coast. Uncle Fredy invited me to come to Bar Harbor for a visit. I had been planning to stay for a whole month. But when I arrived at the airport last night, he was not there to greet me as we had arranged. I waited and waited outside the terminal for hours. I tried calling him many times, but I just got his voice mail. Finally, this morning, when the sun was coming up, I took a taxi into town. I did not know his home address, just that he worked at a hospital, and since this is the only hospital in town, I had the taxi driver drop me off here."

Hayley could not ignore the sense of dread building up inside her, but she tried her best to maintain a mask of calm in front of Christy, who was so visibly distraught and shaken. She lightly patted Christy on the back, trying to offer her some comfort.

Christy wiped her nose with the tissue. "Uncle Fredy was hoping I might move here and get a job. You see, I am a U.S. citizen, I was born here. My mother was Honduran, my father American. Shortly after I was born, they broke up, and my mother moved us back to Honduras to be near her family. That's where I grew up. Uncle Fredy has been here in the States since he was seventeen, and when he would come visit us, he would constantly tell me about all the opportunities here, how I should study to be a nurse just like him. I have a business administration degree back home, but I could not find work. Although my mother did not want me to leave Honduras, I decided to at least come and see what it was like, and if there was a chance I could be happy here."

"Is your father still in the States?"

"No," Christy said, her voice cracking. "He died about ten years ago. He never came to see me. I never knew him. Uncle Fredy was my only family outside of Honduras."

Christy fell silent, eyes downcast on the floor. Then, after a few moments, she muttered, "I am so worried about him."

"Let me help you," Hayley said, standing up.

Christy raised her gaze up at Hayley, expectantly. "Did you know my uncle?"

"Not well. But he took excellent care of my brother, who has been here for an operation, so I think I should return the favor and look after you, at least until we can locate him."

"But how? No one seems to know where he is."

"We can start by going to his residence. I'm certain Nurse Tilly has his home address on file. There is no reason she can't give it to a family member. Come on, let's go."

"Thank you, Hayley," Christy whispered as she stood up and tossed the wadded-up tissue in a nearby trash can.

As Christy followed close behind Hayley back to the nurses' station, Hayley was confident her usual dogged determination to find answers would serve them well, but there was a deep, unsettling fear in the pit of her stomach about what exactly they might find.

And that made her shudder.

# Chapter 19

Hayley smirked as she and Christy marched up the stained carpeted stairs of the two-story building on lower Rodick Street adjacent to the town pier, behind Norman Hubbell, the acting landlord. Norman was only "acting" landlord because his father was the one who actually owned the structure. But since Norman Sr. had recently suffered a stroke and was home recovering, Norman Jr. had taken over as manager, responsible for collecting rent, overseeing appliance repairs, and generally keeping watch over the place. Norman relished this new role, because at twenty-eight years old, he was still living at home with his parents, with no girlfriend or job. Finally, with this tiny modicum of responsibility, he had a real sense of purpose and a firm grasp on what little power his new position afforded him.

Norman, who boasted a beer gut and was hopelessly out of shape, huffed and puffed his way up the steps, leaning forward to grab the rail in order to assist in the task of heaving his bulky body upward. Unfortunately for Hayley and Christy, who were close on his tail, Norman's saggy jeans slipped down enough to expose a huge butt crack.

Hayley turned to Christy and whispered under her breath, "I promise the views in Acadia National Park will be far more picturesque."

Christy stifled a chuckle.

When Norman, with great effort, finally hoisted himself up from the last step to the second-floor landing, he had to stop a moment to catch his breath.

"I told Dad he should install an elevator. Maybe now that I'm in charge, we'll finally get that done," Norman sputtered, breathing heavily.

"We really appreciate you doing this, Norman," Hayley said.

Norman nodded, waiting until he could breathe in and out without gulping for air before responding. "Well, normally we have a strict rule not to allow anyone into an apartment without the tenant present, but since Fredy told me his niece was coming for a visit, and he did show me a picture of Christy—you're even prettier in person, by the way—I don't see the harm in letting her in to wait until Fredy comes home." Norman attempted a seductive wink, but closed both eyes instead of just one. He tried one more time, failing again. Closing one eye while leaving the other open, apparently, was not one of Norman's innate superpowers.

"Thank you so much," Christy said gratefully.

Norman stared at her with a longing gaze that was bor-

derline creepy, more Norman Bates than the usual harmless, socially awkward Norman Hubbell.

They all stood on the landing, Norman scratching his
backside while still locked in on Christy like a rifle-toting
hunter focused on an unsuspecting deer innocently graz-
ing in a meadow.

Hayley cleared her throat. "Norman?"

Norman snapped out of his reverie, reached into his
pocket for a key ring, and rifled through all the keys until
he found the right one. He unlocked the door and swung
it open, ushering Hayley and Christy inside.

The blinds were drawn and it was dark inside and a
musty odor permeated the air. Hayley flipped a switch on
the wall next to the door and the kitchen and living area
of the modest one-bedroom was suddenly bathed in light.
Mail was scattered on the floor that the postman had
pushed through the slot on the door, at least several days'
worth of letters, bills, and flyers.

Hayley walked into the small kitchen as Christy bent
down to inspect the mail. There were unwashed dishes in
the sink, a plate, some silverware, one glass, and a cooking pot caked with what looked like gooey cheese. Hayley
glanced into the small plastic trash can in the cupboard
underneath the sink and saw a torn-open box of Kraft
macaroni & cheese. Hayley guessed that this may have
been Fredy's quick dinner before his shift started on the
night he disappeared.

Christy moved to the small kitchen table and sat down
as she rummaged through Fredy's stack of mail.

Hayley then checked the bedroom. The bed was made,
although hastily; there were some underwear briefs flung
on the floor, the bathroom was in need of a cleaning,
toothpaste smeared the countertop, and the mirror was

smudged with streaks of soap. A used toothbrush stuck out of a plastic drinking cup next to a nearly empty bottle of mouthwash. It didn't look like Fredy had had time to clean the apartment before his niece had been scheduled to arrive.

Hayley walked back out to the living area where Christy was finished going through the mail. That's when she noticed Norman still hovering in the doorway, staring hungrily at the back of Christy's unsuspecting head.

"We don't want to keep you any longer, Norman. We know how busy you must be," Hayley said evenly, crossing to the door.

"Huh? Oh, yeah. With Dad out of commission due to his stroke and all, everything's been laid at my doorstep. You have no idea how much pressure I've been under running things—"

"It must be very hard," Hayley said, resisting the urge to add, . . . *for someone who hasn't worked a day in his life*.

Norman ignored her and kept his eyes glued on the lovely visitor from Honduras. "If you need anything, Christy, don't hesitate to call me, day or night. I live just a few blocks away, so I can be here in no time at all."

Christy spun around in the chair and gave him a friendly, but disconcerted smile. "You're very kind. I will do that, Norman. Thank you."

She might as well have said, *I want to marry you right now and bear your children, Norman*, the way the young man's chubby face suddenly lit up, his fleshy cheeks rising so high they nearly swallowed his eyes whole.

"O—okay, then, right," Norman sputtered, seemingly trying in vain to think of a reason not to leave, but failing that, he finally turned his bulky frame around, giving them one more unsolicited look at his half-naked backside. Hayley quickly shut the door to block out the sight.

"Do not call him for any reason," Hayley warned. "That is serious stalker material."

Christy grinned. "I promise."

"Find anything?"

Christy solemnly shook her head. "No, some bills, mostly junk mail, flyers with coupons, that sort of thing."

Hayley noticed a calendar stuck to the side of the refrigerator with a *Golden Girls* magnet. She walked over and noticed yesterday's date circled with *Christy, 10:30 PM* scribbled above it. She removed the calendar and magnet and set it down on the kitchen table for Christy to see.

Christy picked up the magnet. "Fredy loved watching the *Golden Girls* reruns on TV when he was growing up. He says that's how he learned to perfect his English. Talking like an old retired lady from Miami."

Hayley smiled and pointed at the note on the calendar. "He didn't forget you were coming."

"Ten-thirty. That's when the last leg of my flight arrived from Boston. He wrote it down so he wouldn't forget." Christy then glanced up at Hayley, distraught. "What could have happened to him?"

"Don't worry, Christy, we will find him," Hayley said reassuringly, although she was still completely stumped on just how they were going to do that.

Christy stood up from the table, her arms wrapped around her waist, hugging herself, and wandered aimlessly into the living area to the window. She stopped and stared out at a back alley. "What am I going to do? My uncle is nowhere to be found. I brought very little money with me because Fredy paid for my travel expenses and promised to take care of me while I was here. What few dollars I did have on me I used to pay for the taxi ride from the airport to the hospital."

"I can give you some money to use while you're here—"

Christy interrupted her. "No, I cannot accept your charity."

"Then think of it as a loan," Hayley said, reaching for her checkbook that was buried in her bag.

Christy vigorously shook her head. "Please, I do not want to borrow money I may not be able to pay back."

Now was not the time for this poor girl to be proud.

She needed help.

"Okay, then how about you get a job?"

"Yes, that seems to be my only option, but I am going to have to apply and interview, and that will take time."

"Well, consider this your interview. Have you waited tables before?"

"Yes, back home at a café during summers."

"Okay, you're hired."

"For what?"

"Chef Romeo's, a delightfully cozy new Italian eatery in town that I have been running the past two nights. It's been nonstop busy and we could use all the help we can get. Fifteen dollars an hour, plus tips. You can start tonight. Interested?"

Christy's sad, mournful eyes suddenly sparkled to life, and she threw her arms around Hayley, squeezing her into a warm hug. "Thank you, Hayley. I am indebted to you. I promise not to disappoint you."

"You're the one doing me a favor," Hayley said.

Christy released her grip and stepped back from Hayley, near tears that at least one of her problems had just been solved. "Is there anything I need to know before tonight?"

"Yes, watch my friend Mona, who has been helping out waiting on customers, and just do the opposite."

Christy crinkled her nose, confused. "Okay."

# Chapter 20

The last thing Hayley had ever expected to see at Chef Romeo's on a Sunday night was a busier dinner rush than the one they had endured on Saturday night, especially when so many in town needed to be up early for work on Monday morning. But sure enough, as Hayley stared out the window, slack-jawed, there was already an overflow crowd outside milling about the parking lot, waiting for tables to open up.

Hayley checked her watch. It was already going on eight-thirty. She had spent most of the evening in the kitchen, cooking and plating the food and doing everything she could to alleviate the stress on Kelton, who had to stop chopping and stirring and tasting every few minutes in order to towel off the sweat beading his brow. Once she was confident Kelton had everything under control, she then did her rounds in the dining room, stopping at all the tables to make sure the guests were satisfied with their meals and had plenty of wine in their glasses.

Hayley watched as Christy glided across the hardwood floor, balancing a tray of five entrées on her shoulder, eyes straight ahead, fully focused. She set it down on a tray stand and with a bright smile on her face, began serving a table of women on a girls' night out.

Hayley had been duly impressed with how quickly Christy adapted to the chaotic environment, following all of Mona's helpful tips, but politely ignoring Mona's habit of barking at the customers and warning them not to make her job any more difficult than it already was.

Hayley spotted Lenny setting up a table with clean silverware and napkins, and signaled Liddy at the hostess station to call the next name on the waiting list.

Hayley started to head back toward the kitchen when a man at a corner table flagged her down. She stopped in her tracks, surprised to see her boss at the *Island Times*, Sal, splitting a mushroom black olive pizza with his wife Rosana. She hustled over to greet them.

"Sal, what are you doing here? It's a work night," Hayley said, wagging her finger.

Sal had a reputation for falling asleep in front of the TV usually well before nine o'clock in the evening, swearing it had nothing to do with his nightly shot of whiskey after dinner.

"I could say the same to you. You told me this little moonlighting gig was not going to interfere with your office manager duties at the paper," Sal said gruffly.

Rosana rolled her eyes, annoyed. "Sal, please don't

start. It's a wonderful thing what Hayley's doing, taking over for Chef Romeo so his staff can keep working and pay their bills. Don't listen to him, Hayley."

"Now don't go jumping down my throat, Rosie. I'm just saying I don't want Hayley overextending herself, you know. I'm worried about her health, that's all."

Hayley suppressed a laugh.

Health had nothing to do with Sal's deep concerns. No, he needed someone at the *Island Times* office eight o'clock sharp every morning in order to make sure the coffeepot was brewing when he rolled in, his typically tired and grumpy self.

Deep down, Hayley fought the urge to come clean to Sal with how dissatisfied she had become at the *Times*, answering the phones and dealing with disgruntled subscribers and planning the office parties and feeling like a glorified secretary. How these past three nights at Romeo's had been a welcome and transformative challenge, and had opened her mind to a plethora of new possibilities. But instead, she chickened out and simply said, "How's the pizza?"

"Crust is a bit chewy, I like it a little thinner, but the sauce is pretty tasty," Sal muttered.

"Coming from Sal, that's like a four-star Michelin review!" Rosana chirped. "We had the fried calamari as an appetizer. Three simple words: To die for."

Swallowing his pizza, Sal barked, "You got anything good here for dessert? I don't like anything fancy, just something simple to cleanse the palate!"

Hayley leaned forward. "I will have Christy bring over some spumoni for you, on the house."

Rosana clapped her hands gleefully, then flicked her eyes back toward her husband and sighed. "I don't know how he does it. He can be a rude discontent, and yet he still manages to score a free dessert!"

Sal sat up in his chair, disgruntled, and snorted, "People expect me to complain. It's who I am."

"Maybe you should think about rebranding," Rosana said, grabbing the last slice of pizza off the silver tray that was sitting on top of a metal rack on the table before Sal had the chance to swipe it for himself.

Sal grimaced. "You usually only have two slices."

Rosana took a big bite of the slice and slowly chewed, speaking with her mouth full. "I'm especially hungry tonight."

"Maybe you could share—"

"No, Sal," Rosana snapped.

Sensing a marriage spat starting to bubble up, Hayley scurried off to the next table on her path back to the kitchen. She was surprised again to see Andrea Cho and her husband Leonard. Andrea was picking at her mushroom risotto while Leonard sopped up the last of the marinara sauce on his plate with a big hunk of buttery garlic bread.

"Andrea, Leonard, I didn't see you on the reservations list for tonight," Hayley said, smiling.

Andrea put down her fork. "Liddy managed to slip us in ahead of a few other parties. I promised to use her as our realtor when I sell my family's waterfront cottage in Castine in the fall."

Hayley made a mental note to remind Liddy not to give preferential treatment to customers willing to bribe her with a real estate commission.

"I hope you enjoyed your dinners," Hayley said, eyeing Andrea's half-eaten risotto.

"Yes, it's quite delicious," Andrea assured her. "I'm

just eating half-portions to lose a little weight and get healthier. I'll have the rest for lunch tomorrow." She then focused her attention on her husband. "Maybe you should do the same, Leonard."

Leonard had been ignoring them as he devoured his garlic bread soaked in marinara sauce. "Huh?"

"Don't talk with your mouth full," Andrea snarled. "I was saying, maybe you should cut down on all the salt and carbs, and then we wouldn't have to rush you to the hospital so much."

Leonard chomped on his garlic bread defiantly, in silence, until he finally swallowed, his Adam's apple jutting out as it went down. He stared daggers at his wife, but then glanced up at Hayley with a friendly smile. "The manicotti was excellent, Hayley. Would you tell our waitress to bring around a dessert menu? I'm in the mood for some tiramisu."

"And maybe you could cut down on the sugar too," Andrea mumbled under her breath.

Hayley thought she might have to go get a steak knife from the kitchen in order to cut through the tension.

"I feel fine," Leonard seethed, reaching into his coat pocket, which was slung over the back of his chair.

"It looks like you've made a remarkable recovery," Hayley noted encouragingly.

"Thank you, Hayley," Leonard said, pulling out a blood pressure monitor and wrapping the cuff snugly around his arm but not too tight.

Andrea's eyes widened, horrified. "Leonard, *what* are you doing?"

"Taking a reading," he said nonchalantly. He opened an app on his phone and pressed a green *start* button and the arm cuff began inflating. He kept his eyes glued to his phone for the result.

"*Here?*" Andrea cried. "You can't wait until we get home?" She looked around, embarrassed, but nobody seemed to be watching, except for one tiny six-year-old girl at a nearby table, who had probably never before seen anyone take their blood pressure and was curious to know what exactly Leonard was doing.

"I like to take it at the same time every night. You were the one who insisted we get out of the house," Leonard argued. He frowned as the arm cuff deflated and the digital numbers appeared on his phone. "It's pink. That's not good. Green means you're good to go, yellow is a warning that it's elevated above normal, and red is basically get yourself to a hospital stat. So pink is obviously *not* good."

"Nobody asked for this tutorial, Leonard! Can't you see that Hayley is busy?" Andrea said.

"Oh, dear, my heart rate is close to a hundred," Leonard fretted before looking pointedly at his wife. "I can't possibly imagine what could be stressing me out so much all the time."

Andrea chose to ignore him.

Christy suddenly appeared at the table and reached out for Leonard's empty plate. "All finished?"

"Yes, thank you, it was delicious," Leonard said, his mood brightening at the pretty server's presence.

Andrea chose to ignore that too. "Would you wrap up the rest of mine to go?"

"Certainly," Christy said, stacking the plate of risotto on top of Leonard's empty one.

"You must be new in town," Leonard said, eyes twin-

kling. "I haven't seen you before. I surely would have remembered spotting such a pretty girl around."

"Stop fawning, Leonard, it can't be helping your heart
rate," Andrea snapped.

"Christy just arrived last night," Hayley explained.
"She's here visiting her uncle."

"Who's that?" Andrea wanted to know.

"Fredy," Christy chimed in. "He's a nurse at the hospital."

"Never met him," Andrea said dismissively.

Leonard sat up in his chair. "I did. He was working the
night you brought me there when I thought I was having
a heart attack."

"Can you be more specific? Your medical emergencies
are pretty much a regular occurrence these days," Andrea
spat out.

"The most recent time, last week," Leonard said, annoyed.

Hayley perked up.

Of course.

Leonard was at the hospital on the same night Fredy
disappeared.

"Did the two of you have any interaction?" Hayley
asked.

Leonard nodded. "Yes, he brought me a fresh pitcher
of water at one point, and a little later he came in while I
was watching Stephen Colbert to check my vitals, and
then . . . Oh, never mind."

Hayley and Christy exchanged quick glances.

"Never mind what?" Hayley pressed.

"It's nothing. I drifted off to sleep at some point and
woke up in the middle of the night, and thought I saw

something, but I was pretty out of it from the drugs they gave me, so when I woke up the next morning I figured it was just a weird dream."

"Why are you wasting our time with another one of your silly dreams, Leonard?" Andrea huffed. She turned to Hayley and Christy. "You would not believe how many hours of my life I have lost listening to him go on about his stupid dreams!"

Hayley wanted to shove a napkin into Andrea's mouth to shut her up, but wisely refrained. "No, Leonard, tell us, what did you think you saw?"

"I like to sleep with a night-light on so it's not completely dark in the room . . ." Leonard started to explain.

"Can you believe my forty-four-year-old husband is afraid of the dark?" Andrea lamented.

"Anyway," Leonard said, bristling. "I asked Fredy to leave my door open a crack so the light from the hallway could come in and he happily obliged. James Corden was on—he comes on after Colbert, and I find his British accent droning and kind of boring, and so I fell asleep not too long after that . . ."

"Get to the point, Leonard!" Andrea cried.

"Will you let me tell the story my way, please, Andrea?" Leonard hissed, cheeks tightening, lips pursed, the base of his neck reddening. Then his face relaxed as he returned his gaze to Hayley and the fetching Christy. "I heard some noise outside my room and when I opened my eyes, that's when I saw them, Fredy and this other guy."

Hayley took a step closer to Leonard. "What guy?"

Leonard shrugged. "Some big dude, I'd say almost twice as large as Fredy. He had Fredy by the arm, like he was taking him somewhere. When they passed by my door, Fredy tried to stop, but the big guy kept pulling him roughly along by the arm, as if he was forcing him."

Christy gasped, alarmed.

"Can you describe this man?" Hayley asked.

Leonard shrugged. "Big. Built like a wrestler, you know, like the Rock."

"His *face*, Leonard!" Andrea yelled, unable to remain quiet any longer. "Did you see his *face*?"

"No," Leonard said. "He was wearing one of those medical masks, so I never got a good look."

"Leonard, you moron, the man is missing! It's all over town! Why didn't you say something sooner?" Andrea wailed.

"I didn't think much about it because like I said, I thought I was dreaming!"

It was obvious to Hayley now that Leonard was describing the same man as Randy had claimed to have seen, which could only mean her brother was absolutely *not* hallucinating due to his post-surgery sedated state.

Despite what the police wanted to believe, Randy had indeed witnessed Chef Romeo's murder.

And Nurse Fredy may have been an unlucky eye-witness.

# Chapter 21

When Hayley dragged her weary bones through the back door into her kitchen after driving home from the restaurant, it was already a few minutes past eleven. Leroy was there to excitedly greet her as she stumbled in. She opened the cupboard, grabbed a box of doggie treats, and tossed one toward him, which he ably caught in his mouth. Then, after trying to call Bruce and getting his voice mail, she slowly made the trek up the staircase, an attention-starved Leroy eagerly scampering behind her, and took a long, hot, scalding shower to wash off the dirt and grime and smell of food in her hair.

She knew her night was far from over.

Usually on the weekends, Hayley would get a head start on her columns for the week so she wasn't so slammed during office hours while tending to her other duties. But with all that had been going on, she had failed to even crack open her computer. Once she toweled off and threw on some gray sweatpants and a ratty pink T-shirt, she climbed into bed with her laptop and popped it open.

She stared at the blank screen, impatiently waiting for inspiration to strike, but it never came.

Leroy snuggled up beside her, instantly falling asleep. As she stared down at him, his little body heaving up and down as he snoozed peacefully, his eyes shut tight, her own eyes became heavy and she couldn't resist setting her computer down on Bruce's empty side of the bed and wiggling deep down underneath the white goose-down comforter, joining her little dog in dreamland.

She had no idea how long she had drifted off to sleep when her buzzing phone on the nightstand next to her suddenly snapped her awake. Hayley shot up in bed as Leroy fitfully shifted his position with a sigh. She grabbed her phone.

It was Bruce returning her call.

"Bruce?"

"Hi, babe. Sorry I missed your call earlier. I was in the middle of a subway tunnel with no service on my way back to Manhattan from Brooklyn."

"Are you at your hotel now?"

"Yeah, I just got back."

"Sounds like a long day."

"It was, and I have to be at the courthouse in the morning by eight."

"I'm sorry," Hayley said guiltily. "I know today was supposed to be your one day off."

"I have a number of ways you can make it up to me when I come home after the trial," Bruce said.

She could picture him in her mind leering.

"Did you find anything useful?"

"Oh, yeah, I had coffee with Alonzo this morning, and he gave me the names of a bunch of people in the neighborhood to talk to, childhood friends, former restaurant employees. I spent most of the day tracking them all down. Some refused to talk to me for whatever reason, but a few turned out to be fountains of information. I just emailed you some news articles that corroborate what I found. But the bottom line is, Luca Esposito, aka Chef Romeo, ran a very successful restaurant in Bensonhurst. He was kind of famous in his old neighborhood. There really was no reason why he should ever leave."

"So what changed?"

"According to just about everybody I spoke to, Luca opened his first restaurant right across the street from another Italian restaurant, an old neighborhood favorite that had been around for years. Luca knew he had to play hardball in order to compete and stay in business, and so in the words of one of his cooks, he went nuclear. He complained to the city council that the rival's building was not up to code and was a fire hazard and needed to be shut down immediately. He called in a favor to an old high school buddy who worked for the New York State Liquor Authority and got him to challenge their license for serving free wine to people waiting outside for a table. He even wrote to U.S. Immigration claiming they were hiring undocumented workers. He was pretty relentless and wore the owner down until he finally closed his doors and went out of business after nearly forty years."

"Do you know anything about the owner?"

"Well, the place was called Caruso's, so I'm assuming that was his name. Apparently, he was an older guy, in his seventies, who grew up in Brooklyn and dedicated his whole life to running his family-style restaurant. But after

Luca began targeting him, he finally just gave up, figuring it just wasn't worth all the aggravation, and so he shut his doors and retired. I tried to track him down, but it turns out Old Man Caruso died earlier this year. His kids filed a lawsuit against Luca, but Luca enlisted the help of another high school chum, now a fancy lawyer, and got the whole case dismissed."

Hayley gently rubbed the top of Leroy's head as she took all of this in. "I don't understand. If he won and drove out competition, then why did he leave Brooklyn?"

"He got greedy," Bruce said. "He was riding high on his success of one restaurant, and decided he wanted to expand and open another, this one in Bay Ridge. But he needed capital to grease the wheels and get it started, so he decided to get a loan. Even though money was coming in, he was still carrying a lot of debt, and he couldn't get a bank to work with him, so he borrowed the cash from a guy by the name of Rocco Mancini."

Hayley only had to hear the name to know where Bruce was going with this. "Uh-oh. Let me guess. Mob-connected?"

"Not just connected. The Mancinis are one of the most notorious New York crime families down here. Everyone tried talking Luca out of it, but he refused to listen, and just plowed ahead full steam. He got himself in hock for about a hundred K. Unfortunately, the Bay Ridge restaurant was in a bad location and went bust not long after the grand opening."

Hayley breathed in slowly. "Leaving him owing the Mafia over a hundred-thousand dollars."

"Which was compounding daily at thirty percent interest," Bruce added. "What his first place was bringing in wasn't nearly enough to cover it, so he kept putting Rocco off, making up excuses, promising to make good on the debt if given a little more time. But you've seen this movie before. Those Mafia loan sharks aren't known for their patience, so Rocco dispatched a couple of his thugs to send a clear message."

"By blowing up his house and the poor innocent old lady who lived next door, according to Alonzo."

"Yeah, she was sadly collateral damage," Bruce said.

"That certainly would be enough to scare him into skipping town, changing his identity, and showing up in a remote part of Maine to start over," Hayley surmised.

Her mind began to race.

Was the big man Randy had seen murdering Romeo and Leonard had seen hustling Nurse Fredy away, one of Rocco Mancini's thugs? Had the Brooklyn Mob family somehow discovered Luca Esposito's whereabouts and sent a coldhearted assassin up to Maine to rub him out? It sounded like a *Sopranos* plotline. Almost too fantastical to believe.

She heard Bruce yawning on the other end of the call.

"Get some sleep, honey. You deserve it. I can't thank you enough for all this," Hayley said.

"Love you, babe."

"Back at you," Hayley said, ending the call and putting the phone back down on the night table. She then reached over and flipped open her laptop, checking her email. Bruce had attached a file, which she immediately downloaded and opened. It contained mostly supplemental information to what Bruce had already informed her about: local advertisements for Luca's two restaurants, the Caruso family lawsuit against him and its dismissal by the court, various articles about the Mancini family, their philanthropic endeavors to the community, perhaps to cover up their other illegal activities.

Hayley came across a gushing article from a local paper about the generosity of the Mancinis donating the money to build a children's playground in nearby Dyker Heights. Accompanying the story was a photo of the Mafia don himself, Rocco Mancini, posing with his wife in front of a freshly painted seesaw and large jungle gym. Hayley chuckled at how much Mancini, in a long coat and wearing a fedora, looked exactly like the Mob bosses in all those old Hollywood movies. He was a foot shorter than his wife and could probably pass as Joe Pesci's younger brother.

That's when Hayley focused on Mrs. Mancini.

Why did she look so familiar?

Towering over her husband, a somewhat forced smile plastered on her face, drowning in a fur coat that was open enough to show off the colorful designer dress she had stuffed herself in. That's when it suddenly hit her. She looked familiar because Hayley had met her—recently, in fact.

Although the photo was probably nine or ten years old, Mrs. Rocco Mancini was not just a dead ringer for Chef Romeo's self-proclaimed paramour and business investor Connie, who had come to see him in the hospital, they were without question one and the same.

# Chapter 22

Hayley had to swallow a frightened gasp at the scary-looking creature who stood in the doorway, gripping a mug of steaming hot coffee. The woman's wild black hair was flying in all different directions. Smudged mascara made her look like an angry raccoon and ruby-red lipstick was smeared across her lips with little thought of stopping at the outer edges. She looked like a clown that had just been mugged. The woman eyed Hayley warily as she raised her mug of coffee and slurped, her abnormally long nails polished to match her lips, a few of them chipped and cracked.

"What do you want?" Connie snarled.

Hayley could see her eyes were watery, as if she had been crying. She sniffed, wiping her nose with a wadded-up tissue in her free hand.

"I was hoping you might have a few minutes to talk to

me," Hayley said pleasantly, trying to ignore the woman's startlingly haggard appearance.

Connie closed the pink sweater she was wearing over a silk cream-colored nightgown in front of her, as it was a chillier than usual morning.

"I'm sorry, I'm not in the mood for visitors right now. Come back later," Connie snapped, moving to shut the door.

Hayley stuck a foot in the doorway to stop her from slamming the door in her face. "Please, Mrs. Mancini, it won't take long, I promise."

The mention of the name Mancini stopped Connie cold. She dropped her mug, which bounced off the floor and splashed coffee everywhere. Her eyes began darting back and forth, as if she was checking to make sure there were no spies hiding in the nearby bushes outside. Then, she grabbed Hayley by the arm and yanked her past the threshold inside the cottage.

Locating Connie Mancini had been easy. Chef Romeo had mentioned that she was just in Bar Harbor for the summer, which suggested to Hayley that she was probably renting a property, and no one was more plugged into the summer rental scene than Liddy. Hayley had called Liddy earlier that morning, waking her up, but it had been worth it. With just a few strokes of her computer keyboard, Liddy had managed to find a quaint seafront cottage just off West Street with a sweeping view of Frenchman Bay and the town pier that had been rented by a Connie Toscano from New York in late April. Toscano, according to the information Bruce had sent her, was Connie's maiden name.

Hayley felt guilty showing up so early in the morning, but she was crunched for time. Randy was scheduled to be released from the hospital later in the day, and she also had to put in an appearance at the office before her boss Sal filed a missing person report.

Connie nervously scanned the surrounding property, as if expecting some kind of imminent military invasion, before she swung the door shut, locked it, and whipped around to Hayley. "How did you know my name was Mancini?"

"I'm looking into the death of Chef Romeo Russo, and my husband happens to be in New York, so I had him do a little digging—"

"Why? Romeo died from a heart attack." Her eyes welled up with fresh tears at the mention of his name.

Hayley explained what Randy had claimed to have seen the night Romeo died.

Connie's mouth dropped open in shock. "Y-you think he was *murdered*?"

"That's what my brother says, and I've never known him to lie," Hayley said quietly.

Ignoring the spilled coffee, Connie wandered over to the bay window and stared out at the stunning ocean view. "And so you've been investigating and found out who I really am, and now you think I may have had something to do with it?"

"N-no, at this point, I—I don't know what to think," Hayley stammered, not wanting to set her off. She had seen just how unhinged Connie Toscano-Mancini could be when she had first met her at the hospital.

Her back still to Hayley, she heard Connie whisper, "I would never do anything to hurt Luca—I mean Romeo." She slowly turned around, tears now streaming down her cheeks. "I loved him . . . And I still can't believe that he's gone."

"Did you follow him up here to Bar Harbor?" Hayley asked.

Connie sighed, then nodded. "Yes. I was hoping to rekindle what we once had. Oh, I was so foolish, so naive. I thought that bankrolling his restaurant here would make him fall in love with me all over again. What an idiot I was."

Chef Romeo had been telling the truth about Connie.

They were not romantically involved.

He had just neglected to mention that they had been once, back in Brooklyn. He also had conveniently left out the part about Connie being the wife of a dangerous and powerful Mob boss, key information that opened a whole boatload of new questions.

"Did your husband find out about your affair with Luca, and that's why he fled Brooklyn and moved here to Maine under a different name?"

"Everybody back home assumed Luca ran because he couldn't pay back the debt he owed Rocco, but that wasn't it at all. Given time, Luca would have managed to pay him back. What really happened was Rocco got suspicious and had one of his goons spy on me, and he got video of me and Luca through the window of the storeroom at his Bay Ridge place. He had set up a mattress and some scented candles; he was always trying to be romantic, which was sweet," Connie said with a wistful smile. "Anyway, once Rocco saw the video, that was basically a death sentence for poor Luca. So he skipped town."

"Did Romeo—I mean Luca—tell you where he was going?"

Connie shook her head. "No, of course not. He was scared to death. He didn't tell anyone. He was literally running for his life. He cut off all contact with me, which of course broke my heart." Connie sniffed again. "I said all the right things to Rocco, how Luca had been just a harmless fling, how I was willing to do anything to regain his trust, be the best wife I could possibly be. I can be very sexy and charming and persuasive when I want to be, which is why Rocco married me in the first place."

Hayley had trouble picturing the sexy and charming part in Connie's current disheveled state, but chose not to question her confident assessment.

"I finally wore him down and he took me back, but I couldn't stop thinking about Luca, and one day a few months ago I was reading a food blog online and I came across a post that mentioned a new Italian restaurant opening in Bar Harbor, and some of the specialty items on the menu. From the moment I read it, I knew in my gut I had found him, that this Chef Romeo was really my Luca, so I got in my car and drove all night to get here so we could be reunited."

"Luca must have been very surprised to see you," Hayley remarked.

Connie chortled. "To say the least. He yelled at me, said he was a dead man walking with me hanging around, which I guess was true, but he also needed my financial help. The bank had just rejected his loan and his restaurant was on the verge of collapsing before it even opened, so he allowed me to become a silent investor. I wrote him a big fat check, and then I decided to rent this place for the summer so we could be together, and hopefully pick up where we left off back in Brooklyn."

"But what about your husband?"

Connie scoffed. "He thinks I'm in Florida looking after my ailing mother, who Rocco can't stomach being around, so there was zero chance he would ever go down south to check on me himself. Besides, I paid my sister Gloria five grand to fly down there in my place and pretend to be me for the summer. She's a dead ringer from a distance. No one would ever be able to tell it wasn't me wheeling my mother around that condo complex, in case Rocco sent one of his gorillas to snoop around and make sure I was telling the truth."

"It sounds like you're playing a very dangerous game. What if your husband found out that he not only paid for Luca's restaurant back in Brooklyn, but thanks to you, he paid for his new place up here too," Hayley said.

"Yeah, his head would basically explode, which is why he can never find out. He thinks I used that money to buy my mother a new condo and full-time nurse for when I eventually come home to Brooklyn after Labor Day."

"But what if he's onto you?"

"He's not!" Connie snapped.

"But what if he is? What if the man Randy saw murdering Romeo was working for your husband?"

Connie hesitated, contemplating the possibility. "Did your brother say what this man looked like?"

"Just that he was large and muscular."

"Did he have a flat nose and a scar on his left cheek?"

"He was wearing a medical mask, so most of his face was covered up," Hayley said.

Connie shivered. "It could be Big Hugo."

"Who?"

"He works for Rocco, very loyal, very dangerous."

Connie scurried from the bay window over to her purse. She rummaged for her phone and scrolled through some photos. "Give me your number so I can text you a photo."

Hayley obliged and within seconds saw a picture of an oversized Mack truck of a man with coal-black eyes, enormous, wide nose, and the aforementioned scar, definitely the kind of nasty character you would want to avoid in a dark alley.

"If Big Hugo is here in Bar Harbor, then there's no doubt I'm next on the list," Connie said, shuddering.

# Chapter 23

Hayley found Randy fully dressed and sitting on the edge of his hospital bed, hands clasped on his lap in front of him, an anxious look on his face.

Hayley chuckled. "You look just like you did when Mom arrived to pick us up at summer camp when you were twelve years old."

"Worst two weeks of my life," Randy moaned.

"Didn't some mean boys in your cabin hang your doll from the ceiling?"

"First of all, it was *not* a doll, it was a G.I. Joe *action figure*, and yes they did. Kids can be stunningly cruel. I hated every minute of summer camp."

"I remember having a great time."

"Well, you liked to be outdoors canoeing on the lake and cooking marshmallows in front of a campfire. I wanted to be home in front of the TV watching *The Price is Right* and reading comic books. I wrote letters every day to Mom, begging her to come get me, threatening to hurt myself if she didn't, but that still wasn't enough! She didn't show up until the two weeks were over!"

"She knew you were bluffing. You wouldn't kill yourself before the fall TV season with all the new shows."

"Well, this agonizing hospital stay has brought back all those bitter, traumatic childhood memories, and I can't get out of here fast enough. I'm just waiting for Dr. Cormack to sign the release papers. I've been ready to leave since five this morning."

"I'm sure he'll be here soon. In the meantime, take a look at this," Hayley said, unlocking her phone and showing her the photo of Big Hugo that Connie had sent her.

Randy studied the man in the picture. "Who am I looking at?"

"His name is Big Hugo. Recognize him?"

"No, should I?"

"So that is not the man you saw in here murdering Chef Romeo that night?"

Randy grabbed the phone from Hayley and brought the screen up closer to his face, eyes intently fixed on Big Hugo. After a few moments, he shrugged. "Could be. He has the same build. But like I said, I was pretty heavily sedated and he was wearing a medical mask." He stared at the photo some more, then sighed, frustrated. "Maybe it's him. I really can't be sure."

Hayley took the phone back from him. "Okay, wait here, I'm going to go show this around to see if it rings any bells with anyone who was here working that night."

"If you see Dr. Cormack, tell him to get his butt in here and spring me from this Alcatraz hellhole!"

"Relax, Randy, you're getting out today, I promise," Hayley said, heading out of the room.

"You also promised not to tease me in front of your friends for acting out episodes of *Melrose Place* in my room when we were kids, and you didn't keep *that* promise!" Randy called out after her.

Hayley snickered as she approached the nurses' station and showed the photo of Big Hugo around to several on-duty nurses and orderlies, none of whom appeared to recognize him.

She glanced around the floor. "Is Nurse Tilly on duty?"

"Yes," a heavyset orderly in his mid-twenties with a shaved head and red goatee answered. "I saw her getting on the elevator with Dr. Cormack. She's probably downstairs somewhere."

"Thank you," Hayley said, smiling, walking briskly toward the bank of elevators.

Down in the lobby, Hayley stepped off the elevator and looked around, but didn't spot Nurse Tilly or Dr. Cormack anywhere. She shuffled down the hall to the cafeteria to see a cluster of people eating breakfast and sipping coffee, but no Tilly. The gift shop next to it was empty, except for a girl at the register absentmindedly flipping through a *People* magazine from the rack in front of the counter. Hayley then sauntered outside to the parking lot, and that's where she finally spotted them, Tilly and Dr. Cormack huddled together in front of Tilly's banged-up Nissan Sentra, engaged in a deep, heavy conversation.

Hayley sauntered over toward them. They didn't notice her at first and continued intently whispering to each other until finally Hayley cleared her throat, surprising both of them. They practically jumped away from each other, deliberately putting a lot of space between them.

"I'm sorry, I didn't mean to interrupt," Hayley said.

"N-no, no, not at all," Dr. Cormack sputtered, nervously straightening his white doctor's coat with his hands, collecting himself.

Hayley noticed Cormack and Tilly exchanging flustered glances, like they had just been caught doing something they shouldn't be doing. Ignoring their odd behavior, Hayley thrust out her phone for them to look at. "Do either of you know this man?"

Both of them barely looked at the photo before Dr. Cormack brushed past Hayley. "No, sorry, I have to get back inside. I have patients to check on."

Hayley cranked her head around. "My brother's waiting in his room for you to sign him out!"

"Tell Randy I will get to him just as soon as I can!" he shouted back, slightly irritated. She watched him rush toward the swinging glass doors into the hospital, furtively glancing back a few times before disappearing inside.

When Hayley turned back around, she caught Tilly staring at the photo on Hayley's phone, a hint of recognition on her face. "You've seen him before, haven't you?"

Tilly reared back, defensively, a pained expression on her face. "No, I have not. I have never seen that man in my life."

"Tilly, why are you acting so secretive?"

"What are you talking about? I'm not being secretive. I can't help it if I don't know the man in that photo. So I would appreciate it if you would stop browbeating me!"

"I'm sorry, I didn't mean to—"

Suddenly, the roar of an engine drowned them out, and Hayley whipped around to see a pickup truck barreling toward them in the parking lot. Hayley and Tilly instinctively stepped closer to Tilly's car, giving the truck more space, but the truck veered to the right, aiming directly toward them, as if intending to mow them down.

Hayley grabbed Tilly by the shoulders and pushed her out of the way just as the truck sped past them. Hayley watched as the driver slammed on the brakes and the truck screeched to a halt, gray smoke pouring out of the tailpipe as it idled. That's when she noticed the license plate had been covered with black masking tape. Suddenly, the truck began backing up, faster and faster, the rear bumper closing in on them.

"Tilly, jump!" Hayley screamed, grabbing Tilly by the arm and leaping up on top of the hood of the nurse's parked Nissan. The truck turned sharply toward them, smashing one of the headlights on Tilly's car and denting the front grille before speeding away, tires squealing, burning rubber, as it careened sharply onto Hancock Street and vanished from view.

Hayley rolled off Tilly, whose whole body was shaking from fright, and called 911. "I'd like to report a hit-and-run!"

Fifteen minutes later, Sergeant Herrold and Officer Earl arrived on the scene. Although a little less lovesick than Donnie, Earl too followed Herrold around like a loyal puppy dog, totally enamored with her strong, no-nonsense demeanor, and in Hayley's opinion, undeterred by her utter lack of charm.

After peppering Hayley and Tilly with a few standard questions, including "Did you see the driver's face?" and

"Did you get a license plate number?" for the report, Sergeant Herrold seemed vexed by having been called out on a hit-and-run, only to be greeted by one broken headlight, a slight dent on the grille, and two apparent "victims" who appeared in perfectly fine health.

Hayley was annoyed by the sergeant's unmitigated lack of interest in what had just happened to them and decided to speak up. "Look, Officer—"

"Sergeant," Herrold corrected her.

"Okay, *Sergeant*, I am sorry Tilly and I are not more banged up, but that truck tried to run us down, whether you want to take this seriously or not."

"You can bet I take *every* call seriously," Herrold said, eyes narrowing, offended. "I am assuming you gave us all the information you have on the truck, so we can be on the lookout. That's all we can do for now. But between you and your brother draining the limited resources of the Bar Harbor police department with your constant calls about midnight marauders and killer monster trucks, I just hope we don't let down the other residents of this fine town, who may require the help of the police."

Hayley could feel her cheeks burning red with rage, and she clenched her fists at her sides, silently telling herself over and over not to engage with this infuriatingly obnoxious woman.

"Come on, Earl," Herrold said, marching back toward the police cruiser.

"I know it's only nine in the morning, but how about Pat's Pizza for lunch? They have the thin crust, just the way you like it," Earl offered eagerly, trailing behind her.

Hayley returned her attention to Nurse Tilly, who was still rattled and upset. "Do you know of anyone who might want to run you down with a truck?"

Tilly hugged herself, eyes downcast, and shook her head. "No, I don't." She glanced up at Hayley. "Do you?"

Hayley shook her head, but couldn't shake the feeling that Nurse Tilly was lying to her. Maybe it was true that she had never seen Big Hugo before, and maybe it was true that she had no idea who might want to harm her, but she was lying about something, and Hayley was determined to find out what it was and why she was so afraid.

# Chapter 24

Hayley stood at the sink, staring at her reflection in the bathroom mirror. Her face looked tired, haggard, and her eyes were puffy. She had not slowed down since taking over Chef Romeo's restaurant, working a full eight hours at the *Island Times*, and looking after her brother while he was recuperating in the hospital. She had exhausted herself.

Hayley picked up a wooden brush and ran it through her hair, slapped on some makeup, and brushed her teeth. Another quick glance. Maybe a slight improvement, but Gisele Bündchen certainly had nothing to worry about. She fluffed out her hair a bit when she noticed a small red stain on her blouse, tomato sauce from the cold slice of pizza she had hastily eaten for supper that had been left over from last night. Hayley ran the water faucet, soaked a washcloth, and tried rubbing it out. The stain disappeared, but she now had a large wet spot above her left breast. She would just leave the car window open to let the wind dry it out on her way to the restaurant.

Hayley winced as she raised her arm and folded up the sleeve of her blouse to reveal a nasty bruise on her elbow from when she jumped up on top of the hood of Tilly's car to avoid getting mowed down by the speeding pickup truck in the hospital parking lot. She knew Bruce would be calling her from New York when she got home later, and she decided on the spot not to share what had happened, lest he worry the rest of the time he was in New York.

She could handle this on her own.

At least she hoped she could.

Besides, she tried telling herself, maybe it was just a drunk driver not paying attention to where he or she was going. Of course, that would explain the first near-miss, but not the truck backing up and trying again. No, despite what Sergeant Herrold was willing to believe, someone seemed to be gunning for her.

Or Nurse Tilly.

Or possibly both of them.

Hayley heard the front door slam open and someone yell, "Where is everybody?"

It was Mona.

Hayley finished up and hustled out of the bathroom, heading for the stairs. She heard Randy calling to her from Gemma's room. "Who's here?"

Hayley shouted from the top of the staircase, "Be right down!" Then she made a beeline for Gemma's bedroom, where she had set Randy up nicely after checking him out of the hospital earlier in the day.

He was sprawled out on top of Gemma's baby-blue

goose-down comforter, fully clothed, wiggling his toes in a pair of wooly socks, watching the local news on a small flat-screen TV mounted on the wall. When Dr. Cormack finally signed the release papers and Hayley had driven Randy home, she could tell he was still in a weakened state from the surgery as she helped him up the stairs to get him settled. But his mood had brightened considerably, knowing he was no longer trapped in a drab, sterile hospital room, feeling vulnerable and exposed, especially after witnessing what he claimed was a murder.

There had been no toxicology or autopsy reports released as of yet. Hayley was certain that if Chief Sergio was not in Brazil and was here in charge of the investigation, they would already know the true cause of Chef Romeo's death, if it had simply been a heart attack or deliberate foul play. But for whatever reason, Sergeant Herrold was remaining tight-lipped and keeping a firm lid on any pertinent information to the case from outsiders, Hayley specifically.

Randy tore his eyes away from the TV and looked at Hayley, eyes blinking. "I heard someone downstairs."

"Mona's here. She's going to look after you tonight while I'm at the restaurant."

"*What?*" Randy tried sitting up in bed, wincing in pain as he gently placed a hand over his abdomen. Hayley scooted over to adjust the pillows he was propped up against. "Why Mona?"

"Because ever since I hired a new waitress, Christy, to wait tables, she's proven herself to be a rock star. The customers love her, she's fast and efficient and courteous, unlike Mona, who tends to scare people. So I decided to have Mona spend the evening here with you instead."

"Oh no," Randy moaned.

"What? You like Mona."

"Yes, sitting at my bar, pounding down her beers, cracking dirty jokes, but not as my nursemaid. She has the patience of a two-year-old."

"You don't give her enough credit," Hayley said. "She's raised seven kids."

"And they're all deathly afraid of her!"

"You're being ridiculous, Randy. Mona will take very good care of you, I promise."

Randy shot her a skeptical look and Hayley bolted out of the bedroom before he could open his mouth to protest some more. She shot down the stairs to find Mona popping the top off a beer with a bottle opener.

"I got up extra early and made a lasagna this morning before I went to the hospital," Hayley said. "All you need to do is preheat the oven to three-fifty and then pop it in for forty-five minutes. There is also a salad in the fridge—you just need to add some dressing—and I brought home a loaf of garlic bread from the restaurant you can heat up."

Mona nodded as she took a swig of her Bud Light and noticed Hayley absentmindedly stroking her injured elbow. "How bad is it?"

Hayley realized what she was doing and stopped. "Oh, this? It's nothing."

"Did you tell Randy what happened?"

Hayley lowered her voice. "No, and I would appreciate you not mentioning it to him. He's worked up enough already about what he saw, and I don't want to make it any worse. Besides, what happened in the parking lot may have had nothing to do with anything."

"You can keep telling yourself that, but we both know it does," Mona said matter-of-factly. "But mum's the word, if that's what you want."

"It is," Hayley said. "Now if you think of anything else you need, just give me a call at Romeo's."

Suddenly a voice boomed out of nowhere. *"Mona?"*

Mona spun around, like a dog chasing his tail, trying to figure out where the disembodied voice was coming from.

"It's Randy," Hayley tried to explain.

Mona stopped spinning around and slammed her bottle of beer down on the kitchen counter. "Where the hell is he?"

"Upstairs."

"Why does he sound like he's right here with us in the kitchen?"

Hayley pointed to a round black device, blue lights glowing around the rim on top next to the breadbasket. "It's Alexa."

"Who?" Mona asked, dumbfounded.

"Alexa. She's a smart assistant. Bruce got one for practically every room in the house. You know what a tech geek he is. It also conveniently serves as an intercom system. Randy is actually talking to you from Gemma's room upstairs."

Mona stared at the device.

*"Mona!"* Randy tried again, this time louder.

"What?" Mona snapped. "What do you want?"

"I'm a little cold. There's a gray velvet quilt blanket on the couch in the living room. Can you bring it up to me, please?"

Mona frowned. "Is this how it's going to be all night?"

"It is a little chilly, Mona," Hayley said with a shrug.

Mona sighed, marched into the living room to grab the blanket, and then trudged up the stairs to Gemma's room.

She could hear Randy yell from his bed, "You don't have to throw it at me!"

A few moments later, Mona came lumbering back down to the kitchen.

She picked up her beer to guzzle the rest of it down when Alexa lit up in blue again.

"Mona?"

"What, Randy? What is it this time?" Mona snapped.

"I'm thirsty. I think there is a pitcher of freshly squeezed orange juice in the fridge. Can you bring a glass up to me, please?"

Mona stared daggers at Hayley.

"He just had surgery, Mona. He really shouldn't be going up and down the stairs, and he did say *please*."

Mona grimaced, yanked the pitcher of juice from the fridge, poured some in a glass from the cupboard, and slogged back up the stairs.

Hayley waited for Mona to return back down to the kitchen again before checking the time on her phone. "I'm running late, I better get going. Thanks again for doing this, Mona. I'm sure Randy appreciates it as much as I do."

Mona mumbled something inaudible, but Hayley had no desire to hear what she said, so she ignored it and turned to go.

Alexa lit up again. *"Mona?"*

"For the love of God!" Mona screamed.

Leroy scurried out of the room, hind legs skittering and slipping across the floor.

"Mona, please don't shout, you're scaring Leroy," Hayley said calmly.

Mona leaned over Alexa and shouted, "What now?"

"Hayley has a can of mixed nuts in the pantry. I was wondering if you could bring them up to me so I can snack on something until dinner," Randy explained.

"No! This isn't the damn Olympics! I'm not running the steeplechase! Now shut up and watch TV and leave me in peace so I can make you dinner!"

"Well, excuse me, Nurse Ratched," Randy sniffed.

"Hold on, Hayley, I'll be right back," Mona said, pushing past her toward the front door.

"Where are you going?" Hayley asked.

"I have to run home for something."

"Mona, no, I have to leave. What's so important that you need to go home and get it?"

"I've been suffering from insomnia lately so the doctor prescribed me some sleeping pills. They're in my medicine cabinet. I can go home and be back in ten minutes."

"Mona, I don't want you falling asleep while you're supposed to be watching Randy."

"Oh, they're not for me. I thought I could crush a few up and spread them around Randy's lasagna to knock him out."

"Mona, I forbid it," Hayley warned.

"But he's going to drive me crazy—"

"No, Mona!" Hayley said forcefully.

Mona sighed. "Okay, fine."

Hayley was about to rush out to her car when she caught a glimpse of Mona reaching to unplug the cord on Alexa.

"Don't even think about it," Hayley said.

Mona dropped the cord and threw up her hands in surrender.

And then, as if on cue, Alexa lit up yet again. "Mona, the juice is a little too sweet. I think Hayley has some herbal tea bags; can you start heating the kettle?"

Hayley dashed out the door before Mona could utter another word.

# Chapter 25

When Hayley pulled into her driveway hours later, the house appeared still and quiet. Mona's pickup truck was still parked in front of the house and Hayley could see the glow from the television flashing through the downstairs living room window. She glanced up at Gemma's bedroom window on the second floor. It was completely dark. She hoped Randy was getting some much-needed rest. Either that, or he and Mona had killed each other and she was about to wander into a grisly crime scene.

The clock on her dashboard read 11:37.

It had been a long, grueling night. Unusually busy for a Monday. Every table full. The staff working their butts off. After ushering the last customers out the door around ten-thirty and sending the staff home after cleaning up, Hayley retired to Chef Romeo's office to go over the books. The restaurant was still in the red and would be for months, but it was definitely on a fast track to making a profit by the end of its first summer in business. The question was, who would be the one to benefit? As an investor, Connie would be entitled to recoup all the money she laid out for Romeo and enjoy a good return on her investment. But who else? As far as she knew, Romeo had no will, no wife or kids, just Cousin Alonzo back in Brooklyn.

Who was she working so hard for?

The answer kept coming back to the staff.

They were very grateful to be making money in this tough economic environment. Every time Hayley tried to dance around the subject of shutting the restaurant down, just the worried looks on their faces was enough for her not to bring it up. But there was no way she could keep up this pace, not considering her other responsibilities. She had initially agreed to run the restaurant just on the weekends; Friday, Saturday, and Sunday evenings, but because of the demand for reservations from both locals and tourists, she now had the place open seven nights a week. It would be foolish to close a business in Bar Harbor that was performing so well.

There was much to think about.

Hayley sat back in her seat and closed her eyes, taking deep breaths, trying to clear her mind and come down from the frenetic, nonstop evening at Chef Romeo's. When she finally opened the door and crawled out of her car, she felt every weary bone in her body aching. She made her way up the wooden steps of her side patio and into the house through the back door.

In the kitchen, some dishes were drying on a towel set out on the counter, and Hayley counted three empty beer cans ready to be disposed of in the recycling bin outside.

Leroy scampered into the room, jumping up and down, happy she was home. But that's the only greeter she was going to get tonight. After feeding him a treat, Hayley wandered into the living room where Stephen Colbert was delivering his nightly monologue on *The Late Show*. Mona was stretched out in Hayley's recliner, mouth open, snoring loudly, sound asleep, her hand splayed open and the TV remote on the floor where she had inadvertently dropped it when she dozed off.

Hayley walked over and bent down, picking up the remote. She shut off the television and Mona slowly stirred awake.

"What time is it?" Mona moaned, wiping the dried spittle from the sides of her mouth with the sleeve of her sweatshirt.

"Going on midnight," Hayley said.

"I better be getting home," Mona said, struggling to lift herself up out of the recliner, but having trouble. Finally, she managed to push down the footrest and haul herself forward.

"How did it go with Randy?"

"It was touch-and-go right after you left. He didn't think his herbal tea was hot enough, and I refused to take it back downstairs and microwave it, but he calmed down once I fed him."

"Our family has a history of low blood sugar that can adversely affect our moods on rare occasions," Hayley said matter-of-factly.

"Oh, is that the excuse you're going with?" Mona asked with an arched eyebrow before continuing her recap. "He was pretty quiet up there while he ate his lasagna, but then he called down for those chocolate oatmeal cookies you had in the Tupperware container next to the coffee maker. Well, I had to break the news to him that I already ate those while I was watching ESPN. How was I supposed to know he even knew they were there? He must have spotted them when they were sitting in the kitchen after you brought him home from the hospital. Anyway, that obviously didn't sit well with him. I told him that maybe he shouldn't be stuffing so many sweets into his face if he's going to be lounging around in bed all day and night with no exercise and packing on the pounds."

"I'm amazed the White House hasn't recruited you to help with world peace," Hayley said, shaking her head.

"I know, right?" Mona agreed, opting to ignore Hayley's intended sarcasm. "Anyway, that just made him madder, but luckily all the yelling finally tuckered him out and he passed out around eight and hasn't made a peep since, thank you, Jesus," Mona said.

"You're a regular angel of mercy, Mona," Hayley cracked.

"I like to think so," Mona said, once again glossing over the sarcasm. Something else popped into Mona's mind. "Oh, I do have to admit I did get a little impatient with him when I served him his lasagna. He wouldn't shut up about what he saw in the hospital, that big dude taking out Chef Romeo, and how he was worried so much time was passing by, and he was concerned nobody but you would ever believe him. So I told him you were on top of it, and if anybody can prove he was right and not just hyped-up on the pain meds, you can."

Hayley felt a twinge of guilt. "Well, so far I've been doing a pretty lousy job of it. I've got two witnesses, Randy and Leonard, both of whom claim to have seen a large man in the hospital that night. But unfortunately, both of them were heavily sedated at the time, and so neither are entirely reliable, not to mention they both said he was wearing a mask that hid most of his face. Sergeant Herrold won't divulge any information about the cause of Romeo's death, so I'm not even sure this is a homicide yet. I showed the photo of a possible suspect, who could be this mysterious man, around the hospital, but no one who was working that night recognized him. So I can't be certain he was ever in the vicinity of the supposed crime. I keep hitting dead ends, nothing I try seems to be working, but I don't have the heart to stop now because Randy will be devastated."

"Who's this suspect you found?"

Hayley shrugged. "Someone connected to Romeo's past in New York. A hired thug working for a man who had it out for Romeo, goes by the name of Big Hugo."

Hayley unlocked her phone and brought up the photo. She turned it around so Mona could see it.

Mona casually took a quick glance, but then her eyes bulged and she snatched Hayley's phone out of her hand. "Wait, let me see that!"

"Mona, what is it?"

"I know him!" Mona cried, tapping her index finger on the screen. "This is the guy I was telling you about!"

"What guy?"

"That night at the restaurant when I was waiting tables, the one who made my life a living hell by sending his entrée back so many times. Don't you remember?"

"Yes, but I spent most of the night in the kitchen. I never saw him."

"This is *definitely* him! I'd swear on my ex-husband Dennis's life! Okay, I know that doesn't mean much since I despise him, but it's the first name that popped into my head!"

Hayley took back her phone from Mona, then suddenly gasped as a wave of panic washed through her. "Connie!"

"Who's Connie?" Mona asked, confused.

Hayley didn't have time to explain. She quickly looked up the number on her phone that Connie had given her in case she needed to contact her, and then frantically called it.

Hayley raised the phone to her ear.

"Hi, this is Connie . . ."

"Connie, it's me, Hayley Powell!"

". . . I'm off living my best life and can't take your call right now . . . So after the beep, you know what to do."

"Voice mail!" Hayley wailed, impatiently tapping her foot, waiting for the beep.

*Beep*.

"Connie, this is Hayley Powell. You were right. I just got confirmation that Big Hugo is here in Bar Harbor. Please, be extremely careful. Your life could be in danger. Call me back just as soon as you get this!"

Hayley prayed Big Hugo would not find Connie until she could be warned, because after seeing all three *Godfather* movies, she knew exactly what to expect.

And the thought sent a shiver up Hayley's spine.

*Island Food & Spirits*
BY HAYLEY POWELL

The recipe I will be sharing today is one of my absolute favorite pasta recipes! This one, I have to say, is very close to my heart, because it includes one of my all-time favorite ingredients in any dish— cheese! And this particular recipe boasts not one, not two, but three— count 'em—three different cheeses! Is your mouth already watering like mine?

I have loved cheese since as far back as I can remember. My mother once said I ate so much cheese, she expected me to sprout whiskers, which reminds me of a story that happened last month. Bruce and I had driven down to Portland for a weekend getaway off the island. A must-stop whenever we take a road trip on the 95 freeway to southern Maine is at the Cheese Shop on Washington Avenue. Whenever I step into that shop, it's like I have died and bypassed God's waiting room, entering directly into heaven! What a wide variety of delectable cheese to choose from! Anyway, on that particular trip, in addition to the twelve blocks for me, I also picked up a nice Gouda for my brother Randy, who loves nothing better than to make a nice comforting Gouda mac-and-cheese casserole every now and then, especially when his husband Sergio is out of town, or working those long overnights at the police department.

I already knew what I was going to make when we got home with my bounty of cheeses. It was no contest: My simple, but life-changing, three-cheese rigatoni. So a few days later, I got Bruce settled into his recliner in the living room with one of his favorite crime novels, so I could have the kitchen all to myself to prepare my rigatoni dish. I had just gathered my ingredients, when my phone started ringing on the counter. It was my brother Randy.

"Hi, Randy! Have you tried the Gouda I brought over for you yet?" I asked into the phone.

All I could hear was heavy breathing.

"Randy, are you there?"

More heavy breathing.

"Hello?"

That's when I heard my brother frantically whisper, "He's coming!"

I was starting to get a little nervous.

"Who, Randy? Who's coming?"

Before he had a chance to answer, there was a short scream and then the phone went dead. I ran for the back door, yelling at Bruce to get his butt out of the recliner and come with me! Something was seriously wrong at Randy's house and we needed to get there right away!

We broke speed records flying across town to Randy's sprawling house off the shore path with breathtaking ocean views. Bruce screeched to a stop on the gravel driveway, and we both jumped out of the car and bolted toward the front door. I didn't bother ringing the bell. We just charged inside, where I ran from room to room, yelling like a madwoman as Bruce tried catching up to me, huffing and puffing.

Suddenly I stopped cold in the middle of the living room.

I heard Randy calling for help from upstairs.

Bruce and I bounded up the steps to the second floor to the main bedroom. The door was shut. Bruce pushed in front of me and tried the knob. It was locked. He began pounding his fist on the door, screaming Randy's name. Before he got an answer, Bruce ordered me to step aside, and then he backed up into the hallway and charged like a bull, full speed ahead with his head down, shoulder out. He hurled his whole body at the door, just as the door was flung open by a relieved-looking Randy, who was so happy to see us. Poor Bruce went flying headfirst right though the doorway and landed with a loud *thud* on the bedroom floor, which unfortunately for Bruce, was made of hardwood.

I hugged Randy, asking him if he was okay and what in the world was going on. Randy said he would explain over coffee, and we were halfway out of the room, when Bruce asked if we would mind helping him up off the floor first. We rushed over and hauled an achy Bruce to his feet before retreating down to the kitchen for pie and coffee and an explanation.

Apparently Randy's saga had begun a few

days earlier, while he was enjoying his morning coffee, sitting on the couch in the living room and watching the morning news. Suddenly, out of the corner of his eye, he thought he spotted something scurry across the floor. When he got up to investigate, his eyes fell upon something very large and furry running around to the other side of the kitchen island.

At this point Bruce interrupted Randy, and asked, "Large and furry?"

Randy sighed. Maybe in hindsight, it wasn't all that large or all that furry, but it really didn't matter because anything running around in his kitchen was terrifying, especially since the house was built like Fort Knox and absolutely no woodland creatures of any kind were ever supposed to get inside.

Randy then went on to explain that he headed around the kitchen island in time to see a tail disappear between the refrigerator and the counter, and that's when he went into a full-blown panic. He grabbed his phone and ran to the bathroom off the pantry and locked himself inside. He stuffed towels under the door for added protection, then called Sergio to tell him he needed to come home immediately to get rid of a gargantuan-sized rodent that had invaded their home.

When it comes to household pests, it's safe to say my brother Randy will never be cast as the lead in a remake of *Braveheart*.

Sergio was having an unusually busy day at the police station, and could not come home to deal with this particular crisis, and so he told Randy he would just have to take care of the problem himself. Now to Sergio, who grew up on a farm in Brazil, this meant that Randy should place a simple trap down and catch the mouse, but in Randy's mind, this was far too big for one person to handle. He needed to call in reinforcements and that meant the best exterminator in town, Mr. Peabody, whose slogan was, "No More Mr. Mice Guy."

Mr. Peabody proved extremely helpful, and after a thorough search of the entire house, summed up the good news. In the whole three-story house, there was only one entry point for a rodent, and that was under the kitchen sink where a board had come loose. So Mr. Peabody set his cheese-baited trap, using some delicious Gouda Randy was happy to provide, and told Randy he would be back in twenty-four hours, once the un-wanted guest was caught, to dispose of it and seal up the point of entry.

Randy asked how he would know if and when the creature was caught. Mr. Peabody gently explained, "If you hear a loud snap un-derneath the sink, then you will know your worries are over!"

This did not calm Randy's nerves, it just freaked him out even more, to the point where he thought moving to a bed-and-breakfast for a few days might be a good idea. But ulti-mately he decided it was just one mouse (yes, by now the large, furry creature had been downgraded to a tiny mouse), so he could tough it out, at least until Sergio got home.

The next day, Mr. Peabody returned on schedule, but when he opened the cupboard underneath the sink, he shook his head in surprise and pulled out the empty trap. Apparently, the mouse managed to eat all the cheese without setting off the trap. Mr. Peabody piled on more Gouda this time on two separate traps, hoping this would finally do the trick, and told Randy to give it a couple more days.

Which brings us to the frantic phone call where this story started.

After Mr. Peabody left, all that talk of cheese had given Randy a craving. He figured a big Gouda mac-and-cheese casserole would relax him and do wonders for his frayed nerves. It would also go a long way toward patching up things between him and Sergio. Apparently, Sergio blew a gasket when he found out Randy hired Mr. Peabody, whose hourly rate was fifty dollars, rather than just set a two-dollar mousetrap! But he adored Randy's Gouda mac-and-cheese, so it was the perfect peace offering.

Randy began gathering his necessary ingredients, first shredding the cheese at the counter. He turned around just for a second to grab a bowl from a cabinet, and when he turned back, right there on the kitchen counter, not six inches away from him, was the unwanted guest, nibbling on a piece of Gouda cheese (Randy swore that little mouse was smirking at him too!). That's when Randy ran upstairs and locked himself in the bedroom and called me!

And as Randy poured us coffee, feeling better that there was safety in numbers and he wasn't going to have to face this ordeal alone, that's right about the time we all heard a loud snap.

After all that excitement, a cocktail was in order. Randy loves his mojitos, but I am not really a big fan of mint. However, that completely changed when my daughter Gemma, aware of my aversion to mojitos, emailed me a recipe using basil instead, which I gave a try. I just loved it! And I am positive you will too! The bonus is I have an overabundance of basil in my fresh herb garden, so now I have something else to make besides pesto for my pasta.

## THE BASITO

**INGREDIENTS**
4 basil leaves
2 teaspoons brown sugar
½ lime cut into wedges
4 ounces white rum
Crushed ice
Carbonated water, tonic, or ginger ale (your
　preference)

In a tumbler, add your basil, brown sugar, and
lime wedges, and mash it all together.

Fill the tumbler up with crushed ice, then add
your rum and top off with a splash or more of
ginger ale. Take a big sip and enjoy!

## THREE-CHEESE RIGATONI

**INGREDIENTS**
One 16-ounce box rigatoni
1 tablespoon olive oil
1 pound ground Italian sausage
1 stick butter
3 cloves minced garlic
½ cup flour
2 teaspoons Italian seasoning
½ teaspoon red pepper flakes (more or less for
   preference)
salt and pepper to taste
3 cups milk
1 cup shredded Gruyère cheese
1 cup shredded fontina cheese
1 cup shredded cheddar cheese

In a large pot, cook your rigatoni to al dente
according to the package directions.

In a large skillet, heat the olive oil at medium-
high heat. Add the sausage and cook, while
breaking up with a wooden spoon, until no
longer pink and cooked through.

Remove the sausage with a slotted spoon and
wipe out the pan of all the grease and return to
heat.

Add the butter to the skillet, and once melted,
add the garlic, red pepper flakes, Italian
seasoning, stirring until fragrant, but do not
burn. Add in the flour combining all together
and cook for 1 minute.

Gradually add in the milk, whisking as you go to remove all lumps, and until smooth and creamy. Sample the sauce and add salt and pepper to taste.

Remove sauce from heat, and add your cheeses a couple handfuls at a time, whisking until smooth.

Add in sausage and rigatoni into the cheese sauce and mix together. Pour into a greased 13 x 9 baking dish and bake at 375 degrees for 30 to 40 minutes, until hot and bubbly. Remove from oven, let rest 10 minutes, then serve. *Buon appetito!*

# Chapter 26

*"Hayley?"*

His voice was timid, but clear, coming through the Alexa device sitting on the kitchen counter. Hayley was well familiar with this tone. She had heard it countless times before, especially growing up, when Randy wanted his mother to buy him something while they were shopping on a Saturday morning at a department store.

*"Mom?"*

It would always come from the toy aisle and involve a newly released Mattel superhero action figure or Parker Brothers board game based on a popular movie or TV show like *Jurassic Park* or *The Simpsons*. If their mother resisted, Randy would always resort to a breathless promise, "I swear I won't ask for anything ever again! But I really, really, really want this!" Their mother would predictably relent as she fished through her wallet for some money. However, if Hayley called to her from the record section, a New Kids on the Block CD, waxing poetically about how this was supposed to be their best album *ever*, destined to change the face of music, her mother would snap back, "Then maybe you should get a summer job and raise the money to buy it yourself!"

Hayley never held any ill will toward her brother for being favored and spoiled—mothers always seemed to dote on their boys more in her eyes—but that was almost thirty years ago. Randy was now a grown-up, over forty, and she knew he was reverting back to when he was that manipulative eleven-year-old at the department store, determined to walk out the door carrying a brand-new toy.

*"Hayley?"*

Same inflection, same tentativeness.

Eleven-year-old Randy was back.

"Yes, Randy?" Hayley sighed, standing at the stove and flipping blueberry pancakes over in the frying pan with a spatula.

"Could you do me a *huge* favor?"

*I swear I won't ask for anything ever again!*

"What is it?"

"Could you iron my shirt?"

Hayley pressed the spatula down on the sizzling pancakes frying in the pan. "Why? Do you have plans to go out somewhere today?"

"No, I don't think I'm well enough to leave the house yet, but I do know I will feel so much better wearing something pressed. It's one of my weird little quirks. If I'm lying around all day in a smelly T-shirt and sweatpants, I will feel like a sick person, but if I am dressed in one of my favorite clean shirts, freshly ironed like I'm ready to go out on the town, I will feel like a totally healthy person."

There was an odd logic to his theory.

But it did not make it any less annoying.

Hayley glanced at the clock on the wall.

Ten minutes to eight.

She barely had time to serve him breakfast if she was going to make it to work on time.

Randy's voice crackled through the Alexa device. *"Hayley?"*

"I'm still here," Hayley said evenly.

"You think I'm being ridiculous, don't you? I shouldn't have asked," Randy said.

"Hold on, I'll be right up with your breakfast," Hayley said, scooping up the two large blueberry pancakes out of the pan and onto a plate, and setting the plate down on a wooden tray with a small bowl of fruit, a steaming cup of coffee, glass of orange juice, a small plate of butter and a bottle of maple syrup. She picked the tray up and trudged up the stairs, wondering if she had time to text Mona and have her rush over with those sleeping pills she had threatened to grind up in Randy's lasagna.

It didn't sound like such a bad idea in hindsight.

Hayley entered Gemma's room, where Randy was propped up against some fluffy pillows in the bed, watching Gayle King interview a senator from one of the southern states on *CBS This Morning*.

She carefully set the tray down on Randy's lap.

"It looks delicious," he crowed, an obvious attempt to butter her up.

"Where's the shirt?"

Randy pointed to a Calvin Klein light-blue dress shirt

draped over the back of a chair in front of Gemma's old desk, where she used to do her homework in years gone by.

As Randy eagerly poured syrup onto his pancakes, Hayley picked up the shirt and inspected the label.

"Randy, it says right here this is a no-iron shirt. It doesn't wrinkle," Hayley said.

"They always say that, but it's just a marketing ploy," Randy retorted. "But don't worry about it, I know I over-reached. You're taking such good care of me; you made this delicious breakfast. I was stupid to even bring it up."

*But I really, really, really want this!*

"I'll iron the shirt, Randy," Hayley said, resigned.

Randy lit up. "Thank you so much, Hayley! I swear I won't ask you for anything ever again!"

Hayley smirked. "I wouldn't say that just yet. It's still very early in the day. Does Sergio know you're this high-maintenance?"

"Why do you think he's in Brazil for three months?"

"I'm starting to understand. Eat your breakfast," Hayley said, scooting out of the room and down the stairs with Randy's shirt. She set it down on the counter and got her iron and board out of the laundry closet, setting it up in the kitchen.

Leroy, sitting next to his now-empty food bowl, blinked at Hayley with a puzzled expression on his face, as if he had never seen her do this kind of housework before. But she had. It was just rare, very rare, which might explain her dog's confusion.

Another glance at the wall clock.

Two minutes to eight.

She was definitely going to be late now, but prayed Sal would stop by the bakery on his way into the office and be his usual indecisive self, debating on whether he should splurge on the cinnamon croissant or the chocolate-covered cruller, and arrive late himself.

Hayley flattened the shirt on the ironing board and sprayed water from a bottle to dampen it as her Sunbeam Steam Master heated up. Just as she picked up the iron and got to work on the shirt, there was a loud, frantic knocking at her front door.

She set the iron down and went to open the door, where she found a wigged-out, frightened Connie Toscano-Mancini on her front porch. She was nervously peering over her shoulder, as if she expected someone to be following her.

"Hayley, I just got your message this morning," Connie explained breathlessly. "I went to bed early last night and turned my phone off. I didn't hear your message until I left the rental this morning to go get some coffee. I raced right over here as fast as I could the moment I heard it."

"Hurry, come inside," Hayley said, quickly ushering Connie inside the house and shutting the door behind her. "I was going to try you again when I got to the office. Did you notice anyone this morning following you?"

Connie shook her head. "No. No one, but I got so panicked after hearing your message, I could barely keep my eyes focused on the road trying to get over here. I almost hit an old lady with a cane in the crosswalk, can you imagine? How do you know Big Hugo is in Bar Harbor?"

Hayley gave her a brief explanation about Mona recognizing the man in the photo Connie had given her, how she had waited on him at Chef Romeo's restaurant, how demanding he was, which was what made Mona remember him.

"That sounds just like Hugo," Connie scoffed. "He's

the size of a Mack truck, but inside he's a spoiled-rotten child. Nobody can feed him like his saint of an Italian grandmother, who died twenty years ago! Whenever Rocco invited him over for dinner, I refused to cook for him."

"Connie, I think you should keep a low profile until we know it's safe. Hugo probably doesn't know where you're staying, so I suggest you go back there and hide out until we can figure all this out. I'll call regularly to check up on you and if you see anything suspicious, anything at all, do not hesitate to call the police. I don't want you taking any chances."

Connie's eyes welled up with tears. "I knew Rocco had a violent side to him, but honestly I believed that was just when it came to his work, you know, like taking out Carmine 'Cigar' Luciano, who was encroaching on his garbage hauling business, or a random witness who saw him plug Chico the Enforcer and might squawk to the feds—"

"Connie, I probably should not be hearing this because I really don't want to have to go into the witness protection program at some point. I have a nice life here in Bar Harbor I am not ready to give up."

Connie ignored her. "But I never thought he would ever come after me, his own *wife*. Not in a million years. I thought I knew him. I figured if he ever found out I strayed again with Luca, he'd try to win me back, like with a twenty-four carat diamond, or a trip to Bali. I never thought he would actually put a hit out on me!"

Connie broke down sobbing and held out her hands for Hayley to hug her. Hayley hesitantly embraced her and patted her on the back awkwardly. Then, as gently as she could, she tried turning Connie around toward the door.

"You really should go back to your rental, Connie, and lock all the doors and windows," Hayley said.

Connie fished through her purse. "Do you have any tissue? I'm fresh out."

"Yes," Hayley said, rushing back to the kitchen and snatching one, two, three tissues, before deciding to just give Connie the whole box. On her way back, she was nearly knocked off her heels by a bloodcurdling scream.

Connie was no longer by the front door.

Hayley ran to the living room where Connie stood, looking out the window, her whole body shaking.

"Connie, what is it?"

"He's found me!" Connie wailed.

"*What?*" Hayley darted to the window to see a black Lincoln town car with a New York license plate parked across the street from her house.

"That's Hugo's car," Connie whispered, her eyes wide with fear, her bottom lip quivering. "I've seen him driving around Brooklyn in it! He's here! He's going to kill us both!"

# Chapter 27

Hayley peered out the window at the town car. There did not appear to be anyone sitting inside it. "Are you sure that car belongs to Big Hugo, Connie?"

Connie, frightened, nodded. "Yes, I'm sure! I mean, I don't have his license number memorized, but it's the same make and model and it has New York plates! Whose else could it be?"

"All right, stay put. I'm going to go outside and check it out," Hayley said, moving toward the front door.

Connie grabbed her by the shirtsleeve, pulling her back. "You can't go out there! What if he's lying in wait, ready to pounce? We should call the police!"

Hayley had considered that, but since she had already received a stern warning from Sergeant Herrold not to abuse calling 911 after the last two times, she had to be sure there was an imminent threat before she brought in the cops. It could be just a coincidence. Maybe one of her neighbors had friends or relatives visiting from New York who just happened to drive a Lincoln town car. That seemed like a plausible theory.

Connie plopped down on the couch, clutching her gaudy, bejeweled handbag to her chest nervously, as Hayley cautiously made her way to the front door and opened it. It was a chilly morning, even with the sun having crested over the top of Cadillac Mountain two hours ago and bringing the town of Bar Harbor into daylight.

Hayley poked her head out, staring across the street at the Lincoln. Her initial assessment proved correct. Unless he had ducked down out of sight, or was hiding in the backseat, there was no one in the vehicle.

Hayley made a decision.

It was better to be absolutely sure. She dashed across the street and peered into the driver's-side window of the Lincoln.

No sign of anyone.

Just a scrunched-up Burger King bag in the passenger's seat and an empty soda and straw in the cupholder.

Hayley glanced down the street. It was deserted, except for Mrs. Levy, an elderly woman in a baby-blue housecoat bringing some empty wine bottles outside to her recycling bin. Nothing suspicious there. Mrs. Levy brought out at least two empty wine bottles every morning of the week. Hayley looked in the opposite direction and saw a teenage boy five houses down cleaning up after his Great Dane with a plastic doggie bag.

Otherwise, nobody else was around.

Hayley tried the door. It was locked. Suddenly the car alarm started blaring, startling her. The Great Dane began barking. Mrs. Levy wandered farther down her driveway to investigate the commotion. Hayley jumped back from the Lincoln, pretending it had not been her who had set off the alarm. She waved innocently at her neighbor in the blue housecoat and shouted over the alarm, "Good morning, Mrs. Levy!"

Mrs. Levy reluctantly waved back and then covered her ears to block out the deafening alarm.

Hayley quickly scurried back across the street, up the front steps of her house, and inside, where Connie anxiously awaited her.

"What's going on? What's happening?" Connie gasped.

"I accidentally set off the car alarm."

Mercifully, the loud blaring finally stopped.

"Did you see him?" Connie asked breathlessly.

"No, I didn't see anything inside the car except for some trash."

"What kind of trash?"

"From Burger King."

Connie shuddered. "I remember Big Hugo going on once about how Burger King was far superior to McDonald's because of their flame-broiled burgers, even though he admitted the French fries at McDonald's tasted better!"

"That doesn't necessarily prove anything—"

Hayley was suddenly interrupted by Leroy on his hind legs, barking at something outside the dining room window.

Connie screamed. "It's him! It's him! He's circling around the side of the house!"

"Connie, please, calm down. I saw a Great Dane down the street when I was outside. I'm sure that's what Leroy's barking at," Hayley said confidently, but when she glanced out the window where Leroy was barking, the boy and his dog were long gone.

Suddenly her soothing reassurances to Connie were no longer convincing even herself.

Hayley marched over and locked the front door. She told Connie to stay seated on the couch, and then she walked to the kitchen to lock the back door out of an abundance of caution. When she reached for the knob, her heart leaped into her throat.

The door was ajar.

She tried not to panic.

Perhaps Mona forgot to close it all the way when she had left last night. But Mona had parked her pickup truck out on the street, not in the driveway. Hayley distinctively recalled Mona leaving out the front door. Hayley closed the door and turned the lock. There was no way Big Hugo could already be inside the house. He was apparently around six feet five inches tall, so he would not be hard to spot.

Hayley stepped back into the kitchen from the side porch and grabbed some dog food to fill Leroy's bowl. "Come here, boy!"

Leroy excitedly bounded in from the dining room, no longer concerned with what he might have spotted lurking outside. But instead of stopping at his bowl to chow down on his breakfast, he hurtled right past it and came to a halt next to the coatrack on the side porch that was piled high with jackets and heavy winter coats belonging to Hayley, Bruce, and even her kids when they were younger that Hayley had been promising for years to donate to Goodwill.

Leroy urgently sniffed around the floor for a few seconds, and then emitted a low growl, his eyes fixed on the coatrack. Hayley took an uneasy step forward, her eyes dropping down to a pair of men's shoes on the floor.

Not just any shoes.

These shoes were huge, size twelve at least.

They could not belong to Bruce. He was a ten and a half.

The only way those shoes could have made it inside her house was if someone was wearing them and that someone was right now hiding behind the coatrack.

She had to come up with a plan and quick.

She would just pretend that she didn't notice the shoes and casually return to the living room, get Connie, and then calmly head out the front door, away from danger, to the street where she could call 911.

But before she had a chance to make a move, suddenly Leroy boldly rushed underneath the coatrack and began tugging on the intruder's pant leg with his teeth. The next thing Hayley knew, the coatrack toppled over, knocking her to the ground, burying her in an avalanche of ski jackets and winter coats. She managed to burrow her way out from underneath the mound of the coats just in time to see a giant man, mean-looking face, buzz cut, barrel chest bursting out of a tight black T-shirt, towering over her. He had the largest hands she had ever seen on a man.

He pointed a threatening finger at her.

"Stay down!" he hissed.

Then he lumbered off past the ironing board toward the living room with Leroy chasing after him, nipping at his heels, which the giant casually ignored.

Hayley struggled out of the pile of coats. "Connie, run!"

She heard a piercing scream and a scuffle.

Hayley climbed to her feet in time to see Big Hugo dragging Connie by the arm toward the front door.

Suddenly Randy's voice crackled through the Alexa device. "Who's there? What's going on?"

The voice from seemingly out of nowhere briefly stopped Big Hugo in his tracks. He looked around, puzzled, giving Connie the opportunity to reach up and scratch the side of his face with her long, sharp, ruby-red nails. Although Big Hugo seemed impervious to pain, barely reacting to the scratches that had barely even drawn blood, he was annoyed enough to shake Connie roughly by the arm and hiss a stern warning, "Stop it, Mrs. Mancini!"

Randy's disembodied voice could be heard again. "Hayley, what's happening? Are you all right?"

Big Hugo looked around. "Who the hell is that?"

Connie tried freeing herself again by biting down hard on Big Hugo's hand. This time her efforts worked. He yelped, more surprised than hurt, and released his grip long enough for Connie to break free and run toward Hayley, who had come around from the kitchen through the dining room and to the living room to confront Connie's would-be kidnapper.

Connie hid behind Hayley, who was obviously no match for the big brute, who stared at his hand a moment before balling it up in a fist and advancing toward the two women.

Hayley frantically glanced around for some kind of weapon, anything she could use to fight him off with, but the only thing she could get her hands on immediately was a Disney figurine of Princess Jasmine from *Aladdin* that she had bought for Gemma as a souvenir when she was twelve and they went on vacation to Disney World.

Hayley hurled the figurine at Big Hugo and it bounced off his right shoulder harmlessly, dropping to the floor and shattering into little pieces.

Big Hugo didn't even blink.

"I'm not here to hurt nobody," Hugo calmly explained. "I just came here for Connie."

"Well, you're going to have to go through me first," Hayley spit out.

"Suit yourself," Big Hugo said with a shrug.

Hayley wanted to kick herself for even thinking that line she had heard so many times watching movies might actually work.

Big Hugo took a menacing step toward them.

Connie stood behind Hayley, her hands fastened to Hayley's waist, using her as a shield as they backed up into the bookshelf with nowhere else to go.

Suddenly Randy came hobbling down the stairs, his eyes widening in surprise at the oversized, Bond-style henchman in the living room. He hurled himself forward, leaping onto Hugo's back. Hugo spun around, trying to get a look at what was suddenly latching onto him. Finally, he reached back with a massive hand and grabbed Randy's pajama top, yanking him off and sending him hurtling to the floor. Randy winced in pain, still in a weakened state.

Big Hugo whipped back around, shot an arm out and grabbed Connie by the wrist, pulling her toward him until he could get a good grip on her. He lifted her up off the ground and threw her over his shoulder like a sack of potatoes and headed for the door.

Leroy was barking wildly now, snapping at Hugo's pant leg.

Hayley knew if she didn't act fast, Big Hugo would escape with Connie, and there was no telling what he would do to her.

She couldn't let that happen.

Hayley sprinted back to the kitchen, scooped her iron off the board, and charged down the hall where Big Hugo was trying to get out the front door with Connie pounding her fists on his back, her legs flailing helplessly in front of him.

Hayley reared back and clocked Big Hugo on the head with the iron, and like a majestic redwood downed by a lumberjack, Hugo fell forward with a loud crash as Connie flew off him and landed butt-first on Hayley's hardwood floor.

Except for Randy's moans and Connie's panicked gasps, there were no other sounds as Hayley gingerly took a step over to Big Hugo's prone body and nudged it with her foot.

There was no doubt he was out cold.

# Chapter 28

Big Hugo squinted as he slowly regained consciousness and tried opening his eyes. A harsh light was pointed at his face, blinding him. He tried to move but couldn't, because he was strapped to a metal chair with a garden hose. He was unable to speak because something had been stuffed into his mouth and secured with duct tape. He was confused and disoriented.

"He's awake, Connie, can I call the police now?" Hayley asked.

"Absolutely not!" Connie said, snapping off the flashlight she had been aiming at Big Hugo's face. "That's exactly what he wants. The police will just put him in cuffs, read him his rights, and place him in a nice jail cell, maybe even give him a ham sandwich while he waits for Rocco to send a fancy, high-priced lawyer up here to spring him. No, we'll get a lot more out of him if we keep him right here with us for the time being."

Big Hugo struggled to free himself to no avail.

"Don't even bother trying, Hugo," Connie said, grinning. "Rocco taught me how to tie someone up real good so they can't move. It's easier that way when he drops them in the East River."

Big Hugo frantically glanced around, trying to figure out where he was.

Connie could practically read his mind. "We brought you down to Hayley's basement." She leaned down, inches from his face, and growled, "So no one can hear you scream."

Hayley had heard enough. "Connie, I really think we've scared him enough. I'm going to call the police—"

"No!" Connie snapped, snatching the phone out of Hayley's hand. "If the situation was reversed, he wouldn't think twice about threatening us, or worse. He needs to know how it *feels*."

After Hayley had conked Hugo on the head with the iron, Connie had insisted on dragging him down to the basement to revive him and question him. Connie had gleefully gathered the necessary items to tie him up, while Hayley hurried back upstairs to help Randy return to bed and put Leroy outside in the backyard pen where he could run around and not be in the way.

Then, when Hayley had come back down to the basement, she had found Hugo expertly trussed up in a chair while Connie sprayed him in the face with the water bottle Hayley used to iron clothes in order to wake him up.

Big Hugo tried talking through the duct tape, which proved impossible. Finally, Connie reached out and forcibly ripped off the duct tape. Big Hugo yelped in pain. Then, Connie removed a giant sponge from his mouth. "Hayley told me she's been using this sponge to clean her dishes all week and gave me a clean one, but I thought, no, he don't deserve a clean sponge, so I used this one."

Hugo crinkled his nose and rolled his tongue around in his mouth with distaste.

"What happened? Every bone in my body aches," he groaned.

"Oh, while we were dragging you down here, I accidentally let go and you tumbled down the stairs headfirst and hit the cement floor pretty hard. Oops. My bad." Connie shrugged.

"Please, untie me. I'm in terrible pain," Hugo begged.

"Don't be such a baby, Hugo!" Connie snapped. "It totally goes against this whole macho swagger you've tried passing off your whole adult life, when we both know you're just a simpering mama's boy with too many muscles and an eggplant for a brain."

Connie turned to Hayley and held out the phone. "How do I turn on the voice recorder?"

Hayley unlocked the phone, opened an app, and pressed a red button. "It's recording."

Connie turned back to Hugo and shoved the phone near his mouth. "Now, talk. I want to know everything."

Hugo shook his head defiantly and remained tight-lipped.

Connie took a step back. "Fine." She thrust the phone at Hayley, who took it back. "You hold this. Does your husband have a drill set around, you know, for household projects, putting up bookshelves, things like that?"

Hayley pointed to Bruce's worktable. "Over there. Why?"

Connie sauntered over to the table and perused the tools. She held up a hammer. "Oh, this certainly could come in handy." She set it back down. Then she picked up a power drill, plugged it in, and turned it on.

"What are you going to do with that?" Hayley asked.

Connie stared at the drill spinning around and around. "What does it look like? I'm going to get him to talk."

"You're going to *torture* him?" Hayley gasped.

"That's what he'd do to us," Connie reasoned. "Before I married Rocco, I went to dental hygienist school, so I know how to use a drill on someone's teeth." She turned off the drill and picked up the hammer again. "But maybe I'll start with this on your kneecaps."

Big Hugo's eyes popped open, full of fear. "Connie— no, please! You know if I say anything, I'm signing my own death warrant. Rocco will have the boys take me out to the woods and put a bullet through my head!"

"Rocco's not here, *I* am," Connie spat out. "And I can be a lot meaner and far more destructive than he could ever dream of being. Just ask his first wife, who tried to squeeze us for more alimony!"

Hayley was about to call 911 whether Connie wanted her to or not—this was getting way out of hand—when Hugo finally caved.

"Okay, okay, Rocco found some emails between you and Luca. He knew you weren't at your mother's in Florida, so he sent me up here to—"

"*Murder* us both!" Connie cried.

"No! He just told me to bring you back to Brooklyn, even if I had to drag you kicking and screaming. He wants you home with him. He misses you, he's willing to forgive you, put the whole mess with Luca behind him, *if* you just promise to behave yourself and stay faithful. He loves you, Connie. He doesn't want to lose you."

Connie glared at Hugo skeptically. "Why should I believe you?"

"I swear on my grandmother Luisa's life! And you know how much I worshipped my grandmother Luisa, the saint she was! I would never disrespect her memory by lying to you!"

Connie cast an eye in Hayley's direction for her opinion.

"I believe him," Hayley said quietly.

Connie turned back to Hugo and considered his story. But then, she slapped Hugo hard across the face. "Why did you have to kill Luca? He didn't want me anymore anyway, even after I invested money into his restaurant! I was about to come home on my own, and then you had to show up here and murder him in cold blood while he was lying helplessly in a hospital bed! I will never forgive you or Rocco for that! Ever!"

"No, Connie, it wasn't me! I was never at the hospital! I never touched Luca! I swear!"

"You match the description of two eyewitnesses!" Connie yelled, raising the hammer menacingly.

"Then it was somebody who *looked* like me! Rocco was willing to forgive Luca's debt, if you agreed to come back. He never ordered me to take him out, that's the God's honest truth!"

Hayley was convinced Connie was going to start pounding Hugo in the head with the hammer, so she quietly snuck up behind her and wisely wrenched it out of her hand. "I don't think we will be needing this anymore."

"You don't want me to torture him? I mean, come on, the man broke into your house, he terrorized us, not to mention your ailing brother and your little dog. That deserves at least a few whacks, don't you think? He'll be bruised but still alive, take my word."

"No, Connie, I'm good, but thank you," Hayley said, casually hiding the hammer behind her back so Connie couldn't make a quick grab for it.

Connie sighed. "Fine. Whatever."

Hayley made a mental note to never, ever get on Connie Toscano-Mancini's bad side.

Connie then whipped back around and moved toward Hugo, who shuddered at her slow, menacing approach. "I will make you a deal, Hugo. If you go back to New York and tell Rocco you couldn't find me, that I had already fled Bar Harbor by the time you got here, then I will consider coming back on my own accord. Rocco needs to stew a little more for this botched kidnapping attempt. I do not want him thinking that I am just some possession he can steal back on a whim. But I will admit, I find it kind of romantic that he would go to such lengths to reclaim me. I've always had a soft spot for strong men who know what they want. So this little episode stays between us. You don't say a word to anyone, do you hear me?"

Hugo nodded his head vigorously. "Yes, deal."

"Hayley, untie him," Connie said flatly.

As Hayley scurried over and began unknotting the garden hose, Connie added, "After you're loose, you have ten minutes to hightail it out of Bar Harbor, or the deal's off."

"Yes, Connie, whatever you say."

Hayley smiled to herself. If they ever did a reboot of *The Sopranos*, they would be wise to flip the gender of Tony and base the show on Connie Toscano-Mancini.

Hayley would be the first to binge-watch it.

# Chapter 29

Dr. Cormack sat staring at his computer screen, a perplexed look on his face. "Your numbers looks good, glucose in the normal range, cholesterol under control. Blood pressure was a little elevated when you came in this morning, but it's nothing to worry about. You've been under a lot of stress lately, from what I understand."

"Yes, it's been a challenging time with Randy's gallbladder attack," Hayley said, seated across the room, hands folded in her lap.

"You didn't have to come in today. We could have easily discussed all this on the phone," Dr. Cormack said, swiveling away from his computer and turning toward Hayley.

"I have been feeling a little run-down these past few days, so when your nurse mentioned you had a cancellation this morning, I thought it would be best to have an in-person appointment."

"What seems to be the problem?"

Hayley shrugged. "I just feel tired all the time. I usually have a lot more energy. Maybe it's chronic fatigue syndrome."

Dr. Cormack shot her a skeptical look. "Or perhaps you have just been taking too much on. In charge of your brother's care post-surgery, running a restaurant on top of your nine-to-five job at the newspaper, chasing after clues to prove Chef Romeo's death involved foul play?"

"Yes, I have been unusually busy lately, but I'm normally quite adept at keeping a lot of balls in the air," Hayley argued.

Dr. Cormack grabbed his stethoscope and stood up. "Please, sit on the table."

Hayley got up and scooted up on top of the white paper covering the exam room table. She unbuttoned the front of her blouse and Dr. Cormack pressed his stethoscope lightly against her chest, then placed it against her back. "Lungs seem clear. Heart rate's a little fast. Must be my aftershave," he said with a wink.

He took a step back, stuffing the stethoscope in the pocket of his white lab coat. "Could this general malaise you've been experiencing be a slight exaggeration?"

Hayley sat up straight. "What do you mean?"

"Was it an excuse to come here to my office and grill me about Chef Romeo's cause of death?"

"Dr. Cormack, I find that highly offensive!" Hayley huffed. "I would never fake a medical condition in order to take up your valuable time simply for some personal mission."

Of course, that was exactly what she was doing.

And Dr. Cormack was not buying a word of what she was peddling. He folded his arms and looked at her with a knowing smirk. "I'm not mad, Hayley. I admire your moxie, your grit and determination, but I am afraid that does not change the fact that your friend Chef Romeo died of complications from his heart attack. Plain and simple."

"I don't believe it," Hayley insisted.

"I'm sorry you feel that way, but the facts are the facts," Dr. Cormack said with a shrug.

"Look, I know my brother Randy was jacked-up on morphine, but he is certain about what he witnessed. How hard would it be to order an autopsy on the body just to be sure there was no poison in Romeo's system at the time of his death?"

Dr. Cormack frowned, eyes downcast. "Unfortunately, that is no longer possible."

"Why not?"

Dr. Cormack cleared his throat. Whatever news he was about to relate, he obviously dreaded delivering it. He crossed back to his desk and picked up a file folder. He opened it and skimmed the top piece of paper before glancing back up at Hayley. "Let me say, the county morgue is overburdened and understaffed, but that's no excuse. They had a John Doe . . ." He glanced back down at the paper. ". . . tagged A1497. Chef Romeo was tagged A1447." He looked up sheepishly. "I guess the second four looked like a nine. Anyway, according to the coroner, somehow the tags got switched."

Hayley gasped. "What are you saying?"

"The A1497, the John Doe, was scheduled for cremation. I guess in the mix-up—"

"Oh my God, they *cremated* Romeo?"

"It was an honest mistake, but the county officials are going to conduct a full investigation."

"So now there is no way we will ever know for sure whether or not Chef Romeo was murdered!" Hayley cried.

"I'm sorry," Dr. Cormack said quietly. "But let me be clear: I stand by the cause of death. Chef Romeo had a faulty ticker, and I believe without a doubt that's what killed him."

"That's a pretty convenient conclusion now that all the evidence has been destroyed," Hayley snapped.

"Don't go looking for a conspiracy where there isn't one, Hayley."

The phone on Dr. Cormack's desk buzzed. He picked it up. "Yes?" He grimaced. "What is she doing here?" He listened for a moment. "Well, tell her I'm with a patient."

Hayley buttoned her blouse back up and slid off the exam room table. "I won't take up any more of your time, Doctor," she said, furious.

"Wait, before you go, I can prescribe something for you to bring down your stress levels."

"No, thank you. I think I would prefer staying high-strung. It will motivate me to find answers, even if no one else wants to!" Hayley snapped.

"That's not fair."

"Goodbye, Doctor!"

Hayley slammed out of the office. She was not so much angry over the colossal mistake at the morgue, but more over the fact that she could not shake the nagging feeling that Dr. Cormack had not been completely leveling with her.

Hayley had always prided herself on how good she was at sensing whenever someone was hiding something, or omitting the full truth. And her radar was currently off the charts when it came to Dr. Cormack. He may not have been the one in the medical mask injecting poison into Chef Romeo's tube that fateful night. He was much too short to be the man Randy described. But there was something the good doctor was not sharing. She could easily tell from the hint of fear in his eyes. And she was not going to rest until she found out exactly what it was.

On her way out of the office, Hayley bumped into Lorraine Cormack, the doctor's wife, an attractive, brassy blonde with flawless makeup and a tight face, the product of aggressive plastic surgery to grasp onto the remaining vestiges of her youth. Although her facial expressions were hard to read since she had had so much work done, it was obvious Mrs. Cormack was visibly upset.

Hayley stopped her in the hallway. "Lorraine, are you okay?"

Lorraine brushed past her and whispered, "Yes, I'm fine."

Then she charged into her husband's office and slammed the door behind her.

Hayley casually lingered outside, hoping to eavesdrop on their conversation.

"Lorraine, what is this? Have you gone mad, busting in here unannounced?" Dr. Cormack admonished.

"Here, take a look!" Lorraine wailed.

"What is this?" Dr. Cormack asked.

"Your credit card statement, the one you always insist on paying yourself. I thought I would be a good, dutiful wife and handle it for you this month. Do you mind explaining the restaurant charges during the time I was visiting my sister in Boston? Two consecutive nights at Havana, another at Mache Bistro, one at Café This Way . . ."

"Oh, for heaven's sake, Lorraine. Did you expect me to stay home the entire time you were away? I went to dinner with a couple of golfing buddies. Is that a crime? And I resent you snooping around, trying to catch me in some imagined act of infidelity."

"*Imagined?* Do you really think I'm that stupid?" Lorraine wailed from behind the closed door.

"I think you're being paranoid and completely over-reacting! Frankly, you're embarrassing yourself."

"Oh, is that your tactic now? Trying to make me feel like I am crazy? I have lived in this town my entire life. I know practically everyone. You didn't think I would call Havana and find out who you were there with?"

"Are you *spying* on me now? Seriously, Lorraine, you need help—"

"Oh, put a sock in it, you disgraceful, lying cheat! I know who you have been stepping out with!"

"Keep your voice down!" he hissed.

There was a brief silence behind the door, followed by intense whispering. Hayley moved closer and pressed her ear up against it. Before she could make out what they were saying, someone tapped Hayley's shoulder. She jumped and spun around to find Betsy Cantwell, Dr. Cormack's loyal nurse, trained for years in the art of effortlessly moving patients in and out of the doctor's office, and obviously keeping a tight lid on all of his personal secrets.

"The exit is this way, Hayley," Nurse Cantwell said sharply.

Hayley looked around, lamely pretending to be lost, then spotting the big exit sign above the door just a few feet away from her. She smiled at the nurse and said brightly, "I always get so turned around in this place. Thanks, Betsy. I'm sure I will see you and Clarence at the music festival next month!"

She made a mad dash for the door.

Nurse Cantwell followed close behind, making certain Hayley left the doctor's office and did not try to sneak back.

# Chapter 30

If Lorraine Cormack was right about her husband's in-fidelity, then there was very little doubt in Hayley's mind who the "other woman" might be.

It had to be Nurse Tilly.

As Hayley jumped in her car and raced over to Tilly's tiny one-story house on Snow Street, just two blocks from the Bar Harbor Hospital where she worked, she re-called the odd encounter she had had with Dr. Cormack and Tilly in the parking lot just before someone had tried to mow her and Tilly down in that pickup truck. When Hayley had first happened upon them, they both appeared caught off guard, startled, almost frightened, as if they had been caught doing something they shouldn't.

It had immediately raised Hayley's suspicions.

Tilly had been acting so skittish, so secretive lately,

Hayley knew there had to be some logical explanation for her strange behavior.

An extramarital affair made perfect sense.

When Tilly opened her front door to find Hayley standing there, dread was suddenly written all over her face. Tilly nervously closed the light Kelly-green sweater she was wearing over her white nurse's uniform and frowned. "Hayley, what are you doing here?"

"I have to talk to you. Can I come in?"

"No, I'm sorry. My shift starts in ten minutes, I need to get to the hospital," Tilly said abruptly, obviously worried about what Hayley might know.

"Tilly, it's very important. I have been thinking about what happened to us in the hospital parking lot—"

"You mean with the truck almost running us down?"

Hayley nodded. "Yes, at first I thought I was the target, but now I have reason to suspect—"

"*Me?* Why on earth would anybody want to hurt me? I'm a nurse! All I have ever done in my entire life is help people feel better!"

There was a tense silence.

Even as the hollow words tumbled out of her mouth, Tilly's whole face betrayed a distinct look of guilt.

Treading delicately, Hayley said quietly, "What about Lorraine Cormack?"

Hayley could see Tilly's body stiffen, her mind frantically racing, wondering exactly what Hayley knew.

"Lorraine? What does she have to do with anything? What exactly are you implying, Hayley?" Tilly asked, defiance in her voice, but unbridled fear written all over her face.

Hayley folded her arms, eyes boring into Tilly, who was growing more jumpy and jittery by the second.

Tilly checked her watch. "I'm going to be late."

"I *know*, Tilly," Hayley said quietly.

"Know about what?"

"You and Dr. Cormack," Hayley said.

Tilly gasped, wrenching her head from side to side to make sure none of her neighbors were out mowing their lawn or checking their mailbox, and then she reached out and grabbed Hayley by the shirtsleeve and pulled her inside the house, slamming the door behind her.

"I don't know what you think you know, Hayley, but you're wrong! Dr. Cormack and I are simply professional colleagues. There is nothing untoward between us, I can assure you."

"Lorraine knows too," Hayley said matter-of-factly.

Tilly looked as if the wind had just been knocked out of her. Her whole body sagged, like a wilting flower. "That—that can't be true."

"I just came from his office. I overheard her yelling at him behind closed doors. She apparently came across some credit card receipts."

Tilly covered her mouth with her shaky hand. "Oh, dear Lord, no . . ."

"There's no point in continuing to deny it."

Hayley knew from her experiences with Tilly that she was basically an honest person, so she knew it was not going to take much longer for her to crack under pressure.

"Two romantic dinners at Havana. Another at Mache Bistro, yet another at Café This Way . . ."

Tilly's mouth dropped open in shock. Her legs were wobbly and she had to sit down on her small leather sofa.

She stared at the floor for some time, processing everything, then slowly raised her head to look at Hayley. "Does Lorraine know it was me?"

Hayley nodded solemnly. "She called Havana and found out who her husband had been dining with."

Tilly gasped, this time covering her mouth with both hands. "I knew I was making a mistake! I kept telling myself, 'Tilly, this is wrong, he's a married man,' but he was just so charming, and relentless. He pursued *me*, Hayley, not the other way around, although in the end, what difference does it really make? It's wrong and I never should have put myself in such a compromising situation. I suppose everyone in town knows now."

"No, just me, and maybe Nurse Cantwell at his office, but you know how loyal she is, she probably won't say a word to anyone. Lorraine, on the other hand . . ."

"He was so scared his wife was going to find out. He used a credit card he thought she didn't know about. Joke's on him, I guess. He made me promise over and over not to tell *anyone* about us. I felt so guilty, sneaking around all the time, it made me feel so dirty, but I couldn't help myself. It's been a while since any man has paid even a little attention to me, not since I broke up with my boyfriend almost four years ago. When Dr. Cormack started showing interest in me, I was flattered; it made me feel good. I thought it was just a harmless flirtation, but then one thing led to another . . . Oh, God, Hayley, I'm such a pathetic cliché! How did I get myself into such a mess?"

"When did the affair start, Tilly?"

"It hasn't even been two months. Dr. Cormack was so paranoid people might find out. Whenever we'd go out to a restaurant, he'd make a big deal about telling everybody how he was treating me to an expensive dinner for my birthday. He loved to show everyone how well he took care of the nursing staff at the hospital, always loudly making the point that our meals together were strictly platonic, nothing to raise any eyebrows over. No one seemed to question it, although if anyone paid close attention, they would probably wonder why I was the only nurse who reaped the benefits of his abundance of generosity. One of the waiters at Havana, who was one of Dr. Cormack's patients, asked why we were there two nights in a row, and without missing a beat, he told him that the previous night had been my birthday and the second night was my five-year anniversary at the hospital. He had no problem lying. He was quite good at it. I, on the other hand, am a terrible liar. And I have been struggling every day with hiding what we have been doing. But he was adamant we keep the affair a secret. That's why he didn't want to tell anyone what we saw the night Chef—" Tilly stopped herself.

Hayley perked up. "The night Chef Romeo what? The night he was murdered?"

"Nothing, just pretend I never said anything."

Hayley wagged an admonishing finger at her. "Tilly . . ."

"I can't. I promised him I would never tell."

"Tilly, if you saw something . . ."

"Dr. Cormack told me there was no murder, Chef Romeo died from a heart attack, so there would be no point in coming forward, if there was no crime."

"But if it does turn out to be murder and you hid key information, then that's obstruction of justice and you could go to jail!"

Tilly's whole body was quivering now.

Hayley felt bad for browbeating poor Tilly so hard, but she knew Tilly was close to breaking and so she had to

DEATH OF AN ITALIAN CHEF

keep up the pressure. "It's all going to come out eventually anyway. You might as well come clean now before it's too late."

Tilly buried her head in her hands and sobbed.

Hayley sat down beside her and gently patted her back.

Tilly took a deep breath and then sat up straight, eyes turning to Hayley, resigned, and finally ready to talk. "That night at the hospital, we both took our break at the same time and met up in the medical supply closet. I know, how silly, right? Acting like irresponsible teenagers! It was pretty quiet on the floor so no one saw us sneak in there. But when we came out, we practically bumped into two men leaving the room."

"What room? The room Chef Romeo was sharing with Randy?"

Tilly nodded grimly.

"Was one of those men Fredy?"

Tilly nodded again.

Andrea Cho's husband Leonard had been right about what he had seen while he had been sedated.

"What about the other man? What did he look like?"

Tilly nervously began wringing her hands.

"You didn't get a good look at his face?"

Tilly's eyes started filling with tears, her bottom lip quivering, her hands trembling.

Hayley pressed harder. "Who was it, Tilly?"

Tilly sighed. "He had a mask on, but it slipped down at one point and I caught a glimpse of his face, and—and I recognized him. It was—it was Chuckie . . . he works as a construction foreman for Vic Spencer."

Vic Spencer.

The contractor who had threatened Chef Romeo after

he refused to pay the remainder of his bill for the shoddy kitchen remodeling job.

"Tilly, do you know if Chuckie and Nurse Fredy were friends?" Hayley asked.

Tilly shrugged. "I don't know. But they both looked very agitated and nervous, and I did happen to notice Chuckie had Fredy by the arm, like he was taking him somewhere."

Did Fredy accidentally walk in on Chuckie dispatching Chef Romeo? If so, he would have been a potential murder witness, and Chuckie more than likely would have taken him by force. He would not risk leaving him behind to tell anyone what he saw.

And if Chuckie had spotted Dr. Cormack and Nurse Tilly coming out of the supply closet during his escape from the crime scene, then perhaps it had been Chuckie behind the wheel of that pickup truck. Maybe he was trying to bump off Tilly. Hayley was just collateral damage.

Hayley grabbed Tilly by the hand. "We need to go!"

"But I have to get to work!" Tilly protested as Hayley dragged her out the door to her car.

"We have to warn Dr. Cormack!" Hayley cried.

If Chuckie was running around trying to tie up loose ends and keep any witnesses from talking, then both Tilly and Dr. Cormack's lives were likely in serious danger.

### Island Food & Spirits
BY HAYLEY POWELL

Once a month, my two besties, Liddy and
Mona, and I get together at one of our
houses for a girls' night home-cooked meal.
Last month it was my turn to host and prepare the main dish while Liddy and Mona
were assigned the cocktail and dessert, re-
spectively. As usual, I was craving pasta so I
knew an Italian meal was in the cards. Liddy
had recently dropped the news that she was
currently a vegetarian. She made a few noises
about how vegetarians saved twenty-five live
animals a year, but Mona and I both knew the
real reason for this new cause was because
she was dating her yoga instructor, who es-
poused the benefits of a plant-based diet.

So out of respect for my BFF (plus my passion for pasta), I decided to whip up my ricotta stuffed shells, a specialty of mine, and
putting modesty aside, they did not disappoint.

After dinner, we were sitting around gos-
siping and sipping on the delicious wine
spritzers that Liddy had brought, when suddenly, out of the blue, Mona sat back, cleared

her throat, and announced, "I went out on a date."

Liddy, who had just taken a sip of her spritzer, literally choked and spit it out. I sat motionless, unable to speak, which as all of you know, is the rarest of occurrences. There was nothing but shocked silence.

Mona sighed and groaned. "I knew you two would make a big deal out of this!" That was our cue. Liddy and I both began talking at once, shouting questions at Mona, who threw her hands in the air and yelled, "If you shut up, I'll tell you!"

I couldn't resist one more question. "Why didn't you mention this before now, when the evening's almost over?"

"I've been working up the nerve all night. I wouldn't be telling you now if it weren't for Officer Donnie!"

Liddy gasped. "You're dating Officer Donnie?"

I could see the veins popping out of Mona's neck, so I grabbed Liddy's hand and squeezed it, signaling her to stop talking, which mercifully she did.

Mona heaved another sigh and continued, explaining that she was not dating Donnie, she had just run into him on the night of her date; he knew all about it, and despite her threatening him with bodily harm if he breathed a word, realistically she knew he would almost certainly tell his boss Sergio, who in turn would tell his husband Randy, who then in turn would tell me, his sister, who would immediately go running to Liddy, so she decided her only option was to get her story out of the way. Obviously, Liddy and I both leaned forward at the same time, on pins and needles.

Mona's lobster shop had served customers, both locals and visiting tourists, for decades (she inherited it from her parents, who inherited it from her grandparents). She had countless repeat customers over the years, but one stood out above all others. His name was Matt (actually, that's not his real name, but Mona refused to allow me to reveal his identity in this column). Matt was from the Philadelphia area, but traveled to the island every year to his summer home. His first stop was always Mona's shop for fresh-caught lobsters, clams, and crabmeat. They always had a flirtatious relationship. Matt would tease Mona, asking why she refused to go on a date with him, Mona replying, "Because I'm a married woman!"

Of course, this year was different, given how Mona and her husband divorced last winter. And so, when Matt predictably asked, as he handed over his credit card to pay for his seafood, "When are you going to come over to my place for dinner?" it was a shock to both of them when Mona blurted out, "How about Sunday?"

Apparently, Matt's eyes nearly popped out of his head. But he said he would pick Mona up at six o'clock, and then grabbed his bags of seafood and dashed off before she could change her mind.

Matt showed up a few days later at six on the dot. Mona, of course, didn't want to give the impression she was trying to impress him or anything, so she answered the door in her sweatshirt and jeans, although she did slap on some deodorant, which for Mona might as well have been a generous spray of Gucci Bloom Eau de Parfum For Her.

She knew from their many chats that Matt's home was located just outside of Bar Harbor, with a sea view, because he had said on more than one occasion how much he loved sitting out on his front lawn, watching the ocean and the many cruise ships, pleasure boats, and lobster boats that passed by.

Matt soon turned off the main road and drove up a long, tree-lined drive until they reached a large clearing. Well, Mona's mouth dropped open in shock as she stared at the most beautiful house, or arguably *mansion*, which she had ever seen, perched high atop the cliff overlooking Frenchman Bay, the Atlantic Ocean stretching out for as far as the eye could see.

"Wow," Mona managed to choke out.

Matt laughed and with warmth in his voice, said, "Yes, I know it's a bit much, but whatever Mother wants, Mother gets."

"Oh, your mother lives here? I don't think I've met her before," Mona said.

"She's here now. I hope you don't mind if I introduce you to her at dinner."

Well, Mona had not planned on meeting Matt's mother on their first date. She found that a bit forward and weird, but since she was already there and hadn't driven herself, she figured she didn't have much of a choice. She forced a smile and shrugged. "Sure."

Matt appeared pleased and jumped out of the car, ran around to the other side to help Mona out, and then led her into his palatial home.

After a tour of the house, which took almost a half hour given the giant size, Matt escorted Mona through enormous glass doors, outside to the back terrace and a beautifully set dinner table for three. After seating Mona, Matt poured her a glass of Chablis from a very expensive-looking bottle, then a glass for himself and one for Mother, whose arrival was imminent.

Mona was starting to get a little nervous about meeting Mother. During the grand tour, when Mona complimented how lovely the rooms were decorated, Matt proudly informed her that Mother did everything herself without any help from an interior designer. The woman had exquisite taste and Mona was starting to worry about making a good first impression.

After a little more wine and some delicious scallops wrapped in bacon, Matt suddenly stood up, smiled, and said, "Mona, I would like to introduce you to my mother, Beverly. Mother, this is Mona, she's the one I've been telling you about."

Mona quickly jumped up and turned around to greet her, but no one was there. Confused, she turned back to Matt. "Where is she?"

Matt laughed. "She's right here, you silly goose!" He pointed to what Mona had thought was a pretty vase decoration in front of his mother's place setting. That's when it suddenly hit her like a ton of bricks that the vase was actually an urn! And Mother was inside it!

Mona managed to mumble, "Nice to meet you," before dropping back down in her seat, while taking slow and steady breaths to get ahold of herself, and trying to devise a quick exit plan.

Fortunately for Mona, Matt did not seem to notice her distress. He was too focused on Mother, saying things like "See, I knew you didn't have to worry about liking her!" "Isn't she great?" "You do like her, don't you, Mother?" "I wish you would say something, Mother!" The more he went on, the more agitated he became as Mona sat frozen in her chair, desperately trying not to appear panic-stricken, which she most certainly was.

That's when Matt suddenly slammed his fist down on the table, and screamed, "Mother, say something! You're being rude to Mona!"

That was all Mona could take. She jumped up, and forcing herself to remain calm, told Matt that she needed to use the powder room, adding, "It looks like you and Mother need a few minutes alone." Matt nodded, then turned to the urn and said, "See, I told you she would understand us. When are you going to trust me?"

Mona slowly walked inside through the open glass doors before breaking into a run straight through the house, out the front door, and down the tree-lined drive to the main road, with no plans to stop until she was in another time zone!

She was just about a half mile from town when she heard a car approaching from behind! Fearing it might be Matt, she ran faster and faster until the blast of a siren startled her and she slid on some gravel on the side of the road and landed hard on her butt. Much to her relief, it was Officer Donnie in his police cruiser, curious to know why Mona Barnes was running alongside the road like an escaped convict.

Mona jumped into the cruiser and ordered Donnie to get her safely to town as she recounted her disturbing date from hell, all the while swearing him to secrecy.

Mona took a swig of her spritzer when she finished her story.

I finally had to ask, "But what happened to Matt?"

Mona sighed. "He had the nerve to call me the next day at my shop and tell me that he and Mother had talked it over and decided that perhaps I wasn't the right girl for him, but they both wished me well, and then he hung up."

At that moment, Mona swore off dating forever.

Liddy had to hold her tongue because she had told me earlier that she already had someone waiting in the wings for Mona, but would press pause on that until Mona was ready.

## SUMMER RED WINE SPRITZER

**INGREDIENTS**
2 strawberries, tops removed and sliced in half
6 blueberries
½ teaspoon honey
Juice of half a lime
3 ounces of your favorite red wine
1½ cups soda water
Mint leaf

In a glass add a few ice cubes, strawberries,
blueberries, honey, and lime juice and stir it well.
Add the wine and carbonated soda and top off
with a mint leaf.

## HAYLEY'S STUFFED SHELLS

**INGREDIENTS**
**SAUCE**
3 cups favorite marinara sauce

**PASTA**
1 box jumbo shells (this recipe will make about
    18 stuffed shells, but throw a few extra shells in
    just in case any rip).
salt and pepper
1 teaspoon garlic powder

**RICOTTA FILLING**
15 ounces whole milk ricotta cheese
8 ounces shredded mozzarella cheese, divided
½ cup fresh grated Parmesan cheese
1 egg
1 tablespoon dried parsley
1 tablespoon dried basil
½ tablespoon dried oregano
½ tablespoon garlic powder
1 teaspoon each salt and pepper

**TO PREPARE**
Preheat oven to 350 degrees and lightly grease or
spray a 13x9 baking dish.

Cook the jumbo pasta shells according to the box
instructions to al dente. You want them slightly
undercooked because they will finish cooking in
the oven. When they are done, drain and set
aside.

In a large bowl, add your ricotta cheese, egg, seasonings, garlic, Parmesan cheese, ½ of the mozzarella cheese and mix well.

Spread the 3 cups of marinara sauce evenly on the bottom of the baking dish.

With a small spoon fill each shell with the cheese mixture and place, cheese-side-up, side by side in your baking dish.

Sprinkle with the rest of the mozzarella and bake for 25 to 30 minutes, then remove, let rest 5 minutes, then plate, serve and enjoy!

# Chapter 31

"Tilly, what on earth are you doing here?" Dr. Cormack hissed, his eyes bulging out at the sight of his mistress standing on his front porch.

Tilly wilted at his harsh tone. "I'm sorry, Hayley made me come."

Dr. Cormack's angry eyes flicked to Hayley. "I don't know what kind of stunt you're trying to pull by bringing her here, but—"

"I'm sorry for showing up unannounced, but this is an emergency!" Hayley insisted.

Dr. Cormack nervously glanced around behind him to make sure his wife Lorraine was nowhere within earshot, then spun back around and tried to slam the door in their faces. "This is not a good time."

Hayley stuck her foot out, using it as a doorjamb, blocking him from closing it. "Your life is in danger!"

"You think I don't already know that, Hayley? I have never seen Lorraine so enraged and spiteful, and quite frankly, there's no telling what she's capable of doing at the moment!"

"This has nothing to do with your wife!" Hayley cried.

Suddenly they heard Lorraine's booming voice coming from inside. "Who is at the door, Robert?"

"Just some Girl Scouts selling cookies, dear!" Dr. Cormack sang brightly before instantly changing his tone to an urgent, panicked whisper. "Please, you have to go now!"

He kept banging the door against Hayley's intractable foot, frantically trying to close it to no avail.

"We refuse to go until you at least hear us out," Hayley said.

Suddenly Lorraine appeared behind her husband's left shoulder and glared at the two women standing on the front porch. "Aren't you two a little old to be selling Girl Scout cookies?"

Dr. Cormack's whole body sagged.

Lorraine immediately zeroed in on Tilly, her eyes wild with fury. "It's bad enough you have been sleeping with my husband, but is it also necessary to show up here and rub my nose in it?" She then turned her rage on her cowering husband. "All I wanted to do was order some mint chocolate chip cookies! I love those cookies! I figured I deserved to enjoy a few extra calories given what you have put me through! But no, instead I am forced into a face-to-face encounter with your secret mistress! When will your cruel need to humiliate me ever end?"

"Lorraine, listen to me, I did not invite them here!" Dr. Cormack shouted.

"Is that supposed to make me feel better?" Lorraine snapped.

Tilly was on the verge of dissolving into a puddle of tears and sputtered, "Please, Dr. Cormack—"

"*Dr. Cormack*? How odd he doesn't even allow you to call him by his first name, especially since you and my husband now obviously know each other in the biblical sense!" Lorraine seethed. "What's that about, Robert?"

Hayley felt as if she was trapped in a never-ending episode of *The Real Housewives of Bar Harbor* and she could not take it anymore. "All right, hold it! I know you're devastated, Lorraine, and it's very awkward with us being here, but we never would have come if it was not vitally important. Dr. Cormack and Tilly are eyewitnesses to a *murder*—"

"*What*?" Lorraine gasped before grabbing her husband by the arm and spinning him toward her. "What is she talking about?"

Dr. Cormack opened his mouth to speak, but nothing came out. He just shook his head, confused, at a loss for how to respond.

Tilly, in a misguided attempt to jog his memory, piped in with, "That night we met in the medical supply closet, when we came out and we saw Nurse Fredy being escorted away by that big man in the mask, don't you remember?"

There was a long, strained pause.

Lorraine squeezed her husband's arm tighter, her sharp nails digging into his skin. "Supply closet?"

Tilly shrank back again, realizing her faux pas.

Dr. Cormack's head drooped.

"Is that where you sneak away for a secret rendezvous

with your mistresses? You can't even spring for a cheap motel?" Lorraine scoffed.

Hayley stepped forward, allowing Tilly to scoot behind her and hide. "Look, Tilly told me she recognized Vic Spencer's construction foreman, Chuckie, when his mask slipped. Did you see him too, Dr. Cormack?"

Dr. Cormack nodded slightly, keeping one eye on his inflamed wife. "Yes, yes, we saw him," he said.

"Why didn't you report that to the police?" Lorraine asked, still gripping his arm.

"Because I-I was afraid . . . if we told anyone what we saw, the police would ask more questions—and—and it might get out that we were—we were—"

"Having an affair!" Lorraine barked. She pushed her husband away. "You pathetic coward!"

And then she furiously marched back inside.

"Lorraine, where are you going?"

"To pack! I'm going to my mother's in Pittsfield!" Lorraine wailed, slamming the bedroom door.

Dr. Cormack whipped around to Hayley and Tilly. "Well, I hope you're satisfied!"

"The sorry state of your marriage is not my concern, Dr. Cormack!" Hayley yelled.

Her angry pushback startled him, and he momentarily shut up and stood in the doorway, briefly docile.

"I don't know how many more ways I can say it, but Chuckie has already tried to run down Tilly here with a truck. I am fairly certain he is planning on coming after you too, so I suggest you lock your door and don't open it for anybody until the police can find him and arrest him."

Although given her track record with Sergeant Herrold, Hayley was not entirely confident the police would take any of this seriously, not without hard evidence, which Hayley still was sorely lacking.

"Fine, I will do that . . . if you will let me," Dr. Cormack said, staring down at Hayley's foot blocking the doorway.

She slowly removed it, allowing him to finally slam the door shut. They heard the bolt click firmly into place from the inside.

Tilly tugged on Hayley's shirt. "What about me? I have a double shift today."

"You should be safe at the hospital. Just don't go anywhere without someone accompanying you. And whatever you do, don't go home. I want you to stay with me at my house tonight. Randy is there. I will call Mona and Liddy to come over. There is safety in numbers."

"Are you going to go to the police?"

"Not just yet. Chuckie doesn't know we are onto him yet. If he was doing Vic Spencer's bidding, then maybe I can dig up a little more information, so Sergeant Herrold has no choice but to bring them both in for questioning."

"Hayley, that sounds dangerous!" Tilly wailed.

"Trust me, if Chief Sergio was here, a couple of eyewitnesses would be more than enough, but that infuriating skeptic in charge while he's gone is going to need a whole lot more, so it is up to me to give it to her. Don't worry, I will be fine," Hayley said reassuringly, trying to convince herself as much as Tilly.

Famous last words.

# Chapter 32

The Seagull House, a seven-bedroom, nine-bathroom estate located just outside of town off route three, adjacent to the College of the Atlantic, had recently been bought by a married couple who co-anchored a popular cable morning news show from New York. The wife had a history on the island. Her parents lived for decades during the summers in tony Northeast Harbor on the other side of the island before they died, and so she wanted to custom design her own fabulous summer residence using her millions of dollars in cable news money. A seaside mansion with spectacular views of Frenchman Bay just wasn't enough. She wanted a pool. Now, most residents, even the millionaires, never bothered with a pool because in the normally chilly climes of Maine, you might get to use an outdoor swimming pool three, four months out of the year, tops. But the Seagull House's new owners were not going to be deterred. They wanted an Olympic-sized pool that stretched almost to the cliff's edge. It took a lot of money greasing the wheels at the town hall, but after a long, protracted fight, they finally secured the necessary building permits, and they hired local contractor Vic Spencer to get the job done.

The pool project was the talk of the town for weeks. A few protesters from the neighboring college concerned about the environmental impact had picketed in front of the property, and there was a standoff with a college student bravely throwing himself in front of Vic Spencer's earthmover that made the front page of the *Island Times*, evoking memories of that lone student in Tiananmen Square facing off with a giant tank. Suffice it to say, public support fell to the students. But ultimately, it was all for naught. Vic had the legal right to proceed and so the local civil unrest ultimately receded.

With the new owners of the Seagull House back in New York busy working on their morning show, Vic took his sweet time with the project, slow-walking progress so he could charge more.

Small towns have a way of knowing everyone else's business, so it was no secret that Vic could be found just about every weekday between eleven and twelve sitting at the counter in Jordan's Restaurant, chowing down on a cheeseburger and onion rings. His foreman Chuckie usually joined him. Hayley had also heard through the grapevine that Chuckie had been staying most nights in Vic's office trailer that was parked on the estate where they were working, after having had a knock-down, drag-out fight with his girlfriend, who kicked him out of their ramshackle house down a dirt road in Tremont.

So when Hayley pulled onto the gravel path leading

down to the Seagull House, she was fairly certain that both Vic and Chuckie were out to lunch. As she pulled up next to the trailer outside the majestic colonial structure, a couple of workmen were shuffling out from behind the house toward their cars. Hayley recognized one, Gary, the son of Rhonda Harris, who had been in her high school class. When Gary spotted Hayley, he lit up with a warm smile, just like his mother's.

He was the spitting image, Hayley thought.

Hayley jumped out of her car and headed toward Gary and the other worker.

"Hey, Hayley, if you're here to see Vic, he's not here," Gary said.

"Oh, darn, when will he be back, do you think?" Hayley asked.

Gary shrugged. "Not for a while. He said he had some errands to run after lunch, so I'm guessing maybe two, three at the latest. Me and Sam here are gonna go grab some lobster rolls up at the Trenton Bridge. See you around."

"Bye," Hayley said, waiting as they climbed into Gary's truck and sped away. She pretended to be walking back toward her own car to leave the property, but once Gary's truck had turned onto the main road and disappeared, Hayley made a beeline for Vic's office trailer.

Surprisingly, it wasn't locked. She stepped inside. The place was messy and disorganized. There was a shoddy wooden desk and metal chair with a computer and cheap printer. Stacks of paper cups, a few dirty mugs, and a coffeepot that had not been cleaned out. In the back of the trailer was a stained mattress with twisted-up sheets and a couple of ratty old pillows. Obviously Chuckie's makeshift bed for the time being.

Hayley was on a mission. Find something, anything that would tie Vic and Chuckie to Chef Romeo's murder. She sat down at the desk, cleared some papers, and glanced around. She opened the desk drawers. More paperwork and work orders and receipts for building materials. She got to the bottom drawer and when she pulled at the handle it didn't budge. This drawer was locked. Hayley noticed a letter opener in a cup holder along with some pens and pencils and a ruler, and used it to jimmy open the lock and get inside the drawer. The first thing Hayley saw was an expensive-looking bottle of scotch. No wonder Vic had kept this one locked. He wanted to keep his booze out of the hands of his workers. But then she noticed, rolled into a dark corner, another bottle, this one much smaller. *Maitotoxin* was printed on the label. Hayley had never heard of it. But after a quick Google search on her phone, she quickly learned that Maitotoxin was a cardiotoxin, which exerted its effects by increasing the flow of calcium ions through the cardiac muscle membrane, causing heart failure.

*Heart failure.*

Hayley gasped. She had just found the murder weapon used to kill Chef Romeo. Vic had had his right-hand man Chuckie do his dirty work by sneaking into the hospital disguised as an orderly and wearing a mask. He had injected Maitotoxin in Chef Romeo's system through the tube that he had been hooked up to, killing him instantly. Because Romeo was already recovering from a heart attack, Vic had counted on that fact to keep the doctor from ordering a full autopsy. What would be the point? It would be obvious that Romeo's condition just naturally worsened before ultimately proving fatal.

Hayley found a musty old rag hanging from the faucet

in the tiny kitchen area and used it to gingerly pick up the bottle of poison and slip it in her bag to avoid getting any fingerprints on it.

She was halfway out the door when she suddenly found herself face-to-face with Chuckie, blocking her exit, a grim look on his face. Gary had mentioned Vic had errands to run after lunch, but not Chuckie.

She had not counted on him returning to the work site earlier.

And she was about to pay for that critical mistake.

"What were you doing in there?" Chuckie growled.

"I was looking for Vic," Hayley said calmly.

Chuckie eyed her suspiciously. "In his office?"

"Yes, I want to talk to him about adding an enclosed patio to my house. Gary said Vic was still at lunch when I showed up, so I decided to wait until he got back, but it's getting late now, and I have to get back to my office before the boss notices my lunch hour has stretched to almost two," Hayley said with a chuckle.

Chuckie didn't crack a smile.

"Can you tell Vic I stopped by and will try and call him later?" Hayley asked casually.

"Why don't you go talk to him yourself?"

She scanned the area.

There was no sign of Vic.

"He's here?" Hayley asked, confused.

Chuckie nodded. "Around back. At the work site."

"But I thought—" Hayley stopped herself and smiled innocently at Chuckie, trying not to tip him off to the fact that she knew from Gary that Vic would be gone for a good chunk of the afternoon.

"Go on, I'm sure he'd be happy to give you a quote,"

Chuckie said flatly, shoving his hands in the front pockets of his jeans.

Hayley hesitated, not sure what to do, but to avoid arousing any more suspicion, she decided to play along. "Well, I guess I'm in luck then."

She headed off around the side of the house and could feel Chuckie's prying, watchful eyes fixed upon her.

She rounded the corner and happened upon the giant hole in the ground where the luxurious swimming pool would be. A massive yellow excavator was parked about fifty feet from the hole next to one of three huge mounds of dirt.

There was still no sign of Vic.

Maybe he was working down in the hole.

Hayley cautiously approached the edge and peered down. There were some discarded tools and a couple of hard hats, but otherwise the hole was empty.

Suddenly, without warning, the deafening sound of the excavator roaring to life drowned everything out. The noise caused some frightened birds to flee from the branches of a nearby tree.

Hayley spun around. The giant earthmover rolled menacingly toward her. She could plainly see Chuckie in the cab operating it.

Her heart sank.

He had lured her back here by lying about Vic being on site.

And his plan was becoming painfully clear.

He wasn't going to use a simple four-wheel truck this time.

He was going to come after her with a giant excavator.

Hayley backed away as far as possible, until her heels

were dangling precariously over the edge of the hole. She could try to dash to the left or right, but the hole was too long and wide. The excavator would reach her before she managed to clear it.

She watched as Chuckie, who appeared so nonchalant and carefree in the cab, shifted one of the levers, which raised up the humungous metal shovel bucket until it was directly over Hayley's head!

He was going to use it to crush her to death.

Sure enough, she saw him pull another level and the bucket began its drop. Hayley, left with no choice, took a flying leap over the edge of the dirt hole, tumbling down the side, until she found herself facedown in the dirt. She rolled over in time to see the bucket crash to the ground near the edge of the hole where she had just been standing.

Hayley closed her eyes, thankful to still be alive. When she opened them again, Chuckie was standing at the edge of the hole, coolly sopping sweat off his brow with a handkerchief and peering down at her lying in the dirt at the bottom.

"Sorry, didn't see you," he said as easily as if he had just bumped her arm slightly, instead of trying to demolish her like a bug with a two-ton piece of construction equipment.

# Chapter 33

Officer Donnie escorted Hayley into Sergeant Herrold's office, where she sat, leaning back in her chair, black boots propped up on top of the desk, casually scrolling through her phone.

Moments earlier, Hayley had driven directly from the Seagull House to the Bar Harbor police station immediately following her disturbing run-in with Chuckie. Officer Donnie had been manning the reception desk when she had arrived, and much to Hayley's irritation, hemmed and hawed after Hayley requested a meeting with Sergeant Herrold. Donnie had claimed she was busy handling other vital police business, an excuse Hayley simply did not buy since there was rarely any "vital police business" to attend to in town. Hayley had refused to budge and insisted it was important, and that it would be a dereliction of duty for Donnie not to at least alert

Sergeant Herrold to the fact that Hayley was here and needed to speak with her urgently.

Donnie sighed, slightly annoyed, as if Hayley was simply here to collect donations for a food drive or complain about a parking ticket. But he did finally scoop up the phone and call Herrold in her office, or rather Sergio's office that she had usurped while he was away.

After Donnie had said in a somewhat derisive tone, "She says it's important," much to Hayley's surprise, Herrold agreed to see her.

Upon finding Herrold looking relaxed and bored while staring at her phone, she knew Donnie had been covering for Herrold and there was no "vital police business" demanding her immediate attention.

"Yes, Hayley," Vanessa said, rubbing her eyes and forcing a polite smile. "How can I help you today?"

"Someone just tried to kill me," Hayley said.

The room fell silent as Herrold and Donnie exchanged skeptical looks.

Sergeant Herrold swung her feet off the desk, planted them on the floor, then leaned forward, clasping her hands in front of her. "Did this person use a truck like last time?"

"No, an earthmover. But this time I got a good look at his face. I know who it was."

"Well, please, don't keep me in suspense," Herrold said, a crooked smile on her face, as if she was just humoring Hayley. "Who was it?"

"Vic Spencer's foreman, Chuckie Rhinehart. I also have three eyewitnesses who saw Chuckie leaving Chef Romeo's hospital room shortly before he died," Hayley said.

Herrold and Donnie exchanged another glance, this

one less mocking and a little more curious. Hayley also noticed Donnie's body shivering slightly every time he made eye contact with Herrold, as if just her offhanded gaze caused some kind of electricity to shoot through him from head to toe.

This boy was more than just smitten.

He was spellbound by this woman.

"Who are your witnesses?" Herrold asked.

"Leonard Cho, for one. He saw Nurse Fredy leaving the room with a man in a mask, who it now turns out was Chuckie."

Donnie piped in. "If he was wearing a mask, how did Leonard know it was Chuckie?"

"Actually, he didn't."

"Because of the mask," Herrold said, rolling her eyes.

"Yes. But the other two witnesses *did* see his face when the mask accidentally slipped down at one point," Hayley explained.

Herrold grabbed a Post-it note and a pen. "And who might they be?"

Hayley frowned. "Well, I'm having a little trouble getting them to come forward. I'm sure they will eventually, they just need a little more time."

"Why?"

"It's a deeply personal matter, but I'm certain with a little more persuading . . ." Hayley said, frustrated.

"I have an idea. Why don't you come back when you've done a little more persuading?" Herrold suggested, shaking her head.

"So the fact that Chuckie Rhinehart just tried to crush me with a giant shovel not ten minutes ago isn't worrying enough to arrest him, or at the very least bring him in for questioning?"

There was a knock on the office door.

They all turned to see Officer Earl standing shyly in the doorway, holding a pink box.

"Yes, Earl?" Herrold asked.

Earl held up the box. "I stopped by the Cookie Crumble Bakery on my way in and bought you a blueberry scone."

"My favorite!" Herrold cooed.

Donnie bristled.

It appeared as if his rival for Sergeant Herrold's affections was suddenly getting the upper hand.

"It looks like you're busy," Earl said, scooting into the office and planting the box down on top of Herrold's desk before slowly backing away. "So I'll just leave that there and let you get back to what you were talking about."

"Thank you, Earl. That was very sweet of you," Herrold said, flashing a rare smile.

At least for Hayley it was a rare sight to see.

Donnie scowled at Earl, who could hardly contain his giddy excitement over pleasing Vanessa Herrold.

"A—anytime, anytime . . . A—anything you need," Earl sputtered as he backed into the wall before managing to stumble his way out the door.

Donnie just stood frozen in place, staring daggers at the now-empty doorway.

Herrold opened the box and peeked inside. "Looks delicious." She raised her eyes back up to Hayley, appearing disappointed over the fact that Hayley was still in her office. "Now, where were we? Oh, yes. The evil, homicidal maniac Chuckie Rhinehart. Where did this alleged murder attempt on your life take place?"

"At the Seagull House. Behind the main structure where they're building a swimming pool. Chuckie sent me back there looking for Vic, who he said was there, but he wasn't, and the next thing I knew, he was driving an excavator and barreling down on me and nearly dropped the shovel right on top of my head! If I hadn't jumped into the dirt pit when I did, I wouldn't be standing here now!"

"How do you know he just didn't see you?" Donnie inquired, folding his arms confidently.

"He *saw* me!" Hayley cried.

"Did you have one of those red vests on like construction workers wear, or a hard hat, or any kind of protective gear?"

"No," Hayley whispered.

"What?" Herrold asked, leaning forward.

"No!" Hayley said louder.

"And after he barely missed you the first time with the giant shovel, did he try again?"

Hayley shook her head, frustrated. "No."

"Did he say *anything* to you?"

"He said . . ."

Herrold raised an eyebrow, curious. "Yes?"

"He said—he said he didn't see me," Hayley mumbled.

Herrold leaned back in her chair again. "Hayley, I want to take your accusations seriously, really, I do."

It was painfully obvious she did not.

"But I am a little confused. If you are not one of the two mystery witnesses who claim they saw Chuckie Rhinehart at the hospital after supposedly murdering Romeo

Russo, why would Chuckie have any reason to come after you?"

"Because he caught me coming out of the company's office trailer at the construction site," Hayley admitted, wincing.

"You broke into Vic Spencer's mobile office?"

Hayley reached for her bag and opened it, rummaging around. "I know I shouldn't have done it, but—"

"Seems to me that you are the only one at risk of being arrested here. There is a little thing we like to call breaking and entering," Herrold said.

Donnie snickered.

Hayley found the bottle, yanked it out of her bag, and dramatically slammed it down on the desk.

Sergeant Herrold stared at the bottle. "What are those, eyedrops?"

"No," Hayley barked. "According to the label, it's Maitotoxin."

Herrold and Donnie both gave her blank looks.

"It's a toxin that stops the heart. I found it in Vic Spencer's trailer, where Chuckie has been staying ever since his girlfriend kicked him out."

Herrold grabbed a tissue from the box on her desk and used it to pick up the bottle and read the label.

Eureka.

She was *finally* showing a modicum of interest.

So was Donnie, who stared wide-eyed at the bottle, clearly wigged-out that he was in such close proximity to a deadly poison.

Herrold gently set the bottle back down and nodded, then slowly raised her eyes to meet Hayley's again. "Okay, thank you. I will look into it."

She had said the right words, but Hayley was still not convinced Sergeant Herrold would actually follow through and launch any kind of serious investigation.

But Hayley had done everything she possibly could for now.

Except pray for Chief Sergio's return from Brazil soon.

# Chapter 34

Hayley hurried out of the police station and hustled to her car. She knew she had to get to the *Island Times* office. She had been missing in action at the paper for an unacceptable amount of time ever since Randy's gall-bladder attack.

Although she was fairly confident Sal would not fire her, given how utterly lost he would be without her, she did not want to endure another one of his earsplitting tirades where he loved to use his favorite cliché, "You're skating on thin ice, missy!" Hayley had no clue why he called her *missy* when he was mad, but she assumed he had picked it up from when he was a kid and his father yelled at one of his five sisters.

As Hayley dashed across the street to her car, she nearly got mowed down by the mail truck. Hayley could see Lonny Chapman through the windshield; a cherubic-faced, rotund postal worker gripping the steering wheel with his chubby hands, panic in his eyes. Hayley waved apologetically as she reached the curb on the other side of the street and called out, "Sorry, Lonny!"

The mail truck kept going, but Hayley spotted Lonny shoot an arm out the driver's-side window and give her a brief thumbs-up.

Jumping behind the wheel of her car, Hayley barely had time to flick the key in the ignition when her phone buzzed and vibrated on the passenger seat where she had just tossed it.

She glanced down at the screen.

It was Tilly.

Hayley left the car idling, still parked at the curb, as she scooped up her phone and tapped the speaker button.

"Hi, Tilly. Listen, I was just about to call you. I found some disturbing evidence in Vic Spencer's office trailer that strongly incriminates both him and Chuckie Rhinehart, so I want you to stay at the hospital and don't go anywhere—"

"I'm not at the hospital, Hayley," Tilly said.

Hayley sprang up in her seat. "What? Where are you?"

"Home."

"Tilly, I specifically told you *not* to go home. I need you to get out of there and drive directly over to my house. I will call Randy and tell him to expect you."

"I can't. Not yet, anyway. I still have to pack a few things and I have a cake in the oven."

"A cake? I don't understand! I thought you had a double shift at the hospital today."

"I did, but I ran into Dr. Cormack in the staff break

room first thing when I punched in, and he deliberately ignored me and refused to make eye contact, pretending like he didn't even know who I was, and I got very upset. My head hurt, I was all thumbs, I dropped a tray of meds all over the floor and they got all mixed up and had to be thrown away. I burst out crying while taking a patient's temperature. The poor man thought he was dying! I have been a complete mess today, so that lovely Shelley Clark, who was just getting off her shift as I was starting mine, offered to cover for me so I could go home and calm down and get some rest. Wasn't that sweet of her?"

"Yes, Tilly, but you shouldn't be home—"

"Don't worry, I am almost done packing. You can tell Randy I will be over there just as soon as my cake is done. Shelley suggested I come home and do something that relaxes me and baking always relaxes me. You will love this cake, Hayley. It's going to be a triple-chocolate layer cake. I still have to make the frosting. I hope I have enough unsweetened cocoa powder left in the cupboard."

"Tilly, please, listen to me—"

But Tilly's mind was unfortunately elsewhere. "We can all have a slice or two together for dessert this evening, you, me, and Randy."

Hayley heard a ringing sound.

"Tilly, what's that sound?"

"Someone's ringing the doorbell."

"Don't answer it!"

"I'm sure it's Lonny the mailman. He always rings the bell when he has a package that's too big to fit in the mail slot. I've been expecting some new kitchen utensils I ordered off Amazon a few days ago. They're supposed to arrive today. Hold on, Hayley."

"Tilly, wait!"

But it was too late.

She could hear Tilly put down the phone and yell, "Coming, Lonny!"

Hayley knew it could not be Lonny the mailman at the door.

She had just nearly been run over by his mail truck not two minutes earlier. There was no way Lonny would already be at Tilly's house on his mail route in that short of a time frame.

"Tilly, don't answer the door!" Hayley yelled as loud as she could, knowing it was pointless because Tilly was too far away from the phone to hear her.

Suddenly Hayley heard a shriek.

Her whole body tensed.

It was Tilly.

Hayley jammed her car into gear and raced as fast as she could over to Tilly's house. When she screeched around the corner onto Tilly's street, she immediately spotted the front door wide open.

Hayley veered into the driveway and screeched to a stop. She leaped out of her car and hurried up the cement walk to Tilly's front porch. She stopped, clutched her phone, ready to call the police.

But what would she say?

She didn't know what had happened. The shriek could have just been Tilly's excitement over the arrival of her new kitchen utensils.

Or at least that's how Sergeant Herrold might interpret it. In Herrold's mind, Hayley was just the Girl Who Cried Wolf, a nuisance with too much time on her hands, definitely not to be taken seriously. No, Hayley had to be absolutely sure Tilly was in real danger before contacting the police yet again.

Hayley poked her head through the door without actually stepping inside. "Tilly?"

No answer.

Hayley took a baby step inside, clinging to the doorframe with one hand, ready to turn around and bolt at the first sign of trouble.

"Tilly?"

Nothing.

Just an eerie, unsettling stillness.

Hayley took another step, this one bigger, until she was past the door and inside the small house, hovering in the tiny foyer.

In the living room, there was an open suitcase on the floor with clothes strewn about, as if it had been dropped and the lock popped open and everything inside had spilled out. She also noticed a porcelain lamp had been knocked off a side table next to the couch and had cracked in half.

These were sure signs of a struggle.

Someone had broken in and dragged poor Tilly away.

She had to call the police now.

Sergeant Herrold was going to hear her out this time, whether she liked it or not, because Tilly's life was now in grave danger.

She was certain of it.

She reached for her phone in her back pants pocket when suddenly the front door slammed shut, startling her. Hayley spun around to see Chuckie Rhinehart with one beefy arm wrapped around Tilly's throat while holding a gun to her head. They had been hiding behind the door all along when she had come in.

Chuckie slowly, menacingly redirected his aim, pointing the gun straight at Hayley, who swallowed hard as she shot her hands up in the air, squinting her eyes fearfully, as she prayed he would not suddenly pull the trigger.

## Island Food & Spirits
BY HAYLEY POWELL

I can't tell you how many nights after work I have stood, staring into my pantry, desperate for some inspiration for what to make for dinner! This particular night, I was saved when I happened to zero in on a box of orecchiette, which literally translates in Italian to "little ears"! I adore this underrated gem of a pasta! Of course, after an exhausting day at the office, I didn't want to have to prepare anything too fancy, just a simple, easy dish that could be whipped up in a half hour. That's when it hit me! Peas and pasta! A long-time staple in my house! I hadn't made it in quite a while, and then I remembered why, which made me chuckle.

Bruce was sitting at the kitchen table and asked me what was so funny, and so I sat down at the table and filled him in on the whole hilarious story.

Back in the day when Mona's kids and mine were still young and rambunctious (they still can be rambunctious, but now most of them are old enough to vote), Mona and I would pack them all up (my two and her seven—no, eight. Honestly, who can keep track?) on hot summer days and trek over to the Glen Mary wading pool, which was located just down the street. All of us, kids included, would load up our arms with beach balls, rubber duck floaties, towels, and even a fold-up chair or two, while Mona's dog King, a monstrous German shepherd, effortlessly pulled a wagon tied to his leash, packed with an ice chest of cold drinks, peanut butter sandwiches, snacks, and sometimes even a kid or two sitting on top of the cooler.

We were quite a sight to see marching down the street. If we waved a few American flags around, passersby would assume we were just part of Bar Harbor's Fourth of July parade!

Now as most parents know, after a whole Saturday afternoon in the sunshine, splashing around in a wading pool, any kid would get pretty worn-out. And that's exactly what Mona and I always counted on! We wanted that pack of wild kids exhausted and barely able to keep their eyes open! The plan was to head home at dusk, park the kids in the living room with a Disney movie—preferably one that took a while to get exciting, so at least a few of the younger ones would pass out early on—then Mona and I could safely retreat to the deck and enjoy a cocktail or two before I would make a simple supper for everyone.

On this particular evening, I decided to make peas and pasta. After refreshing Mona's Paloma cocktail, I headed to the kitchen and took out a bag of frozen peas from the freezer, and then set it out on the counter to

defrost a bit before joining Mona back outside on the deck.

We were howling about some embarrassing story from our middle school years when
my daughter Gemma suddenly came rushing
out, in her dramatic seven-year-old way, and
exclaimed, "Aunt Mona, I think you need to
come inside because Dennis Jr. told Dougie
that if he put peas up his nose, they would
come out his eyeballs! I told Dougie that
Dennis was just fooling him, but he didn't believe me."

That's when Gemma took a long pause for
dramatic effect (something I'm sorry to say
she picked up from her mother) before continuing, "Of course they didn't come out of
his eyeballs, but they did get stuck in his nose
and now he can't breathe very good."

As you can imagine, Mona and I jumped to
our feet and dashed inside to the living room,
where poor little Dougie was standing in the
middle of the floor, crying his eyes out, a
spilled bag of peas all around his feet. Dennis
Jr. was huddled in the corner, trying to will
himself invisible so his frantic mother would
not see him.

Mona grabbed Dougie and tilted his head
toward the ceiling to take a quick peek up his
nose. Then she turned to me and mouthed
the words, "I don't know what to do!"

I scurried to the kitchen, grabbed my bag,
and fumbled around for a pair of tweezers before rushing back to the living room, handing them to Mona, and cried, "Try these!"

Mona had barely got the tweezers past the

opening of the nostrils before Dougie was screaming and squirming and trying to free himself from his mother's grasp. Mona sighed. "I guess we're going to have to take him to the emergency room!"

"No! I don't want to go to the hospital!" Dougie wailed.

Mona picked little Dougie up in her arms, his tiny arms and legs flailing, and headed for the door, giving Dennis Jr. a little side-eye and silent warning that he was in big trouble.

Suddenly, without warning, with Dougie's mouth wide open as he was crying, the boy let out a loud hiccup, followed by a big sneeze, and peas shot out of his nose and across the room, one bouncing off the top of my forehead.

All the other kids thought the flying peas out of Dougie's cannon nose were the coolest thing they had ever seen, except for Gemma, who found the whole pea trick "gross."

After another check up Dougie's nostrils to make certain all the peas had been dislodged, Mona ordered Dennis Jr. to go wait in the truck while she gathered up the rest of her brood to go home.

After they left, I took in the sight of all those peas on my kitchen floor (I hadn't mopped in a week), and turned to my own kids, Gemma and Dustin, and said with a smile, "How about pizza?"

After that incident, I lost my appetite for peas and pasta for quite some time, that is until recently. I even updated it for Bruce's taste, and I am happy to report that it has now become a favorite weeknight staple for the two of us on busy days when we don't feel much like cooking and want something easy to make. Trust me: This is sure to be one of your favorites too, especially with the Paloma cocktail, Mona's preferred drink of choice, even today.

## PALOMA COCKTAIL

**INGREDIENTS:**
2 ounces grapefruit juice
2 ounces simple syrup
1 ounce lime juice (fresh is best)
2 ounces club soda
2 ounces tequila
Lime wedge

Rub a lime wedge around the rim of a cocktail glass, then dip the glass in coarse salt and fill with ice.

Pour into the glass your grapefruit juice, simple syrup, and lime juice and stir to combine, then top off with your club soda.

## SIMPLE ORECCHIETTE WITH PEAS AND GORGONZOLA

### INGREDIENTS

2½ cups of orecchiette (if you can't find them,
   medium-sized shells will work)
¾ cup peas, fresh or frozen
¼ cup half-and-half
¼ cup Gorgonzola, crumbled
½ cup fresh basil (more if you like)
Salt and pepper to taste
Parmesan (optional)

Boil your orecchiette as package instructs.

In a large pan add the butter and melt on
medium heat.

When melted, add your peas and give them a stir.

Add the half-and-half and stir.

Add the cooked orecchiette and mix well, coating
the pasta.

Remove from heat and serve. Feel free to add
some freshly grated Parmesan at the end because
you can never have too much cheese!

# Chapter 35

Hayley could see the panic in Chuckie's eyes as he appeared to contemplate his next move. Tilly looked like a helpless rag doll he was clutching against his chest.

She sobbed softly.

"Tilly, are you all right?" Hayley asked gently.

Tilly nodded slightly, sniffling, her mouth almost covered by Chuckie's massive muscled forearm.

Hayley kept her hands high in the air as she softly spoke to Chuckie. "Don't you think this has gotten way out of hand, Chuckie? Not only do you have two eyewitnesses who saw you slipping out of the hospital after you killed Chef Romeo, you now also have me to contend with, and I've been talking. More people know now. You might as well stop trying to cover up your crimes. You need to turn yourself in. It's over."

"I'll be the one to decide when it's over!" Chuckie spat

out, squeezing the gun so tightly his knuckles were a ghostly white.

"How many more people do you have to hurt in order to protect your boss, Vic Spencer? He's not worth it," Hayley said, trying to stay measured and calm but not quite succeeding.

Chuckie stared at her, puzzled. "What are you talking about?"

"Doing Vic's dirty work for him. Don't expect him to stay loyal to you. Once everything is out in the open, you can bet he'll cut a deal to protect himself and let you take all the blame," Hayley said.

Another blank look from Chuckie.

And then he laughed.

"You got it all wrong. I didn't take out Chef Romeo for Vic. I did it for me . . . for my father!"

"Your *father*?"

What did Chuckie mean by that?

And then it hit her like a thunderstrike.

Bruce's legwork in Brooklyn.

The rival Italian restaurant Chef Romeo had put out of business.

"Your last name isn't Rhinehart, is it, Chuckie?"

Chuckie shook his head. "Nope. Rhinehart is the last name of an old girlfriend I decided to use when I moved up here."

"Your real name is Caruso."

"Well, she's finally getting somewhere," Chuckie sneered.

"I—I don't understand," Tilly squeaked.

"Chuckie's father, Gio Caruso, had a successful local family-run Italian restaurant in Brooklyn. That is, until

Chef Romeo opened his own restaurant right across the street and put him out of business."

"Everyone in the neighborhood loved our place. We were busy with a line out the door every night of the week. I grew up busing tables for my dad. He wanted me to take over some day when he retired. We got rated Brooklyn's best pizza in *New York* magazine. Dad was on top of the world. He even got offers to go on the Food Network and the Cooking Channel and make his famous manicotti. But then Chef Romeo came along and ruined everything!"

"You can't blame him for opening a popular new restaurant. That's just business."

"No, but what about the underhanded scare tactics he pulled? He started spreading vicious rumors about my father's place, using fake social media accounts to invent incidents of food poisoning, writing one-star Yelp reviews, even joking in a YouTube video that people would be risking their lives if they ate at our restaurant. We honestly didn't think people would believe his lies, but after a while, the rumors started to stick, and pretty soon business was way down and Dad was forced to raise the prices on the menu just to stay afloat, which caused his loyal customers, after so many years, to flock across the street to Chef Romeo's. He eventually had to lay off staff that had been with him for decades, and then, finally, after almost forty years in business, he had to close the doors for good. It devastated him and he never recovered. Running that place was his life's work and thanks to that smug, despicable jerk, my father was left with *nothing*. He sank into a deep depression and could never get himself out of it . . . until the day he died from a broken heart."

Revenge.

This was all about a son's revenge.

"How did you find him all the way up here in Maine?" Hayley asked.

"I followed him. It was common knowledge around the neighborhood that the Mob was after him for squelching on a loan. I knew the walls were closing in on him, and that he'd try and make a run for it, so I began staking him out. And one night I was parked right outside his town house when he packed up and got out of Dodge. I tailed him ten-and-a-half hours all the way up here to Maine. He never met me, didn't know who I was, so it was easy to change my last name and pretend to be new in town. Vic hired me for his construction company, and then I just bided my time, waiting for the right opportunity."

"And poor Nurse Fredy just happened to be in the wrong place at the wrong time," Hayley lamented.

Chuckie grimaced, a hint of guilt on his face. "He walked in and saw everything: me injecting the toxin in the tube, your brother passed out on the floor. I had no choice. I had to take him with me at gunpoint."

"Where is he, Chuckie?" Hayley demanded to know. "Did you *kill* him?"

A sinister smile crept across Chuckie's face. "Not yet."

Hayley gasped, hopeful. "Fredy's still alive?"

Chuckie nodded. "I got him on ice, handcuffed to a pipe in the basement of the Seagull House. It's empty, the owners are in New York, so he can't bother anyone."

"How long were you planning to keep him down there?" Hayley gasped.

"Not long. Vic's scheduled to lay the foundation for the new swimming pool out back tomorrow, fill the whole thing with cement, so I'm going to make sure Fredy's body is buried in that hole tonight. With all that hardened cement poured over his grave, there's not much of a chance he'll ever be found. I couldn't do it earlier, it was too risky. What if Vic or one of the crew accidentally stumbled across the body?" Chuckie explained in a cold, detached tone.

Hayley suddenly smelled smoke.

Chuckie sniffed the air.

He apparently smelled it too.

"What is that?" Chuckie barked.

"Something's burning," Hayley said.

Tilly's eyes popped open. "My cake!"

Chuckie held her tighter, his gun still aimed at Hayley, as he growled in Tilly's ear, "*What?*"

"I forgot I have a cake in the oven!" Tilly wailed. "I need to take it out before it starts a fire and burns the whole house down!"

Chuckie debated with himself about what to do.

Hayley remained frozen in place, hands still up in the air.

Finally, Chuckie released his grip on Tilly and shoved her toward Hayley. "Okay, both of you, in the kitchen, now!"

He prodded them along with the gun in his hand until they were all standing in the kitchen as black smoke billowed out of the corners of the oven door.

"Don't just stand there! Take it out!" Chuckie commanded.

Tilly, flustered and terrified, grabbed her oven mitts and yanked open the oven door. The entire kitchen quickly filled with thick, choking black smoke. Tilly coughed and gagged as she picked up the burning cake tin with her mitts. Chuckie grabbed a dishrag off the counter to cover his face.

Hayley snatched another towel to protect her hands and reached out for the tin. "Here, Tilly, I'll put it in the sink and run some cold water over it!"

Tilly handed the smoking tin to Hayley, who then glanced out the kitchen window. "Dr. Cormack just pulled into the driveway!"

"What?" Tilly gasped.

Distracted, Chuckie lowered the rag from his face and spun around to peer out the window.

And that's when Hayley shoved the black, burned, smoking cake right into Chuckie's face.

He howled in pain, dropping the gun, which clattered to the floor as he frantically tried wiping his face clean with the rag. There were splotches of red on his cheeks and forehead.

Hayley bent down and scooped up the gun. When Chuckie finally managed to open his eyes again, he saw Hayley gripping the gun, holding him at bay, now firmly in control of the situation.

"Tilly, call 911," Hayley ordered.

Tilly marched over to her landline phone hanging on the kitchen wall, picked up the receiver, and in an almost trancelike state, punched the numbers. She waited. "Yes, I would like to report a break-in . . . and a murder. Am I forgetting anything, Hayley?"

"That's enough to start with," she said.

Hayley was confident that this time, Sergeant Herrold would have no choice but to take her seriously.

She had all the evidence she needed.

Not to mention a confession from the killer.

She was finally going to get justice for Chef Romeo.

# Chapter 36

When Hayley looked out the window to see the police cruiser pull up and Sergeant Herrold get out, she was surprised not to see Officers Donnie and Earl chasing after her like a pair of devoted beagles.

She was alone.

Chuckie was slumped over on the couch, gingerly touching the red welts on his face. Hayley had allowed him to wash the chunks of burned cake off his face in the kitchen sink, before parking him in the living room and keeping his gun trained squarely on him to discourage him from making some kind of sudden move to try and regain control of the situation.

When the doorbell rang, Hayley instructed Tilly, who was a nervous wreck at this point, to let the sergeant in. Tilly scampered to the front door to open it, greeting the sergeant, who brusquely swept past her and into the living room where Hayley was holding Chuckie at bay.

"What happened?" Herrold asked.

Hayley quickly brought the sergeant up to speed by re-counting the details of Chuckie's real identity and motive for killing Chef Romeo, aka Luca, stemming from the events that transpired back in Brooklyn.

Herrold listened curiously at first, then intently, a troubled look on her face, and Hayley believed that she was finally making some headway with the usually intractable and ornery sergeant. When she was finished, Herrold slowly turned around to confront Chuckie on the couch.

"Is this true?"

Chuckie, who for some inexplicable reason had a strange, crooked smile on his face—odd for a man about to be arrested for murder—nodded and grunted, "Every word."

"Okay, then, Hayley, I guess your suspicions were right all along," Herrold said calmly, before reaching out a hand toward her. "Good job. Why don't you let me take over from here?"

"Yes, thank you." Hayley sighed, handing the sergeant the gun she was holding, relieved that she no longer had to brandish a deadly weapon.

Herrold addressed Chuckie on the couch. "Stand up."

He did as he was instructed.

The sergeant stared at him for a long time.

Then slowly, eerily, Sergeant Vanessa Herrold broke out into a wide smile.

Chuckie smiled back at her.

And Hayley suddenly realized that she had made a colossal error.

Poor Tilly was still in the dark.

Sergeant Herrold turned the gun on Hayley and Tilly, as Chuckie walked over and joined her.

Tilly, utterly confused, sputtered, "I—I don't understand what's happening. Why isn't she arresting him?"

"Because I am guessing they know each other, quite well in fact," Hayley groaned, wanting to kick herself, just now noticing the clear physical resemblance. "They're siblings. Brother and sister."

Tilly gasped, stunned. "*What?*"

"Chuckie didn't follow Chef Romeo all the way to Bar Harbor to stalk him and kill him on his own. He had his sister helping him," Hayley explained.

It had all been meticulously documented in Bruce's research he had sent to her from Brooklyn. Chef Romeo's rival, who he drove out of business, had left behind two adult children after committing suicide. A son and a daughter. And in their sick, twisted minds, justice had finally been done in their father's name.

"Actually, she devised the whole plan to take out Chef Romeo at the hospital while he was recovering from his heart attack," Chuckie offered. "I just carried it out."

"Rather sloppily, I might add," Herrold snapped, shaking her head, still a bit peeved. "Now we have a big mess to clean up."

"It all makes sense now why you refused to take Randy's story seriously, about what he saw that night, why you kept dismissing me as a nuisance. You were protecting Chuckie. You didn't want the trail of clues leading back to your brother," Hayley said as Tilly squeezed her hand, on the verge of fainting away from fright.

"B-but your name is Herrold," Tilly managed to squeak out.

"That's my married name, from a brief, ill-fated marriage in Manchester, New Hampshire. I think when this is all over, I'll probably go back to my maiden name, Caruso. Vanessa Caruso, what do you think?"

"I think you are not going to get away with this," Hayley said defiantly.

Sergeant Herrold raised the gun in a threatening manner, almost as if she had decided to shoot Hayley right here on the spot. "You have been a constant thorn in my side from the moment I got here, with your poking and prodding and endless questions and theories, playing the infinitely annoying role of plucky heroine out for justice. I don't know how your brother-in-law can stand it. But fortunately, he's not around to save your butt this time. I'll be doing this town a huge favor."

"But everyone loves Hayley!" Tilly choked out.

"You don't have to defend my honor, Tilly. She doesn't care," Hayley said softly.

The radio attached to Herrold's belt crackled to life and they could hear Officer Donnie's somewhat distorted voice. "Sergeant Herrold, are you there?"

Herrold handed the gun to her brother. "Keep an eye on them."

She stepped into the hallway and spoke into her walkie-talkie radio. "Yes, Donnie, what is it?"

"I responded to the shoplifting call at the Big Apple. It was a twelve-year-old, Tommy Eaton. He tried pocketing a pack of bubble gum and some Twizzlers. Ed Levitt, the manager, didn't want to press charges, just shake him up a little; you know, scare him straight by calling the cops on him, so I just gave him a stern warning and sent him home."

"Okay, I'll see you back at the station," Herrold said.

"Where are you?" Donnie asked.

"I had to answer a call, which turned out to be a false

alarm. An old lady thought she saw a prowler outside her kitchen window, but it turned out to be her gardener. She forgot it was Thursday."

They could hear Donnie chuckle over the radio.

Hayley wanted to scream for help, but knew Chuckie would happily pull the trigger if she made the slightest sound.

"I'm going to run a personal errand, so I will be out for another hour or so," Herrold said into the radio.

There was a pause before Donnie spoke again.

"Is Earl with you?"

"That's a negative," Herrold said.

"Because he left shortly after you did and I haven't seen him since, and normally you and I are partners on patrol, so I don't understand why he would think he could just take my place whenever he felt like it when we get more than one call—"

Herrold threw her head back in frustration, then spoke firmly into the walkie-talkie. "Earl is not with me, Donnie. I promise you. Over and out!" She turned off the radio. "God, he is so jealous! Like I would *ever*!"

"We going to run that personal errand now, sis?" Chuckie asked, giving her a wink.

Herrold then crossed to the window and peered out. "No one seems to be out and about in the neighborhood, so now might be a good time for us to leave. We wouldn't want to give anyone the false impression that you two have been arrested."

"Where are you taking us?" Tilly cried.

"Like I said, my brother and I have a little mess to clean up," Herrold said ominously, a wicked smile on her face as Chuckie prodded Hayley and Tilly out the door with the gun.

The street was empty. No one could be seen in their yards. There wasn't even a loose dog sniffing around any bushes. Chuckie hurriedly stuffed the two women in the back of the cruiser and slammed the door shut, jumping in the front passenger seat as Herrold got behind the wheel and they sped away.

Hayley and Tilly were trapped. There was a combination of steel mesh and bulletproof glass separating them from their captors. No latch on the doors to try to wrench open and escape. Nothing to use as a weapon. Their situation was bleak.

Tilly sobbed softly, the cold, hard reality of their predicament slowly sinking in as they were whisked away toward the entrance to Acadia National Park, where Hayley suspected they would be shot and buried deep inside the forest and quite possibly never to be found.

# Chapter 37

The radio up front in the cruiser crackled again and Donnie's voice came through, his tone now more agitated. "Sergeant Herrold, I'm back at the station. What's your ETA?"

Hayley could see Herrold shaking her head, even more irritated, as she snatched up the radio and spoke into it. "I don't know, Donnie, and I'm getting really tired of having to report my whereabouts to you every five minutes!"

There was silence except for some radio static before Donnie spoke again. "It's just that there's no sign of Earl yet. Can't imagine where he could've gone, but I'm free to come meet you, if you'll give me your location."

It didn't take a deductive mind to pick up on the fact that Donnie feared Earl might be with his beloved sergeant at this very moment, the two of them sneaking behind poor Donnie's back.

Herrold took a deep breath to calm herself before speaking into the radio again. "Look, Donnie, I don't need a babysitter, so will you please stop hounding me?"

Chuckie jolted up in his seat. "Uh-oh. Trouble ahead."

A park ranger truck was approaching from the opposite direction. At the sight of the police cruiser on a park road, outside its jurisdiction, the ranger flashed his green lights for the cruiser to slow down so he could talk to them.

Donnie's voice on the radio was suddenly more tense. "Who was that? Was that Earl? I heard a man's voice!"

"I have to go, Donnie. Stop bugging me! You're worse than my ex-husband! Now I told you, I'll come back to the station when I'm done with my errand!" Herrold snapped.

She shut off the radio as Chuckie turned around and waved the gun threateningly at Hayley and Tilly in the back. "Not a peep from either of you, you hear me?"

They both nodded.

Tilly covered her mouth with her hand to muffle her crying.

The park ranger truck rolled to a stop next to Herrold's window, which she rolled down before instantly adopting a calm, friendly demeanor. "Howdy."

"Ma'am," the ranger said, tipping his hat. "Everything all right?"

"Yes, we got a call from some tourists that a couple of kids were setting off firecrackers in the park. We picked them up and are transporting them back to the station now so we can call their parents."

Hayley could see the ranger glance toward the back-seat windows, but they were tinted so he could not see who was in there, and there was no reason for him to doubt what the sergeant was telling him.

He shook his head. "Kids . . ."

"It could have been a lot more serious. They could have started a fire. Sorry I didn't call ahead, but we were already near the area and decided to take care of it."

Hayley could see the ranger eyeing Chuckie in the passenger seat curiously; no uniform, obviously a civilian, but it didn't spark enough concern for him to ask any further questions.

"No worries, I appreciate you handling it. You have a great day," the ranger said, smiling.

"Likewise," Herrold said, quickly rolling the window back up and speeding off.

Hayley cranked her head around to see the park ranger truck disappearing around a bend, along with any hope she had of him coming to their rescue.

They drove another six or seven miles.

Hayley flung a protective arm around Tilly, who had long abandoned trying to keep up a brave face, and was constantly wiping the tears off her face with her shirtsleeve.

Finally, the cruiser pulled over to the side of the road next to a park trail. Hayley knew this trail. There was hardly ever any foot traffic and it stretched through the woods for miles past a pond and a marsh. Plenty of ideal places to bury a body or two. A sense of dread was growing inside her. Their options at this point were severely limited. She had no clue how she was going to get herself and Tilly out of this one.

Chuckie jumped out of the cruiser first and opened the back door on Hayley's side, menacingly shoving the gun at her and ordering her and Tilly to get out of the car.

Herrold raised her hand to shield her eyes from the blazing sun, making sure there were no cars approaching from either direction, before ordering Hayley and Tilly to start marching down the trail. Herrold and Chuckie followed close behind, Chuckie pointing the gun straight at their backs, ready to shoot if either one of them tried to make a run for it.

They were heading for the swampy marsh. There was little doubt in Hayley's mind now what the plan was. Herrold and Chuckie were going to shoot them, and then somehow weigh them down with heavy rocks so they would sink deep down to the bottom into a watery grave. She had to do something fast to save herself and Tilly.

But what?

*Think, Hayley, think*, she told herself.

"This way, off to the right," Herrold ordered.

They were leaving the park trail, heading deeper into the woods, farther from any sign of civilization. Just over the ridge was the marsh, Hayley guessed.

As they plodded along, Tilly suddenly tripped over a tree root sticking out the ground and hurtled forward, landing facedown in the dirt.

Herrold sighed, annoyed. "Get up."

Hayley looked up ahead. There was a large white pine in front of them, its long branches waving in the light breeze. She noticed one branch with its bluish-green needles and baseball-sized cones hanging in front of them, about twenty feet ahead.

Chuckie bent down, grabbed Tilly's arm, and roughly hauled her to her feet, pushing her ahead of them. "Keep going," he snarled. "We're almost there."

Hayley spun back around and marched at a clip ahead of them until they were near enough to the tree where

Hayley could snag the swinging branch in her hand and pull it forward as she kept walking. She stretched it as far as she could, bending it back farther and farther, slowing her pace until Herrold and Chuckie were right behind them.

Then, with her free hand, she placed it on top of Tilly's head and shoved her down. "Tilly, duck!"

They both dropped down to their knees as Hayley released her grip on the branch. It snapped back violently, whacking both Herrold and Chuckie in the face.

"My eye! My eye!" Chuckie screeched after a pinecone nailed him in the face.

"Run!" Hayley yelled, seizing Tilly by the hand and dragging her through the woods behind her toward the marsh. Hayley knew she had only bought them a few precious seconds, and they had to make the most of it because Herrold and Chuckie still had possession of a firearm.

They arrived at the marsh in just a few seconds and stood at the water's edge. There was nowhere else to go. They could hear twigs snapping and brush rustling as Herrold and Chuckie chased after them.

Hayley squeezed Tilly's hand. "Take a deep breath, Tilly."

"What?" Tilly gasped.

"Trust me," Hayley said, snapping off a hollow weed and guiding Tilly into the swampy marsh until they were waist-deep. Pulling Tilly down with her, they both submerged beneath the water, alternately using the hollow reed, the top of it just above the swamp's surface as a makeshift breathing tube. They remained there for what seemed like an eternity, taking turns breathing through the reed until finally Hayley, slowly, inch by inch, raised her head above the water, just until her nostrils were slightly above the surface where she listened intently.

A wave of relief washed over her when there was no immediate sign of Herrold and Chuckie, at least near where they were hiding. A couple birds squawked. There was a splashing sound, probably a duck, not far away. And then, she heard faint voices. She poked her head up farther until she was standing. She reached down and pulled Tilly up out of the water with one hand while signaling her to keep quiet by pressing a finger to her lips. Tilly nodded and they both stood in the middle of the marsh, shivering from the cold, listening.

The voices, which sounded like Herrold and Chuckie, grew fainter and fainter, as if they were heading away from them, which meant it was probably safe for Hayley and Tilly to head back to the trail and to the main road, where hopefully they might be able to flag down a tourist or park ranger.

Trudging out of the marsh, Hayley and Tilly retraced their steps until they found themselves mercifully back on a paved road. The police cruiser was still parked off on the side next to the trail.

That was a good sign.

Hayley and Tilly walked along the side of the road, hoping to hitch a ride with the first car that came along, but it was about twenty minutes before Tilly spotted a vehicle approaching.

She pointed excitedly. "It looks like the park ranger!"

She waved her arms frantically as the vehicle approached, but as it got closer, coming more sharply into view, it turned out not to be the park ranger truck, but a police cruiser!

"No!" Tilly wailed. "It's them! They found us!"

Tilly made a break for the woods, but Hayley remained firmly planted in the middle of the road, facing the vehicle down as it approached.

"Tilly, wait!"

The squad car slowed to a stop just a few feet from Hayley and Officer Donnie jumped out.

Tilly collapsed in a heap on the side of the road.

Hayley wanted to kiss him, she was so relieved to see his face. "Donnie, what are you doing out here?"

"Don't tell Sergeant Herrold, but the chief's car has a GPS system installed, and all I had to do was use this app on my phone to track it. I just had to know who she was all the way out in the park with, because Earl knows how much I care for Vanessa, and it would be a betrayal of our friendship if he's been going behind my back—"

"I can you assure you, Donnie, the sergeant is not out here with Earl. You have nothing to worry about. But trust me when I tell you, you and Earl both just dodged a bullet. Actually, we *all* have today."

Officer Donnie had no clue what she was talking about.

Tilly rushed forward and grabbed Donnie around the neck and planted a big, wet, sloppy kiss on his lips. "Thank you, Donnie, you saved our lives! You're a hero!"

Donnie made no move to extricate himself from Tilly's unexpected embrace. "I did? How?"

"We'll explain everything on the way back to town," Hayley said. "But let's please just get out of here. And radio someone to head over to the Seagull House! They'll find Nurse Fredy alive and well in the basement!"

Another puzzled look from Donnie.

Hayley hurried to the safety of the squad car as Donnie assisted Tilly, who was limping, exhausted by her terrifying ordeal. Even though Donnie remained clueless about what had happened to them, it didn't matter because Hayley could tell that he was more than happy to take any credit they were willing to give. In Officer Donnie's mind, being called a selfless hero was long overdue and well deserved. He even had a pretty damsel in distress on his arm to complete the picture. For him, it had turned out to be a pretty great day. And his huge crush on Sergeant Herrold didn't seem so monumental and all-consuming anymore.

# Chapter 38

When Hayley had announced on Facebook that tonight would be the last night Chef Romeo's would be open for business before closing for good, she had not expected such an outpouring of support. They had to shut down online reservations because there were so many requests, the sheer volume threatened to overload the website.

Or at least that was what Liddy had told her.

Liddy wasn't exactly a key member of the Geek Squad when it came to her tech prowess. She had just been making her wishes clear, saying time and time again, "It makes no sense to close when you're this popular and the restaurant is making so much money!"

Hayley agreed, but this business did not belong to her, and with the legal owner now deceased, she could not see how it could remain her responsibility to keep it going.

"So you change the name to Hayley's House of Pizza, make a few tweaks to the menu, and I guarantee you people will come," Liddy argued before they opened the doors to the public at Chef Romeo's one last time. "I know Kip Massey, who owns this building. He owes me big for getting his asking price on his lake house last month. I'm sure I can get you a sweet deal on the rent."

"Liddy, I know you mean well, but enough is enough. I can't run a restaurant. I already have a full-time job," Hayley said.

"Yes, one you're bored with as you've told me and Mona time and time again. This could be the big change you're looking for. I have never seen you with more energy, ever since you temporarily took over this place."

Nurse Fredy's sister, Christy, who was finishing setting a nearby table with some silverware and wineglasses, spoke up. "Please, Hayley. This job has been a godsend. Fredy has convinced me to extend my stay. He's trying to talk me into enrolling in nursing school so we can work together at the hospital. But I'm going to need to earn money to pay for it. Besides, I told you, back in Honduras I got a degree in business administration, so I could help you out with the books!"

"That's kind of you to offer, Christy, I really appreciate everyone's enthusiasm, but—"

There was a pounding on the front door.

Liddy sighed. "See, they can't even wait until five o'clock for us to open. This is the sign of a successful business!"

"It's two minutes past five. You're late unlocking the door," Hayley said, shooting Liddy a withering look. "And that's just Mona banging on the door. You know how she gets when she's hungry and her blood sugar drops. Watch out!"

Liddy circled around the hostess station and unlocked the door. She swung it open and Mona was the first to charge in, Randy following close on her heels.

"What kind of place are you people running here?" Mona bellowed as she tramped toward her favorite table in the back. "The early-bird special only lasts until six-thirty!"

"Maybe if you hadn't quit on me, Mona, you would have made sure we opened on time."

"Look, I make no bones about it: I have zero interest in having to stand around listening to impossible-to-please out-of-towners complain about everything!" Mona barked. "*I* like to be the one complaining!"

"Truer words were never spoken," Liddy cracked, before turning to Randy. "It's nice to see you out of bed. How are you feeling?"

"Strong enough to devour a full portion of the chicken Parmesan," Randy said, beaming, following behind Mona to their table.

Instead of hiding out in the kitchen to supervise, Hayley had decided to hang back to greet her first rush of customers. She was surprised to see Officer Donnie and Nurse Tilly, Donnie looking dapper in a suede brown jacket and open-collared shirt, Tilly pretty in a demure floral-print dress that accentuated her nicely curved hips. They pranced into the restaurant, holding hands.

"You two look very nice tonight," Hayley remarked.

"Thank you," Tilly gushed. "I have never seen Donnie look so handsome, have you?"

"Not in recent memory, no," Hayley said, smiling. "Are you two . . . ? Is this a . . ."

They both looked at Hayley expectantly.

"Date?"

Donnie and Tilly exchanged knowing glances and then erupted in giggles, like they were sharing a secret joke between just the two of them.

Donnie was the first to nod in the affirmative. "Yes. Our *first* date."

"Well, we'll try to make it special," Hayley said, turning to Liddy, who had just come back from dropping menus off at Mona and Randy's table. "Liddy, would you show Donnie and Tilly to that nice private table near the fireplace? It's a special occasion."

"Right this way, please," Liddy sang, grinning, winking conspiratorially at the happy couple, going way overboard as usual.

Hayley was not surprised that Donnie and Tilly had become romantically involved. In her opinion, they made the perfect couple. And it certainly helped when Donnie had bravely swooped in and single-handedly rescued them from a brother-and-sister team of treacherous killers. At least that was the scenario that had settled in Tilly's mind and Hayley had no intention of disavowing her of that exaggerated impression.

Not as long as it brought the wide-eyed nurse and the loyal, young police officer together.

Luckily, Donnie's relationship with his best buddy Earl was already on the mend. Once Donnie had become aware that Sergeant Herrold and Chuckie Rhinehart were siblings and had been behind the murder of Chef Romeo, he had wasted no time putting out an APB to the entire New England area so the state police could be on the watch for them.

As it turned out, Officer Earl, who Donnie feared had been sneaking around with the object of his affection, was at the time on his way back from Ellsworth. He had taken the afternoon off to pick up a pair of blue and purple pearl-drop stone earrings, retail price $7.50, at Walmart, and had them gift-wrapped so he could present this little token of devotion to his paramour Sergeant Herrold before his rival Donnie got a similar idea into his head.

The APB came over Earl's radio just as he was crossing the Trenton Bridge onto the island and passing Herrold and Chuckie, who at that exact moment were speeding out of town in the chief's cruiser. Earl turned his car around and gave chase until the fugitives were stopped by a roadblock set up across route three near the Home Depot in Ellsworth. They were currently sitting in a cell at the Hancock County jail awaiting arraignment. Earl made sure everyone knew that he had kept the receipt for the earrings from Walmart so he would be able to get a full refund, or at least a store credit.

Soon Chef Romeo's was packed with patrons, and the madness continued unabated for the next four hours. Hayley powered through the night, ignoring her aching feet as she toggled back and forth between the dining room and the kitchen, making sure everything was running smoothly.

When there were only a smattering of customers left a few minutes past nine, including a google-eyed Donnie and Tilly, who fed each other forkfuls of a tiramisu they were sharing on the house, Hayley finally took a break, plopping down at Mona and Randy's table, where they were enjoying a post-dinner shot of Chef Romeo's personal favorite, sambuca.

Nurse Fredy strolled over to the table, in a white linen shirt and khaki dress shorts, looking particularly relaxed and handsome.

"Fredy!" Hayley exclaimed. "It's so good to see you."

"Alive?" he said with an arched brow.

"Yes!" Hayley cried.

"Thank you for looking after my niece. She considers you family now, Hayley. We both do."

"Are you dining alone?" Randy asked.

Fredy smiled. "Why, yes I am. I just came for a little pasta and to watch my niece in action."

"Well, please, sit down," Randy offered, a bit too enthusiastically. "Mona and I would love to have you join us!"

Mona was blissfully chewing on a piece of garlic bread when she heard her name mentioned. "Huh? Oh, yeah, sure . . ."

Randy excitedly moved over so there was room for Fredy to grab a chair and sit down next to him on the same side of the table.

"I want to thank you for giving Christy a job here, Hayley. We're both very grateful," Fredy said.

"She's a rock star! And believe me, we're all grateful to see you safe and sound!"

"Thank you," Fredy said, before turning to Randy. "It's nice to see you outside of the hospital, looking so handsome and healthy."

"You're too sweet," Randy cooed flirtatiously, as he impulsively reached out and gingerly touched the top of Fredy's hand with his own.

"Randy got some wonderful news today," Hayley quickly interjected.

Fredy turned to him. "Oh?"

"I did?" Randy asked, perplexed.

"Yes. Now that Sergeant Herrold has been arrested, the Bar Harbor police department is shorthanded, so Randy's husband Sergio, the chief, is flying back from Brazil early. He'll be home tomorrow!"

"Yes, thank you for reminding me, Hayley," Randy said through gritted teeth, nonchalantly removing his hand from Fredy's. "I'm very happy about that."

There was an awkward pause.

Except for Mona snickering.

"I can't believe we're almost done, all of this is finally going to be over," Hayley said, glancing around the busy restaurant, before grabbing the last piece of garlic bread from a red basket on the table and shoveling it into her mouth.

"It doesn't have to be," Randy reminded her.

Hayley threw her head back, laughing. "Will you stop already? I told you, I know nothing about running a restaurant."

"Come on, Hayley, you've told me at least a dozen times while sitting at my bar that having your own restaurant has always been a dream of yours."

"Yes, but I was at a bar. People say a lot of things when they're drinking alcohol," Hayley argued.

Mona sat back in her chair and folded her arms. "Your kids are grown up and gone and living their own lives. You know Bruce would be supportive. Are you really the last person around here to notice just how much you seem to enjoy doing this?"

Randy leaned forward, locking eyes with Hayley. "Why should you just sit in an office and describe food when you can actually be the one to create it by running your own place?"

Hayley laughed. "Because I'm way beyond such a major career change at this point in my life!"

Mona, Randy, and Fredy, along with Liddy, who had wandered over to the table, all stared at her skeptically.

None of them were buying it.

And deep down, neither was Hayley.

# Chapter 39

Hayley's eyes fluttered open. The early-morning sun was already beating through her bedroom window. Yawning and stretching, she rolled over to see a large suitcase next to the door.

It belonged to Bruce.

A smile crept across her face.

He was finally home.

As she flung the wadded-up sheets and her goose-down comforter off her, and sat up on the edge of the bed, sliding her feet into a pair of cushy moccasin slippers, she could smell the aroma of bacon in the air. She closed her eyes, picturing it sizzling in a frying pan on the stovetop downstairs.

Her husband was making her breakfast.

She knew she had married him for a reason.

Hayley stood up, threw on some baggy sweatpants and

a wrinkled T-shirt, and stopped by the bathroom to inspect her face and hair. Bruce had seen her at her worst. But if he was going to the trouble of cooking for her, the least she could do was make sure she didn't have any sleepy seeds in her eyes when she welcomed him home. She tied her frizzy hair in a ponytail, splashed water on her face, and padded down the stairs.

Bruce was in the kitchen, standing by the stove, scrambling some eggs, adding a dash of pepper, a pinch of basil. Leroy noisily lapped up the wet food in his doggie bowl near the back door, completely oblivious. Bruce didn't see her at first. By the time she reached the archway to the kitchen, he had finally sensed her presence, and broke into a wide grin. "Well, hello, beautiful."

Hayley held up a hand. "Stop. You don't have to overdo it. You're feeding me. You've already scored major points."

Bruce bounded over and enveloped her in a big bear hug, then kissed her softly on the lips. "Miss me?"

Hayley pretended she had to think about it. "I suppose so. Cold cereal and a banana just weren't cutting it."

He kissed her again, then returned to his eggs.

"I didn't hear you come home," she said.

"Flight was early. I was tiptoeing around, trying not to wake you. You looked so serene when I got in. It's so rare that you're not talking, so I didn't want to disturb the peace and quiet."

Hayley playfully picked up an oven mitt and threw it at him. It bounced off his shoulder and landed on the counter.

"What happened with the trial?" Hayley asked, snatching a piece of bacon from a plate on the counter and taking a bite.

"Hung jury, can you believe it? I may have to go back to New York all over again next spring. The prosecutor is promising to refile the charges."

Bruce plated the eggs, bacon, and wheat toast and poured two mugs of coffee, and they sat down at the kitchen table together to enjoy his efforts.

Bruce recounted aspects of the trial for a few minutes, but he could tell something was on his wife's mind. "Okay, what's up?"

"I've been doing a lot of thinking—"

"Uh-oh."

Hayley chuckled. "I know, whenever I get an idea in my head, your life is usually upended."

"I knew marrying you would never be boring," Bruce said, scooping up a forkful of scrambled eggs and shoveling them into his mouth. "What is it this time?"

Hayley took a deep breath. "How would you feel about me completely changing course?"

"You want pancakes instead?" Bruce cracked.

"No," Hayley said, smiling. "I want to stop working at the paper, do something new, maybe start my own business."

Bruce leaned forward, intrigued. "What kind of business are you thinking about?"

"How does Hayley's Kitchen sound?"

"Aren't we in Hayley's Kitchen right now?"

"I am imagining something a little bigger."

Bruce nodded knowingly. "I see."

"Liddy says she could get me a good deal to rent Chef Romeo's space. I'm sure I could get approved for a small business loan for start-up costs, I pretty much have a staff already in place . . ." She stopped, anticipating Bruce's reaction.

He seemed to be mulling it over, not sure.

Hayley braced herself. "You think it's a terrible idea, don't you?"

"That depends."

"On what?"

"Can I be in charge of the wine list?"

Hayley finally exhaled, jumped up from the table and wrapped her arms around her husband's neck, showering him with kisses on his head and face before she stopped and said, "Just make sure to keep your day job in case I'm a spectacular failure!"

"That's never going to happen," Bruce said reassuringly.

Hayley grabbed her phone.

"Who are you calling?" Bruce asked, chewing on a piece of toast with strawberry jam.

"Sal, before I lose my nerve."

She heard Sal's gruff voice after the first ring. "You better not be calling in sick! I have two reporters out with the flu already!"

"No, I'll be in soon, Sal, but we need to have a talk—"

"Can you pick me up a cinnamon bun on your way?"

"Yes, I can do that, Sal, but—"

"I'm going to need a little comfort food, if you're going to up and quit on me!"

Hayley gasped. "Sal, how did you know?"

"Please, Rosana's been preparing me for this ever since you took over for Chef Romeo. She said, 'Sal, it's only a matter of time. Hayley needs to spread her wings'—whatever the hell that means. You know how flowery my wife can get with her words! 'She's a natural chef who needs an outlet for her innate talents,' she told me, so I'm guessing she's right. She's always right. At least that's what she tells me day in and day out."

"She's right, Sal," Hayley said, smirking.

"I can find a new office manager, but what about your column? You have a lot of fans around here. I'd hate for you to just walk away from them."

Hayley had not even thought about that. She had just assumed that if she left the *Island Times*, then she would also have to leave behind her column. She loved writing that column and if there was any way . . .

"So do you think you could run your new restaurant and still write for me? Think of it this way, Hayley: The column would be free advertising. People could read your recipes and then come and taste them the same day at your restaurant?"

"Of course I could still write my column. Sal, thank you!"

"Now don't go leaving me in the lurch! I expect two weeks' notice, enough time to train your replacement!"

"Yes! Yes, Sal, whatever you say!"

Bruce beamed, excited for her.

"And I expect given our history, how magnanimous I have been—I'm not always this supportive and under-standing—I expect that my wife and I will get preferential treatment when we come in to your joint. Guaranteed reservation, good table, maybe a free dessert every now and then!"

"You got it!" Hayley cried.

"Oh, and Hayley, one more thing," Sal said, lowering his voice, appearing to get serious.

Sal had always been like a father to her.

She suspected what was coming.

He was going to tell her how proud he was of her.

"Don't forget my cinnamon bun!" he yelled.

Close enough.

"I won't. Thank you, Sal," Hayley said before ending the call.

Bruce was already on his feet, giving her another hug.

Her mind was already racing, full of thoughts and ideas.

There was so much to do.

A new chapter in Hayley Powell's life was about to begin.

## Island Food & Spirits
BY HAYLEY POWELL

News travels fast in a small town and Bar Harbor is no exception.

As I'm sure many of you have heard by now, I will be leaving my office manager position at the *Island Times* to pursue a new career path, which I am very excited about, and I will let you know all the details just as soon as I can.

And for those readers who have been asking me about the future of my column, well, let me reassure you, thanks to the best boss in the world, *Island Times* editor-in-chief Sal Moretti, I will be continuing my daily column uninterrupted, coming up with new and exciting recipes to share with you for the foreseeable future.

As I make this transition, I cannot help but look back at all the fond memories I have accumulated as office manager at this newspaper. I have developed lifelong friendships with so many talented reporters and photographers, copy editors and columnists. And although I've known my husband Bruce since high school, our whirlwind romance that led to us finally tying the knot really got started right here at the *Times* office where we were both employed. However, of all the wonderful people this newspaper has brought into my orbit, there is one person who really stands out above all—my boss, Sal Moretti.

Sal is a one-of-a-kind character, to be sure. True to his Italian heritage, he likes to yell and wave his hands around, and that can sometimes be a little intimidating, but deep down he's a pussycat. Now, that does not mean his moods can't be a little challenging to navigate. I've known plenty of pussycats whose personalities are, shall we say, mercurial. So as Sal interviews possible replacements to take over my duties as office manager, I would like to share a little advice to the lucky person who ultimately lands at my old desk in the front office of the *Times*. It might make your trial period go a lot smoother!

The first time I ever stepped foot into Sal's office for my own interview, I was a struggling mother of two small children, in desperate need of a job, with a husband who was once again out of work and a marriage that was, to be blunt, quickly heading down the toilet.

Sal was on the phone with his back to me, barking at some poor soul on the other end of the call. His booming voice could be heard through the entire building. I pitied the poor person who was on the receiving end of his earsplitting tirade, and as I stood there, I began to reconsider my decision to apply for this job. I was about to spin around and high-tail it out of there, when suddenly this giant of a man slammed the phone down in its cradle, and without even turning around, bellowed, "Well, get in here and sit down because I don't have all day!" I glanced around my shoulder, hoping he might be talking to someone else, but unfortunately no one else was around, so I scooted in and plopped down in the chair in front of his desk, my stomach doing flip-flops.

Finally, Sal slowly swiveled his chair around and stared hard at me for a few seconds, then growled, "You got a car?"

Words failed me, but I managed a nod.

"Good. Where can you get the best bagel in town?"

This was a curveball.

I thought his first question might be about my references. I was prepared to hand him a letter of recommendation from the First National Bank, where I had worked briefly as a teller some years ago.

I cleared my throat, hesitating out of fear this might be a trick question. Then I figured I might as well just plow ahead with an honest answer. "Well, the Eden Bakery claims to have the best bagels in town, but in my opinion, the Morning Glory's taste better, hands down." He glared at me in silence, and nervously I repeated, "In my opinion . . ."

Still no reaction.

He just continued glaring so I continued talking, or more pointedly, rambling. "I personally love their cheddar bagel with the jalapeño-cilantro cream cheese spread, it's really to die for. I mean, it's so good you don't

even need to get it toasted. One day last week
they were out of them, and my whole day was
ruined . . ."

I wanted to kick myself.

Why couldn't I stop talking?

Sal rubbed his chin with his chubby hands
and stared at me. I could feel myself starting
to sweat a little. He slammed both hands
down on his desk and pushed himself up into
a standing position. He looked me square in
the eyes for another full minute. Now I was so
nervous I could feel trickles of perspiration
sliding down from the top of my forehead. I
just wanted to get out of there.

Then suddenly, in his loud and booming
voice, he said, "Be here at eight AM sharp tomorrow morning, don't be late, and I'll have
a cheddar bagel with jalapeño-cilantro cream
cheese."

Did this mean I had the job?

Without taking some time to process, I figured it was best just to get out of there before
he changed his mind. I jumped up and made
a beeline for the door when he hollered my
name, which stopped me dead in my tracks.
Without turning around, I managed to squeak
out, "Yes?"

"I want mine toasted!"

"Okay," I whispered, rushing out.

I was halfway home before I realized he
had never even asked if I could type.

That was our first meeting.

I've learned lots of little things about Sal
over the many years we've worked together,
and I'm sure whomever you are who ultimately takes over as office manager, you will

too. However, just allow me to fill you in on a few key details that might make your life easier. I don't want you to make the same mistakes I did in the beginning.

First, when attending the annual August work picnic, a green salad with summer veggies has no place on the table. I know you're probably thinking that others might enjoy it. Well, don't! According to your new boss, only salads loaded with pasta and mayo are acceptable, so save yourself the trouble and bring a dessert. A yummy, sugar-loaded caloric dessert will always be a win-win!

Second, and this is very important, when Sal mentions that his wife has him on a diet (and this will occur at minimum three times a year), do not under any circumstances bring any baked goods like brownies, cookies, or muffins to the office, even if they are wrapped in heavy tinfoil, stuffed in your brown-bag lunch, and hidden in a drawer of your desk. Sal Moretti has an uncanny sense of smell when any baked good is within a hundred-yard vicinity! He will find it and it will be gone when you return from your midmorning break. If this happens, do not, I repeat, do *not* confront the man. It will only turn ugly and your day will become endless torture, filled with cranky grumblings and carrot sticks flying through the air like heat-seeking missiles.

Third, when Sal mentions yet again that his wife has him on another new diet (usually postholidays in January, late spring before the summer season, and early fall after most of the restaurants close for the season), try to schedule some time off to avoid the stress. If vacation days are not possible, then your best bet is to eat your lunch away from the office. The last thing you want to happen (which I learned the hard way), is to warm up your pasta puttanesca leftovers from dinner the night before in the microwave and eat in the break room next to a hungry bear eyeing you with contempt as he crunches angrily on a rice cake with peanut butter.

And finally, always remember, if you are running late for work and decide to stop at one of the bakeries for a delicious treat to enjoy with your morning coffee when you get to the office, always, always buy two. Trust me on this.

Oh, I almost forgot! A good bottle of scotch goes a long way at the secret Santa Christmas party! Sal loves his scotch!

You may have noticed that I never mentioned the actual job duties, but I'm sure you'll learn along the way, and I'm always available if you have any questions. I'm sure I will be stopping by frequently with some yummy pasta puttanesca leftovers and a few delicious baked goods to share with my old boss and dear friend Sal.

## SAL'S GO-TO COCKTAIL

**INGREDIENTS**
One bottle of good scotch, your choice, and a
   short cocktail glass.

Add 2 ounces of scotch to the glass! Simple, but
gets the job done!

## SAL'S FAVORITE PASTA PUTTANESCA

### INGREDIENTS
2 tablespoons extra-virgin olive oil
½ cup finely chopped onion
3 cloves garlic, minced
2 tablespoons tomato paste
2 to 4 anchovies, chopped up
1 teaspoon crushed red pepper flakes
1 28-ounce can crushed tomatoes
2 teaspoons dried oregano
2 tablespoons capers
¾ cup pitted black olives, chopped roughly
1 pound spaghetti
Salt
Extra-virgin olive oil for drizzling
Freshly grated Parmesan for topping (optional)

In a large pot, bring salted water to a boil and cook your spaghetti al dente.

In a large pan, heat your oil and add the onions, anchovies to the oil and sauté until soft. Add garlic and sauté 2 minutes until very fragrant.

Add in your tomato paste and stir together. Then add crushed tomatoes, oregano, crushed red pepper flakes, olives, and capers and mix well.

Bring sauce to a simmer on medium-high heat, then lower to low and simmer slowly for 15 minutes.

If your sauce is too thick, add some pasta water to thin it.

Reserve a cup of pasta water in case needed to thin sauce, then drain your pasta. Place in a large bowl and add a cup of sauce to the pasta and mix, then fix yourself a bowl of pasta and add more sauce to the pasta on top. Sprinkle Parmesan if using, then dig in and prepare to swoon!

# Index of Recipes

# Connect with U s

Visit us online at
**KensingtonBooks.com**
to read more from your favorite authors, see books
by series, view reading group guides, and more.

**Join us on social media**

for sneak peeks, chances to win books and prize packs,
and to share your thoughts with other readers.

facebook.com/kensingtonpublishing
twitter.com/kensingtonbooks

## Tell us what you think!

To share your thoughts, submit a review,
or sign up for our eNewsletters, please visit:
**KensingtonBooks.com/TellUs.**